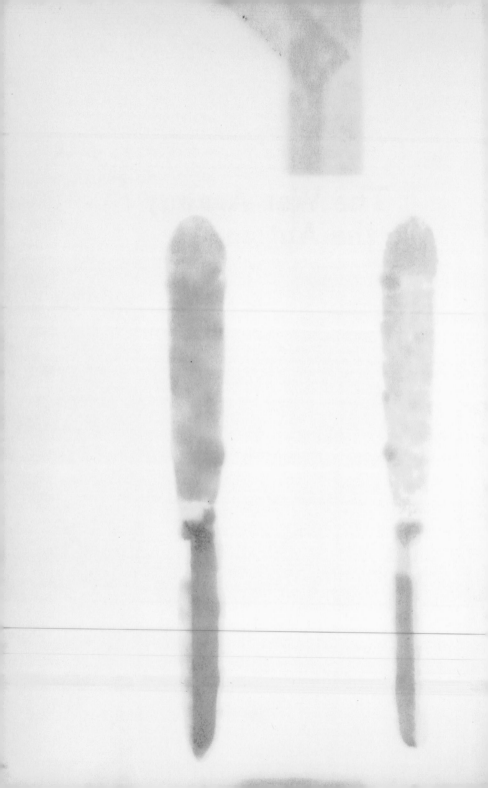

The War Against the Automobile

The War Against the Automobile

B. BRUCE-BRIGGS

E. P. DUTTON | NEW YORK

An earlier version of some of this material appeared in *The Public Interest,* summer 1975. I am indebted to its editor Irving Kristol for his editing of the original version and to its managing editor Robert Asahina for editing the original and this book. Ruth Ann (Mrs. John) Crow drew the graphics; Carolann (Mrs. Louis) Roussel typed the manuscript.

Library of Congress Cataloging in Publication Data
Bruce-Briggs, B
The war against the automobile.
Bibliography: p.
1. Transportation, Automotive—United States.
2. Automobiles—Social aspects—United States.
I. Title.
HE5623.B77   1977   388.3'0973   77-3909
ISBN: 0-525-23008-4
Published simultaneously in Canada by Clarke, Irwin & Company
Limited, Toronto and Vancouver

10 9 8 7 6 5 4 3 2 1

First Edition

"Americans are in the habit of never walking if they can ride."
—*Louis Philippe, Duc d'Orleans, 1798*

"Before the war, cars were for the rich; afterwards, everybody could have one."
—*Canadian Pacific Dining Car Waiter, 1976*

"What Englishman would give his mind to politics as long as he can afford to keep a motor car?"
—*George Bernard Shaw, circa 1930*

"For the lovers of odd, ineffectual, and labyrinthine legislation there is almost nothing to touch the odd successions of statutes trying to enforce transport on wheels three, six, nine, and even sixteen inches wide. Preferential tolls and arbitrary penalties were tried in vain to secure popularity for such strange vehicles. W. T. Jackman . . . devoted many pages to describing the folly of legislators who insisted on concentrating on the wheels, rather than on the surface of the road."
—*J. Carswell, 1973*

Contents

1.

Introduction

America has the best mass transportation system in the world. Almost every country envies us our system, and attempts to imitate it. The increased public concern and national government action regarding mass transportation that began in the late 1950s is a tribute to our high national standards, which so often lead us to see problems in success. Authors, journalists, academics, and politicians would have us believe that intraurban personal transportation, commonly called mass transportation, is a "problem," indeed, a serious one, and that major action is desired and required. Currently, there is considerable concern about the prospects for the future of mass transportation, including some worry about whether present private and government policies will continue to provide us with the mobility we want. There has been much dispute on the issues—some very heated —yet it seems to me that achieving the most desired goals of most Americans is fairly simple and that the necessary private and public funds are easy to acquire.

In order to have an efficient and equitable mass transportation system, we must begin with a clear understanding of our present system and what is wrong with it—but more important, what is *right* about it. Once this is established, appropriate action follows relatively easily.

The existing American mass transportation system moves people with a speed, convenience, comfort, and flexibility quite beyond comparison. It is difficult even to conceive of a system better than the existing one, save only the present arrangement with its costs reduced. So let me first describe the present complex in some detail.

The American mass transportation system consists of three principal elements. First, part of the land area of the nation is dedicated as rights-of-way for the system. Sometimes these are unimproved dirt, but more often they are covered with gravel, concrete, and/or very low quality liquid hydrocarbons. Most of these thoroughfares are publicly owned—by municipalities, counties, and states—and locally maintained. Almost all are open to the public; indeed they could be described as "communist" in their political economy—anyone may use them at will. Others are owned by public corporations that restrict access to users who pay for the privilege. There are about 3.8 million miles of these thoroughfares and they give access to almost all the land in the United States. Still others are privately owned, and therefore subject to the normal rights of private property; however, in custom and practice any person who wishes may normally use them, because such public use is usually considered to be in the interest of the owner. The total length of the privately owned thoroughfares is not known—it probably approaches a million miles.

The second element in our mass transportation system is the 130 million individually operated vehicles. Almost all of these have four wheels with synthetic rubber tires and are individually powered by mechanisms that mix air and liquid hydrocarbons carried in the vehicles to produce kinetic energy. These vehicles can operate on any of the thoroughfares of the system, so that they have great flexibility of movement. In addition, they have modest capabilities to operate cross-country off the thoroughfares. The vehicle is operated by one person who, sometimes after negotiation with the other people in the vehicle (they can also carry up to eight passengers, but usually one to four), decides where it shall go. He has control of the speed—between zero and one hundred miles an hour—acceleration, deceleration, route, destination, time of departure, and time of arrival. Provided a modest annual fee is paid to a state government, any vehicle can be operated on any thoroughfare.

Most individually operated vehicles are privately owned and maintained; that is to say, individual Americans actually possess these machines, paying for them with cash or through installment credit. The owners purchase the liquid hydrocarbons required to fuel them and the rubber tires necessary to make them roll, and are responsible for maintaining the machinery. Either the owners themselves do the maintenance or they engage independent small businessmen to do the work.

The third element in the American mass transportation system are the operators themselves. Approximately 125 million Americans, which is almost all adult Americans, have a reasonable degree of competence in negotiating these vehicles on thoroughfares. Since they are performing this "labor," they do not charge themselves for it. The states consider it a privilege to be an operator of a vehicle—a privilege limited only to those individuals they license. However, this licensing procedure is very liberal (some say too liberal), and very few people are unable to learn the minimum skills necessary to operate the vehicles in a manner satisfactory to the state authorities. The operators are mostly trained by their family and friends, so there is very little economic cost involved in this educational process. Public schools and private firms also train them.

The entire system is financed from a mixture of sources. The thoroughfares, being state owned, are almost entirely paid for by direct levies on their users—fees for operators' licenses, fees for licensing vehicles, and taxes on liquid hydrocarbons and other products necessary to operate and maintain the vehicles. Public corporations collect fees for the use of certain water crossings and a few high-quality thoroughfares, particularly in the northeastern states.

The vehicles themselves are individually purchased through small businessmen who have franchises from the manufacturers of the vehicles. There are four major North American manufacturers and dozens of foreign manufacturers in Europe, Mexico, and Japan, whose vehicles are imported. Replacement parts and other supplies for the vehicles are provided by tens of thousands of manufacturers, distributors, and retailers.

The total cost of the system is enormous—no one knows how much nor can it even be accurately estimated. There are too many factors involved; for example, the thoroughfares, in addition to serving the needs of the operators of the vehicles, also act as yards and buffers for abutting property owners. The vehicles are used primarily for transportation, but also for recreation as well, and many of them have artistic or aesthetic value. The vehicles also serve as private rooms in motion picture theaters and restaurants—and even, it is said, as bedrooms. The operators themselves also have many other functions.

Moreover, the system is not merely an intracity personal transportation system, but an intercity system as well. To further complicate the arrangement, the thoroughfares are used by many other sorts of vehicles—for moving goods and for carrying large groups of people within or between cities.

The financial cost of this complex is huge: one can guess 10 percent of GNP. This, however, would not appear too high, because the system described carries 94 percent of all intracity trips, 85 percent of all intercity trips, and 80 percent of all trips to work. This is the American mass transportation system. Of course, this is the auto-highway-driver complex. What is ordinarily called "mass transportation"—buses, subways, and railroads, which I call "collective transit"—moves only a tiny percentage of Americans. Every other method of moving people in or between cities is trivial by comparison. It is the automobile that moves the great mass of Americans, yet it is under attack today from a number of sources, informed and uninformed, idealistic and selfish.

The automobile-highway system is an unequaled complex of structures, machines, and techniques for maximizing the mobility of the individual American and American families. Everyone knows how good it is; in fact, most of us take it for granted. So it seems strange that over the last generation a concerted and comprehensive attack has been made on the auto-highway system by a small band of publicists and politicians. The number of these opponents of the automobile is very tiny, but they have been powerfully placed, and have strongly influenced—indeed dominated—public discussions of personal transportation in general, and the automobile in particular. As far as I can tell, no major publishing house in the United States has produced a book in favor of the car during the last generation. Published books have been uniformly hostile, sometimes virulently so. (Some of the more notorious of these will be mentioned later.) Similarly, the intellectual or highbrow media as well as academia have been, on the whole, anti-car. And the popular press, which should know better, has accepted the general anti-auto line promulgated by what I see as the enemies of American mobility.

What a few journalists and professors write is not of any particular interest in the wider scheme of things, except that their perceptions have strongly influenced, even driven, politicians and public transportation policy. There has been, as I hope to demonstrate in this book, a "war against the automobile." The purpose of this book is to refute the fallacious arguments of the critics and to put the legitimate complaints in their proper perspectives of the actual costs and benefits of the auto-highway system, and to bring into focus the realization that the criticisms represent not an objective analysis of reality but only the interests of privileged classes in America. The war against the automobile and the myths of mass transportation are merely one campaign in an upper-class struggle against the standard of living, individual freedom, and pride of the great mass of the American people.

The organization of the argument is straightforward. First I will set forth what everybody knows—what a wonderful system the automobile-highway complex is and how it came to be. Then

I will refute some of the phony costs, monetary and otherwise, assigned to the automobile, and then discuss the real costs—which are considerable, but more than justified by the enormous benefits cars procure for society. Then there will be a description of the disastrous course of federal policy over the past fifteen years, followed by an explanation of why this nonsense was foisted on the public. Then there will be a concluding section on what ought to be done to improve the transportation of our people and to reduce all of the costs of the system. The proposals made will deviate considerably from the conventional wisdom promulgated by most transportation "experts" and politicians.

Climb in and let's go.

2.

The Transportation Revolution

Imagine that we had no transportation system in the United States and that we had the means to design one from scratch. The first question to ask is whether we need such a system at all. The answer would have to be—yes. The distribution of the world's resources and goods requires either that they be moved to us or that we move to them. Rarely can we live and work at the same location. Rarely are fuel, minerals, food, and leisure resources found in the same place.

So we need a system, but in this hypothetical case we may choose its configuration. Obviously, a principal consideration is its range—how far it can go—but as important is how far it can go in a given amount of time. In a transit system distance and speed are the same. We often express this equivalence in everyday conversation—when somebody asks how far is it to Joe's place, we'll say, "Oh, about ten minutes." So our transportation system requires speed, and the faster the better.

Our system must have capacity. It is useless unless it can handle what needs to be transported. It must be safe. What good is a system that will crash before reaching its destination?

It must be reliable. There is no point to a system that will break down.

Availability is another useful criterion—the more people who can use the system, the better it is for everyone (or almost everybody, as will be evident later). We must also consider the cost to the users. Obviously, if few can afford it, it serves little purpose.

And last, but certainly not least, the transit system must provide accessibility. This feature is often ignored by even the best transportation planners. The best system is the one giving access to as many places as possible.

Having considered these requirements, we must recognize that many of them are to some degree mutually exclusive. Adults know—or should know—that everything costs something. Speed must be traded off against economy and safety. And everything conflicts with lower cost.

We must also be limited by the laws of physics, which constrain the potential of any system. Higher speeds increase air resistance, as well as use more power and raise noise levels. Because of friction, everything eventually wears out. Because of inertia, damage results when two vehicles come into contact. Given these and other considerations, we have to balance the different criteria that we consider necessary in our transportation system.

Given these limitations, I think it is indisputable that our present system—the auto-highway system—admirably satisfies the desirable criteria. What is even more remarkable is that it has done so even though nobody really planned it. It just worked out that way through the myriad individual decisions of hundreds of millions of people, past and present.

In the real world we could not plan such a system from scratch. We must build upon what has come down to us from the past. Although the origins of much that exists now are lost in obscurity and are the subject of speculation by even the most learned historians, the auto-highway system is less than one hundred years old—and we know how it came about. Its history is copiously documented, and there is a wonderful logic to its development.

Nobody knows how long man has been on this earth, but we do know that for most of that time he got along reasonably well without the automobile. The precursors of the present auto-mobile were built by inventive Germans in the 1880s. The device that they designed was hardly more than a toy until about 1910. And the automobile as a mass transportation system really did not emerge until the early 1920s in North America, the 1950s in Europe, and the 1960s in Japan. Most of the world is still not auto-mobile, and the most advanced societies have been so for only a few decades—a mere moment in the history of mankind.

For most of history, people managed with the natural trans-portation system—walking. It pleased the Good Lord to provide us with legs and feet to propel us from place to place. Walking is an excellent system, used almost universally, and we could not get along without it. Unfortunately, it has grave drawbacks, the most important being the lack of speed. An average walker can cover a mile in twenty minutes. Accelerated walking—"run-ning"—is much faster, but at the cost of range; the mechanism tires rapidly. Walking, however, permits incredible range. Men have crossed continents on foot—but the time required is mea-sured in months, and even years. The range and speed increase somewhat if the feet are provided with artificial protection—shoes. Another serious drawback is that only a very small load can be carried. A man in good condition can pack up to his own weight and cover long distances, but few do this willingly. To modern man, the most familiar load consists of a helmet, knap-sack, rifle, and ammunition—and only a few carry them volun-tarily.

Walking will certainly always be with us, if only for recrea-tional purposes, but it must be considered an inadequate system for covering more than the shortest of distances. Its shortcomings are evident from the fact that throughout history hardly any-body ever walked when he could travel by some other means. When man first domesticated large animals about 3,000 years ago, he rapidly found that it was possible to use them for transportation, at first by attaching them to some wheeled vehicle and later by sitting astride them—"riding." The use of animals for transportation was based on the very simple principle of letting them do the walking. Unfortunately, although riding was an obvious improvement over walking, it also had certain grave drawbacks. The animals were terribly expensive largely because they were unhealthy. They had somewhat of a mind of their own so they had to be watched and controlled; it was very easy to lose them. Their scarcity gave them great value. Possession of animals, and thus the potential for riding, was always limited to a very narrow class of people: riding was for the rich; the rest walked. This still remains true in underdeveloped areas of the world. In the Middle East I have seen one young man assigned to watch over a single camel—the camel is worth a lot, the young man very little. A system based on domestic animals requires large disparities in income and power between the classes. The riding of animals is a perfectly appropriate system for a "feudal" society of the very rich and the very poor, but not for an economic democracy with mass prosperity.

Animals have other drawbacks. They are so large that they take up a great deal of road space when hitched to a vehicle. Moreover, at a different level they have much the same kinds of problems in walking that men do. The faster they go, the shorter the time they can go fast. And their top speed is decidedly limited—in prime condition, a thoroughbred horse is capable of doing thirty miles an hour for only a mile.

Animals present another enormous disadvantage that we tend to forget today. Those quaint photographs of nineteenth-century cities fail to impress us with what the streets smelled like. Animals produce an enormous quantity of emissions, so much that if the rate of horsepower increase in the nineteenth century had continued into the twentieth century, by now the entire United States would be covered with several yards of horse manure. Fortunately, the automobile came along; one of its immediately heralded advantages was that it would eliminate these emissions from cities.

But we should not disregard the horse altogether. It did provide the single greatest asset of a universal transportation system —it gave access to nearly every point. Should we be obliged to get rid of the automobile, for whatever reason, most of the slack would necessarily be picked up by horses. If we are coming to the end of the age of the horseless carriage, as some commentators have proclaimed, we must expect to return to the day of the horse. Fortunately, the prognosis of the death of the automobile is premature, to say the least.

It was noticed very early in history that waterways provided excellent transportation. Wood and reeds could float on water and move with a minimum amount of friction. Much less energy was required to propel things over water than over land. In running waters, the force of gravity was enough to move a vessel downstream. In shallow water a man could propel a raft with a pole; in narrow waterways a vessel could be pulled from the shore; and the oar was invented early on. Not much later it was found that the wind could be harnessed to move waterborn vessels. Several thousand years of incremental development culminated in the mid-nineteenth century with reliable passenger and cargo ships, which linked together the entire world for the first time.

During the time when walking and riding were the dominant modes of land transportation, people preferred to go by water instead, whenever possible. The best road with the best mode of power available was infinitely inferior to a waterway. Ports and river towns were the great cities. While seafaring people were linked together by waterways, their country cousins were cut off from one another. Consider an example from the American revolution: Although it was colonized by New Englanders extremely sympathetic to the patriotic cause, Nova Scotia, through its principal port, Halifax, was closer to England, who controlled the seas, than to New Hampshire, cross-country. British power could be brought by sea, and the Americans could not get to the province overland, so Nova Scotia was held for the empire. Throughout the world only the merchant peoples had sea mobility, and only the very rich had land mobility. The rest—the more than 90 percent who were peasants and artisans—were immobile and unfree.

The evolution of transportation in the modern age closely parallels and indeed was a principal element in the industrial revolution. The first major breakthrough was the eighteenth-century canal, which successfully extended inland the advantages of waterborne transportation. Rivers were adapted and canals dug by hand throughout Europe and America. A few are still in use, but canals were quickly made obsolete by the second major breakthrough of the industrial revolution—the railroad. The invention of the steam engine in the eighteenth century quickly led people to conceive of the possibility of harnessing its power to a moving vehicle. The first idea was to accommodate a steam engine to a stagecoach, and there were many such experiments in the late eighteenth and early nineteenth centuries. But these were frustrated because the available technology was not yet up to the task: The engines were too large and awkward and required highly skilled crews to keep them operating, resulting in vehicles so heavy and bulky that the primitive dirt roads could not support them. The steam coaches quickly bogged down both literally and figuratively, and the early transportation pioneers turned to an alternative scheme. They hit on the bright idea of building special roads for steam vehicles, out of the strongest materials then available—iron rail roads.

Beginning in the 1830s, the railroads began to revolutionize world transportation. Their record of reliability and safety was originally dismal. With our talk of safety today, we forget how incredibly dangerous were these early railroads. Folk songs like the one about "Casey Jones" are filled with bloody crashes. Early bridge-building technology was primitive, and entire trains were lost. But railroad technology gradually improved, and by the end of the nineteenth century trains were achieving speeds in excess of 100 miles an hour. Mile-a-minute service was taken for granted, a speed faster than any horse, any ship, or any other way that any man had traveled before. For the first time in history, interior points were closer to one another than seaports were. While shipping (now steam shipping) retained its advantage for very large cargoes, the train was preferred for its speed. Railroads were so much better than their competitors that stagecoach companies and coastal shipping lines collapsed. Railroads were immensely profitable, and thus their promoters could afford to bridge previously impassable rivers, cross deserts and mountain ranges, and fill in swamps. Such was the imagination, vigor, and optimism of the railroad builders that their lines extended as far as the Arctic Circle and across the Florida Keys.

But the railroad always had distinct disadvantages as a transportation system. Although the lines seemed to go everywhere, in point of fact the number of places in the country within walking distance of a train station was only a trivial percentage of the land area. Worse, the traveler was controlled by schedules and routes: He could go only where the railroads ran lines and when the railroads chose to schedule trains. Of course, despite a somewhat monopolistic situation, the companies did try to locate lines and operate schedules according to their best estimates of the demand of real and potential customers. Nevertheless, their projections, however good, never exactly suited everybody. So people adjusted their lives to fit the timetables of the railroad, just as suburban commuters do until this day. Travelers were obliged to wait between trains when making a transfer. They did not mind this very much, because the train was so much faster than any alternative means and so much less expensive, in time as well as in money, that they saw little cost in adjusting their lives to suit the regimen of the railroad.

Trains were intended for intercity transportation—to link one city with another—but they soon had some very interesting spinoffs that profoundly affected intracity transportation (which is the principal subject of this book). Almost from the very beginning, the railroad lines intended to link cities had a commercial

by-product with profound implications for urban development:
A few pioneers discovered the possibility of living in a small
village near a main line and using the train every day to go to
work in the big city. Commodore Perry, commonly known as
the man who opened up Japan, was commuting from Tarrytown
to his work as naval commandant of New York as early as the
1840s. The railroads recognized the potential of this development
and encouraged the use of the lines for this purpose by reducing
—or "commuting"—the price of tickets bought on a monthly basis.

Some railroads went one step farther and went into real estate
speculation. They promoted what we now call "suburban development," in order to increase the railway use. Thus, for example,
was Philadelphia's "Main Line" born of the Pennsylvania Railroad. In those days, no one except the rich had any personal
transportation other than their own feet, so the early suburbs
clustered closely around the railroad stations. In many of the
older suburbs, particularly in eastern American cities, large
houses are found on small lots; that design was intended to give
the maximum number of upper-middle-class dwellings direct
access to the station. Most of these communities still exist, most
of them are prospering, and most are still serviced by the rail
lines. However, this system was intended for the prosperous.
The masses of Americans were still scattered and isolated on
farms and in small towns, and most of the minority who were
city dwellers still lived in a teeming squalor within walking distance of work.

But this condition was quickly modified by another spin-off
of the trains. Some bright people spotted the potential of the
rails for urban use. Soon the big cities were covered with trolleys
—primitive cars drawn by horses—much faster, more reliable, and
safer than the primitive horse-drawn "omnibuses" that had to
jostle over uneven streets.

Another spin-off was the short-lived attempt to bring railroads
into the city itself. Miniature engines and trains were developed
to carry passengers within large cities. But to take advantage of
the potential speed of the railroad, it was not possible to build

at grade level in the crowded cities, so separate rights-of-ways had to be established. Steam engines with their smoke could not traverse long tunnels, so the city railroads went up in the air, thus earning the label "elevateds." They were noisy and covered the city with soot, but in those halcyon days this was of little consequence, compared with the delights of industrial progress.

The high point of the transportation revolution came toward the end of the nineteenth century. Within a generation the fundamental systems that move us today were invented. The leading edge of technology in those times was electricity. And one of its first applications was to power trolleys.* The horsecar lines quickly converted to electricity. Large amounts of money were invested and huge profits made by traction magnates who covered cities with rails and the overhead cables to provide electricity to the trolleys. By present-day standards, these were terribly ugly (which was one reason that a trolley line was not permitted on New York's swank Fifth Avenue) and potentially unsafe—those hot wires occasionally did come down. As one who used to ride trolleys in my youth, I can personally attest to the splendor of this transit mode. Electric trolleys are smooth, quiet, and luxurious, with only the modest tick-tick of the steel wheels on the rails violating the tranquility. Few lines remain in existence, and I strongly urge the reader to enjoy them while they still last. There are still excellent lines in Philadelphia, particularly the Red Arrow service from Upper Darby cross-country to Media.

The trolley had a distinct advantage over the steam engine, even for commuter work. Since the mode of power was much smaller and lighter, more compact units could be built, riding

* An earlier way to move vehicles was to use electric or some other form of power to drive a moving cable, laid under the roadway, to which a car could be connected or disconnected at will. This was a particularly suitable method of powering vehicles in very hilly cities, where normal trolleys had trouble gaining traction, particularly in inclement weather. These cable cars survive today only in San Francisco, where they are maintained primarily as historical artifacts and tourist attractions.

on much lighter and cheaper rails. Trolley lines not only criss-crossed cities, they fanned out to nearby towns, and there was a time around the turn of the century when one could travel across a good part of the United States by making judicious connections among the various interurban lines. But they did not go every-where, and the rider was at the mercy of the scheduling of the managers of the systems.

The electric motor was also adaptable to larger vehicles. Be-cause electricity did not produce smoke, it became possible to put urban lines underground. So the subway was born and flourished for the first two decades of the twentieth century. The elevated lines were electrified and the lines integrated. The subway was efficient, rapid, and capable of carrying enormous numbers of passengers. As the subway lines spread out from the cores of the great cities, urban development followed, and so what are now the outer reaches of New York, Philadelphia, and Chicago were thus born.

This "rapid transit"—as it came to be known*—was a marvel-ous achievement. With subterranean lines in the center and elevated or grade lines in the outskirts, it could link together a large city with a speed and range hitherto inconceivable. Un-fortunately, rapid transit was enormously expensive and required a major capital investment before large sums of money could be made. If a city was more or less linear, like Manhattan Island, it was easy to design a "line-haul" facility. For example, the first line in Manhattan was from the Wall Street district up what is now the Lexington Avenue IRT to Grand Central Station, then west along what is now the 42nd Street Shuttle, then north up what is now the Seventh Avenue IRT. (If you look carefully at either end of the shuttle you can still see where the tracks connect to the other lines.) With such a linear arrangement it was pos-sible to build lines one at a time. But most cities spread out from a hub, so that a web of lines was necessary to provide access

---

* Apparently the name derives from Commodore Vanderbilt's abor-tive Rapid Transit Company of 1872. It was intended to be "rapid," compared with the horsecar.

to the entire system. It was very difficult to make money on rapid transit unless the whole system was established at once, hence the capital requirements were crippling for private enterprise. Despite the great hopes of promoters, very little money was made on these early investments. Most of them were either begun by or rapidly taken over by government. New York's IRT, BMT, and IND subway systems were soon absorbed into what is now the New York City Transit Authority.

While rapid transit systems of this type became the symbol (along with skyscrapers) of the great city and were installed in London, Paris, Berlin, Tokyo, they did not spread to smaller cities. In the United States, more than half of the rapid transit mileage was in New York City. There were also the "Hudson Tubes" linking Manhattan with Jersey City and Newark, a short line in Newark itself, an important system in Chicago, a partial system mixed with underground trolley cars in Boston, a similar complex in Philadelphia, and a single line in Cleveland. The crucial period of the development of rapid transit in North America was the first two decades of the twentieth century. Almost by inertia, construction continued into the 1920s, and then petered out in the 1930s.

One reason for the waning of rapid transit construction was growing affluence. The lines originally had relatively high fares and were used mainly by the "better sort" in the cities. With the increased living standard of the urban working classes, the subway trains began to fill up with the lower orders, and the more prosperous sought other means of transportation. The more prosperous were also tending to move to the suburbs and had no desire to provide transportation that would serve their inferiors. But the most important reason for the stagnation of rapid transit was that it came up against crushing competition.

During the same period, another marvelous, revolutionary device appeared—the bicycle. Its principles are so simple, it is at first surprising that no one thought of it before. But in fact the technology was not available. To function effectively, a bicycle must be light, well balanced, and easily controlled, and it was not until the late nineteenth century that metallurgy was developed to the point where lightweight frames, wire-spoked wheels, and precision wheel and steering bearings were available. First the "high-wheeler" and then the "safety" bicycles—their design remains substantially unchanged today—swept the industrial world. Bicycles were an incredibly successful fad. In retrospect, the reason was obvious—for the first time in history the urban working man had an individual transportation unit. He could achieve a speed approaching that of the horse; more important, the speed, faster than walking or running, could be maintained for long periods of time. The bicycle was relatively cheap, easy to service, and easy to learn to operate.

But the bicycle did have and still has some basic drawbacks. Unless it is "built-for-two" it cannot carry a passenger, and two-man bicycles were too heavy for one rider to operate efficiently. The bicyclist is also exposed to the elements. The vehicle is ill suited for places with steep hills or consistently rolling terrain; the downhill side is great, but coming up again takes away most of the fun. Less important to the people at the turn of the century, but a more serious drawback today, is that the fundamental design principle of the bicycle imposes a serious safety cost. Like any "single-track" vehicle, it requires forward movement to retain its stability. Unless the rider is exceptionally skilled, loss of speed or stability results in an upset. In the late nineteenth century, the trolley lines were a particular hazard to the bicyclist; once a wheel got caught in the groove of a trolley rail, the rider went down.

But the importance of the bicycle in the transportation revolution is just beginning to be properly appreciated. It was the bicyclists' demand for good roads that led to the first serious effort at highway improvement in the United States. Without the road system begun for the bicyclists, the developing motor vehicle would have had a great difficulty getting underway. The needs of the bicyclists for some way of absorbing road shock, even on the smoothest roads, gave impetus to the development of the rubber tire and later the pneumatic tire, afterward developed for use by other vehicles. Perhaps most important of all, the bicycle industry, ranging from manufacturers to shops, created a cadre of aggressive promoters, engineers, tinkerers, and en. thusiasts for human motion.*

At last, we come to the star of this book—the motorcar. The idea of the self-propelling vehicle operating from its own power source was an old one; Leonardo Da Vinci made some interesting sketches. But there was no device that could provide the energy until the end of the nineteenth century, when three major methods of propelling a vehicle by its own energy—three means of making a vehicle self-moving or auto-mobile—were developed.

Early experiments at adapting steam power to motor vehicles were a failure because of the complexity and unreliability of the machinery. But after a great deal of time, steam cars finally appeared, and very popular and promising they were. The steam car was solid, smooth, fast, and had considerable range; it was also easy to operate. It looked like a potent contender for mastery of the road.

An opponent was the electric automobile—also smooth, very silent, and easy to operate. But because of the relatively small amount of energy that could be accumulated in batteries, the electric car was severely limited in speed and range. (But since it was reliable and capable of instant starting, it was particularly popular with city doctors.)

The third contender for an effective power source for a horseless carriage was the internal-combustion engine. It had been noticed very early in the industrial revolution that a mixture of certain volatile fluids with air produced an explosion, and thousands of inventors attempted to find some means of harnessing this force for practical use. In 1876, the German engineer Nikolaus Otto patented an engine that operated by mixing air

* Remember that the Wright Brothers were bicycle manufacturers in Dayton? The transportation revolution also produced the airplane, but because it is rarely used for intraurban transportation, we will leave it outside the purview of this book.

with a petroleum distillate—"gasoline"—which could deliver large amounts of energy from a relatively light power plant. In the mid-1880s two German inventors, Gottlieb Daimler and Karl Benz, working independently put Otto-type engines into small carriages. Their successful innovation was widely reported and reproduced worldwide. In the early 1890s American imitators achieved the same results, and very shortly the internal-combustion or gasoline engine was a formidable competitor to its steam and electric counterparts. Although it was characterized by high output per unit weight, it was noisy and unreliable. The inventors persevered, and reliability, power, and economy were greatly improved.

Although a complex device, the motorcar was simpler than its major rival, the steam car. The electric auto was never a real competitor, except for limited urban use, because of its very low power-to-weight output. And when the gasoline automobile was equipped with the self-starter, the main advantage of the electric—that it could be started rapidly and easily, even by a woman—was nullified, and the electric was driven off the market. The steam car also suffered from poor fuel economy and from the lengthy start-up time required to get the steam up, but its more important faults were complexity and cost, and it also quickly faded from the road. Of the three principal builders of steam cars, White and Locomobile soon switched to gasoline-powered cars, and Stanley went broke.

The internal-combustion engine was also fitted to other types of vehicles. Contemporary with the first automobiles were bicycles fitted with engines—motorcycles, which were a great improvement over bicycles in terms of speed and range, but not in economy and safety; the two-wheeled vehicle was never a serious threat to the automobile. Gasoline engines on a wagon resulted in the truck. In cities, the trolley had never completely displaced the horse-drawn omnibus, and the gasoline engine provided a suitable replacement for the horse in an auto-mobile multiple-passenger vehicle. Thus the omnibus became the motor bus, which began to replace the trolley in the 1920s.

By the end of the 1920s, the transportation revolution completed its first stage. Obviously, the horse was finished. But the handwriting was on the wall for other systems as well. Commuter railroad, trolley, and rapid transit growth had slowed, while auto and truck sales soared.

The Great Depression was a time of crisis for all of America's transportation systems. Automobile sales collapsed, and almost all of the smaller automakers went into bankruptcy. At the beginning of the Depression there were perhaps fifty independent car manufacturers; at the end there were nine. The Depression hit just as heavily mass transit, which relied mostly on commuter traffic, as well as discretionary trips. With 25 percent unemployed, rides to work dropped precipitously, as did shopping trips and excursions. Hardest hit were the interurban and urban trolley lines. They simply could not afford to maintain their roadbeds, power lines, and stations. The more progressive of them converted to buses, which like automobiles had been improved in efficiency, reliability, and comfort over the years. Because buses could be operated at much lower cost, trolley lines that converted to buses were saved. Nonetheless, the 1930s were slim days for everyone.

Perhaps the most remarkable social effect of the Great Depression, however, was that although automobile sales collapsed, automobile ownership did not. It turned out that among the last things that families would give up was their personal mobility. Rather than buy new cars, people kept the old cars running longer. (The automobile parts market has always been a strong "counter-cyclical" industry; in hard times more people will repair rather than buy new.) The car was second only to the house as the most important possession of the American family.

This was confirmed by World War II. Mass transit underwent its last and greatest boom because automobiles were severely restricted by rationing. The oil, rubber, raw materials, and productive capacity that normally went into manufacturing and operating automobiles were devoted to the war effort. Detroit had a commendable record in supplying the Allied forces with trucks, tanks, and aircraft, and no private automobiles were built for almost five years. The individual citizen was given a paltry ration of tires and oil; on the home front, access to the rights to rubber and oil became one of the most precious commodities. The black market was extensive.

When the war ended in 1945, there was reason to believe that the experience of the preceding twenty-five years established how personal transportation should be allocated. Here was how Americans got around in 1945: Rural people, except the lowest level of agricultural workers in the South, had cars. The type depended upon their income, but most folks in the backwoods owned or had access to a car of some sort. In the cities there was a different pattern—only the more prosperous owned automobiles, and the rest used some sort of collective transit facility—buses, trolleys, or rapid transit. In 1945 only about 55 percent of American families owned automobiles. This may strike the reader as incredibly low, but remember that the contemporary image of the past in the United States is based upon a middle-class perception. Remember those old Van Johnson and June Allyson movies with the girl in the swing on the porch of the big old frame house in the small town—so central to our nostalgic image of the good life in the good old days? Well, that was a reality only for the middle classes. As late as 1930, only 40 percent of American families owned their own homes; even fewer owned their own cars. The past was delightful for only a relatively privileged few. It is only in the last generation, only in the era since World War II, that the mass prosperity that we take for granted was expanded to the rural poor and the urban working classes.

The achievement of a "bourgeois" standard of living for the working people of America has had two important material manifestations—the suburban single-family tract house and the mass-produced automobile. The late 1940s and 1950s saw an absolute orgy of home and auto production. Part of this was merely catching up with the suppressed demand of 1930 to 1945, and the rest reflected the remarkable growth of the productive capacity and the wealth of our economy. The 1950s were the second golden age of the automobile. This was the period when family automobile ownership went from 55 percent to 80 percent of the population. This was the period when the announcement of new car models was a major news event, when the sales race between Ford, Chevrolet, and Plymouth was watched with the interest of a World Series game, when ferocious competition drove Kaiser, Willys, Hudson, and Packard to the wall, when the horsepower race and the tail fin race were cause for excitement. The enactment of the National Defense Highway Act to finance the long-discussed national expressway system marked the high-water mark of the automobile culture in America, when the transportation revolution was almost completed, and the counterrevolution began.

Keep in mind that these are events that occurred only 20 to 100 years ago. All of the transportation systems described are still with us—or could be with us if we cared to have them. Yet they are either nonexistent or trivial in importance compared with the automobile. The commuter railroad, the elevated railroad, the subway, the trolley, the bicycle, the motorcycle, and the bus all fought in head-to-head competition with the automobile, and all lost. The reason is not at all difficult to understand—the automobile was the superior system. No one planned that the car should dominate. Indeed, if its victory had been anticipated, it undoubtedly would have been suppressed by government action in the interests of the robber barons who controlled the transit systems of the past. The use of state action to protect established transportation interests goes back a long way. In the mid-nineteenth century the English stagecoach operators succeeded in passing the infamous "red flag act," which required that any steam coach be preceded by a man on foot with a red flag—thus discouraging the development of steam carriages for half a century.

The fundamental concept to keep in mind is this: The automobile is, so far, the most perfect method of intraurban personal transportation yet devised. Other systems may have advantages according to individual parameters—for instance, electric power is necessarily quieter and smoother. But by the criteria of economy, speed, comfort, convenience, and always most important of all, point-to-point delivery, the automobile was, is, and will be far superior.

The advantages of the auto-highway system are so manifold that they are taken for granted, and often forgotten. Let me try to list them, always comparing them with alternative systems —either other personal transportation systems (walking, the bicycle, the motorcycle), or collective transit systems (taxi, bus, or rail transportation systems of various kinds).

To begin with, the automobile is fast. It can usually achieve speeds in excess of 100 miles an hour or more, but in practice is usually limited to a maximum of 80 by driver preference. A corollary of speed is acceleration; the auto can reach the desired rate of speed rapidly—almost every car on the road can achieve 60 miles per hour in less than twenty seconds. The auto also has great range—300 miles on a tank of gas. With refueling, it can go continuously for days.

The automobile is inexpensive. Almost every American family can afford to buy one. Maintenance is usually cheap; indeed, most is performed by the owners themselves. The ordinary parts for conventional upkeep and repairs are readily available and mass-produced in such quantities that the prices are low.

The automobile is comfortable. The riders are protected from the weather (unlike a walker or a cyclist). The internal temperature of the automobile is controlled. Almost every car has a heater for the winter, and in increasing numbers, air conditioning for the summer. The internal temperature is individually controlled to suit the requirements of the few occupants, and this temperature control rarely fails—which is not the case with collective transit systems.

Those who frequently ride collective transportation systems also appreciate the fact that riders in an automobile always have a place to sit—a nicely padded seat, designed by scientific ergonomics. Furthermore, the occupants of an automobile have their own entertainment systems. Almost every car has a radio, with dozens of stations to choose from, and increasing numbers have a tape-playing device with thousands of cassettes available.

The automobile provides security. When locked in his car the rider is safe from hoodlums and muggers. This security is apparent from the fact that many people will drive through hazardous areas—windows up, doors locked—where they would not dare venture on foot. The automobile gives the driver a means of flight from danger, and in a severe crisis, it can be a deadly weapon. Although the circumstances are fortunately rare, the automobile can provide shelter from thrown projectiles, and even some marginal protection from bullets—highway patrolmen use heavy-duty .357 magnum ammunition because normal pistol bullets cannot be relied upon to reach the interior of a vehicle.

The rider in an automobile has privacy. He can drive alone, or at least choose his companions. He is not troubled by the presence of numerous strangers, many of whom he might consider obnoxious or even dangerous. This privacy has other aspects as well. At a time when public authorities are increasingly harassing various types of presumably antisocial behavior, the driver can order his own life reasonably well in his car. As an important example, public authorities are hassling smokers. The more that smoking is prohibited in "public" transportation systems, the more attractive the automobile is to nicotine addicts. In addition, for many people, the time spent driving is the only extended opportunity for contemplation. You can talk to yourself, or sing. The female driver is not ogled or caressed as the female transit passenger is.

Moreover, the operator can gain pleasure from the very act of driving which is a form of athletics, requiring the coordination of man and machine and offering the satisfaction of doing something well. To some, speed, rapid acceleration, or swift cornering provide pleasure. There is even some modest intellectual satisfaction in selecting the most rapid route and adjusting for temporary shortfalls in the system. (To many drivers, however, driving is at best a bore and at worst a chore.)

Nonetheless, it is easy to learn to drive a car in a reasonably adequate manner. Anyone who travels our roads knows there is a great range of driving skills, but it is unchallengeable that almost everybody can learn to drive in a safe fashion. (This is particularly true when people begin to drive very young.)

The automobile is a suitable transportation system for crippled people. Obviously, the blind cannot drive, but they can ride. The deaf and dumb can easily drive, as can those who have lost the use of some of their limbs. It is not difficult to design a car—many are in use—for people who have partial use of only two limbs; if you can manipulate some part of two arms, or one arm and one leg, you can drive. Driving does not require the stairs or escalators that make public transportation systems extremely difficult for cripples.

The auto-highway system is extremely reliable. The highway is a very simple machine with no moving parts. Failures can occur through washouts, landslides, and a rare design failure resulting in the collapse of a bridge, culvert, or viaduct. In practice, though, such failures are so rare as to be almost acts of nature, like tornadoes or hurricanes.

The car itself fails much more often, but rarely resulting in more than annoyance to the driver. Most frequent is the failure of the car to start, thus temporarily stranding the motorist out of the traffic stream. Road failures usually result in a noticeable loss of power or control, signaling the driver to immediately seek a stopping place. Most important, however, the breakdown of an individual car usually inconveniences only the occupants of that vehicle. Failures of collective transit systems hold up dozens, sometimes hundreds of people; in the case of a train, breakdowns are particularly nasty because they block the entire track. The most annoying type of auto failure is the breakdown on a freeway during rush hour, which occurs altogether too often (partially because there are no legal sanctions to penalize its happening—if there were a fine for blocking traffic, drivers would be more careful to make sure the gas tanks are filled, or to get onto the shoulder of the road, even at the risk of damaging the carcass of their tire). As we shall see later, auto failures leading to death, injury, or serious damage to other vehicles are rare.

The operator of a car is also extremely dependable. When he fails, he rarely does so behind the wheel. We have no idea how many accidents are caused by sudden heart attacks—perhaps a few thousand a year, which amounts to practically zero probability, given the billions of trips taken every year.

Consider the organizational dependability of the driver. Since the operator is driving himself, he has high incentives to perform reliably. He is not organized against himself, and he does not go on strike.

We have been looking at the automobile as an intracity transportation system; let us consider it for intercity and rural transportation as well. In rural areas where people are widely scattered, the automobile is the only transportation system. Before the car, farmers were isolated and led terribly constrained lives; the auto has given them access to the town. Conversely, the city dweller can reach the great countryside. For the first time in history, the enormous gap between town and country has almost been closed.

For intercity use, the automobile is challenged only by the airplane, with its vastly greater speed and its comparable cost. But where speed is not the primary consideration, the automobile has it all over alternative systems. You go where you want when you want, you stop when you want, you eat when you want, you answer calls of nature when you must, you select your own route, you are not controlled by the timetable, and you need not make connections. You don't run for a train. You carry your luggage with you in the trunk. There is no need to look for a porter, or to tip one. Your child can sleep in the back. You can carry your pets. All costs considered, the car is cheaper than train or bus.

And the automobile has some secondary nontransportation uses as well. It offers many people pride of possession. To millions of Americans, cars are a hobby, ranging from a trivial interest to a fanatic enthusiasm. Several hundreds of thousands participate in competitions, and tens of millions watch motor racing.

Apparently, to most people to some degree the car is an aesthetic artifact. They like to look at it; they admire its lines and the detail. New York's Museum of Modern Art has had shows of this form of moving sculpture.

Millions enjoy working with their cars as a hobby. At a less esoteric level, there is even some satisfaction in seeing one's own car well cleaned and polished.

With the automobile so ubiquitous, all manner of institutions and diversions have grown up around it—drive-in restaurants, movies, even church services. And last, but certainly not least, who can ever forget the opportunities the automobile offers young people as a boudoir?

In addition to its passenger-carrying capability, the automobile can haul substantial amounts of luggage and packages—a boon to shoppers. It is no longer necessary for women to shop every day, limiting themselves to those few pounds that they can carry home in their arms. Nor is it necessary, except for very large items, to endure the uncertainties and expense of delivery by the store.

We should not limit our consideration merely to personal use of the car. Its business uses are almost too numerous to mention —just think of the salesman. Its service function is also enormous. The range and reaction speed of policemen are immensely increased. The doctor can reach the patient swiftly (that is, if he makes house calls—but it is not Cadillac's fault if he does not).

Although we are considering the benefits of the automobile, do not forget the advantages of its brother on the road, the truck —the goods-carrying vehicle that supplies us all with economic life. There are few material commodities in this country that are not delivered by truck. Trucks also provide us with services. We take it for granted that a small van will come to our door to bring a man and tools to fix our telephone, our TV, or our plumbing.

The truck offers an excellent analogy to the automobile in terms of its adaptability and decentralization. There is no question that the railroad is much cheaper in moving goods per unit of distance, but it loses out to the truck's flexibility of operation and freedom from connections or transfers. Even a compromise solution that seemed so promising back in the 1950s—"piggy-backing" trailers on railroad flatcars—has not worked out as well as its promoters had expected. In almost all cases it is faster and more efficient, economical, and reliable to drive each trailer individually from its origin to its destination with single truck-tractor units than to drive the trailers to a railroad station, load them on flatcars, ship the flatcars to the terminal, unload and hitch the trailers to new tractor units, and drive them to the final destination. There are too many complications in that system. Point-to-point, door-to-door, is the way to go.

But I have been saving the biggest advantage of the auto-highway system for last: It gives personalized flexibility. It goes where you want, when you want, by the route you select. You do not have to wait for it on a street corner or in a railroad station. You do not have to wonder if it is going to show up at all. You do not have to adjust your time of departure or arrival to suit the plans of some employee of a private corporation or a public authority. You do not have to limit the choice of your place of living, working, visiting, or playing because of the limited service provided by a collective transportation system. You do not have to leave early to catch the last train or bus.

Because the highway system provides access to almost every point, you can go almost anywhere in these United States. If the preferred route is blocked or congested by some failure or by heavy traffic, you can select an alternate route. In theory, as well as in practice, the number of routes between any two points in the United States approaches infinity. In selecting a route, you are not committed in advance—you can change your mind. Furthermore, you may elect to make several stops along the way. In other words, you have control over your own mobility—this is the clincher. There are few things in our society, and fewer with each passing year, that offer us so much individual freedom.

3.

Phony Costs of the Automobile

I think the last chapter ended with a very impressive list of the benefits of the automobile. Perhaps you never thought about them in exactly those terms, but more likely than not you were familiar with them. In fact, there probably is nothing on the list that you did not know already. Perhaps one reason that you never stopped to consider all the advantages of the car is that it has increasingly been under attack in recent years—despite the patent advantages the auto has over all other modes of transportation, advantages demonstrated by the affection the American people hold for it and by the fact that it has utterly defeated all rival systems. People who dislike the auto-highway system prefer to denigrate or disregard its obvious benefits and concentrate instead on its costs. Almost all public literature produced in the United States during the last twenty years has been hostile to the automobile. Some of the auto's shortcomings are quite considerable and serious, but critics have also invented or distorted facts to make the auto-highway system seem more costly than it really is. Let me lay out and refute some of the phony costs attributed to the car.

The auto-highway system discriminates
against the poor.

Although 85 percent of Americans have an automobile available to their household, some 15 percent do not. Some of this 15 percent are wealthy urban cosmopolitans who prefer to invest their luxury income in other goods and services, and either rent cars, take taxis, or perhaps occasionally deign to use collective transportation; such people would not seem to constitute a severe social problem (although as we shall see later, they are a key group in determining our attitudes toward the automobile). In addition, however, a small percentage of the population simply cannot afford to own a car. Because the automobile is the dominant system, this latter group is said to be immobilized—and therefore the car itself is bad.

Well, this argument can only be characterized as mindless egalitarianism. Suppose that a doctor invented a cure for the common cold that was too expensive for 10 to 20 percent of the population. Would we then prohibit its use because it was not available to a small portion at the bottom of our society? Obviously not; those concerned with equity would demand that it be made available to the poor through some sort of public support. Indeed, this is what has historically been done with medicine—those who can pay, do—and the rest get "charity" care. The contention that the auto-highway system discriminates against the poor is specious.

The automobile-highway system discriminates
against minority groups.

Since there are relatively more poor people in minority groups than in the majority white population, any system distributed on the basis of ability to pay is bound to "discriminate against" minority groups. It is a statistical fact that black Americans, as well as Mexican-Americans and Indians, have fewer cars than the majority white population. These groups are simply less prosperous on the whole; you would expect them to own fewer cars. The answer to this particular problem would be to arrange matters so that these people have more money and therefore easier access to cars, if they want them—not to do away with autos altogether.

The automobile system particularly discriminates against the inner-city poor.

This thesis is just silly. Those parts of the United States best served by alternatives to the auto—best equipped with collective transportation systems—are the inner cities where the poor live. These high-density areas were built around streetcar, bus, and rapid transit lines. The poor are concentrated in such places because most Americans want suburban living with cars; those with money moved out to the suburbs while the poor moved from rural areas into the less desirable and therefore less expensive city housing. For the bulk of these in-migrants, relocating thus resulted in an improvement in personal mobility. It is a lot easier to get around downtown Detroit or Philadelphia than rural Mississippi or Georgia.

Moreover, emphasizing the poverty and immobility of the inner-city poor embodies a fundamentally racist attitude. Every study, all available data, and ordinary observation reveal that most people who live in the so-called inner cities or ghettos are not poor. They are working-class people who, of course, have cars. Anybody with a steady job can afford to and usually does buy a car.

Ah, but the inner-city poor are caught in a vicious circle, according to the critics of the automobile. They can afford a car only if they can find work, and the jobs are out in the suburbs where the poor cannot get to them. This is a nasty form of illogic. Most jobs are not yet in the suburbs—employment in almost all cities has grown faster than the population, or grown while population was dropping, or dropped less rapidly than population. Most American cities—with the obvious exceptions of the supercities, such as New York, Los Angeles, and Chicago—are also rather small, and it is not very far from the central city to the suburbs. Indeed, in most places the inner-city dweller is better located to select a job than the suburban resident is. The inner-city resident lives at the hub of the wheel, and he can commute outward in any direction. He has the added advantage of going against the dominant traffic patterns. The most casual observation of urban freeways in any major center reveals large amounts of out-commutation. Consider the relative disadvantage of the suburban dweller, who has to fight his way downtown from a peripheral location through the rush-hour traffic.

The notion that a potential jobholder cannot get work because he lacks the brains or initiative to find his way to an employment interview slanders the urban worker; it is an insult that cannot be explained except as ordinary racism. Despite all the sociologists' talk about the disruptions of urban life, most inner-city dwellers do have family and friends who would lend them a car or give them a lift. Failing that, there is public transportation available. If a man is not working, he has time to take the bus out to the factory or wherever the job is, and if there is no bus he can take a taxicab.

Some of these foolish prejudices so captured the minds of some big thinkers in the bureaucracy that experiments were actually conducted. The Ford Motor Company, which should have known better, actually went to the trouble of offering free bus service from central Detroit to its River Rouge plant in the suburbs. The venture was a flop. Why? Everybody in the inner city who could work or would work already had a job. They had somehow managed to find their way, without special help, out to River Rouge or elsewhere, or to the hundreds of thousands of jobs within the city of Detroit. Similar experiments were held in Watts and St. Louis, with equally dismal results.

Now, I hope that the reader is very tough, because I am going to call attention to some rather unfashionable evidence. First, the traditionally lowest paid members in the urban labor force—

the domestic servants—have managed to get to work for generations without automobiles. Second, if anyone has any illusions
about the immobility of the urban poor in America, I strongly
suggest that he spend a few hours in front of a welfare center
in a major city and watch the quality and variety of vehicles
dropping off applicants and recipients.

This is not the place to discuss the causes and cures of unemployment. Let me merely say that people are unemployed
because jobs are unavailable, or because they do not wish to
work, for whatever reason—not because they are too dumb to
find their way to the job or because the employer is too dumb
to know where to recruit them.

The automobile discriminates against the elderly.

Absolutely right. People who are too old to drive are considerably immobilized. So are those too old to climb the steps of a
bus, and those too old to walk. Age reduces abilities at differing
rates for different people and for different faculties. But this is
a problem of age, not of the automobile. Fortunately, many old
people have relatives to drive them around. Unfortunately, because of increased longevity, larger and larger numbers of the
aged are not living with relatives. This is a terrible social problem affecting all parts of our society. We really do not know
what to do with many old people, and we feel guilty. But there
is no way that the automobile can be blamed. Before the automobile, everybody was immobile. Now only some of the aged
are.

The auto-highway system has flattened
vast areas of our cities.

This is the argument that highways, particularly expressways,
have been driven through poor areas, shattering neighborhoods,
and causing grave hardship to the urban poor and benefiting
prosperous suburbanites. There *was* (note the past tense) some

truth to this, but it was grossly exaggerated. It is difficult to imagine anything that benefits most of society without harming some parts of it, but in the case of expressway construction the narrow training of the highway engineers has minimized the social cost. The engineers sought the cheapest route between point A and point B, and the least expensive route normally caused the least dislocation. Most new urban highways were built on vacant or underutilized land, such as decaying or abandoned waterfronts. Residential areas were normally skirted, and when it was necessary to cut through them, the cheapest and therefore worst were selected.

Happily, the post–World War II era saw the greatest improvement of the quality of working-class housing in human history. The old inner-city areas were rapidly being depopulated and abandoned as their former residents moved up and out to better housing. In most cases, highway construction was a form of slum removal; construction was preceded by demolishing areas that for the most part would have been liquidated shortly anyway, mostly by individual choice. Often, the owners (who were usually resident owners) got more from condemnation by the state than they would have from a private buyer. Needless to say, in some cases, highway construction was imperfectly matched to necessary demolition; there were some serious mistakes and some unnecessary hardship.

The engineers were also guilty of other gross errors—and those good people who fought off attempts to build expressways along San Francisco's and New Orleans' waterfronts have done the nation a great service. It is excellent that someone is keeping a critical eye on the highway builders, but it should not be forgotten that the great bulk of highway mileage in this country did not have dislocating effects; most was laid on vacant land. Building expressways in existing high-density areas is an excellent example of the difficulties of retrofit, of fixing something already established; fortunately, the era of this kind of construction is over. Almost all of the necessary inner-city expressways are now in place. There are a few more that would be desirable from the point of view of their metropolitan regions, though these are unlikely to be built now because of neighborhood resistance. But this is a local problem. Almost all new mileage will be built on undeveloped land to open up new areas for urban development.

If you suspect that my use of qualifiers such as "almost all" is covering many horrible atrocities, let me suggest that you get a map of your city, and measure as roughly as you want the total area of whatever you care to define as the "inner city" or "neighborhoods" or "residential areas." Then measure the length of expressways that cross those areas, making sure you know which expressways were put in after those areas were built. Assume that the right-of-way of an expressway is roughly 100 feet wide; since there are 5,280 feet in a mile, an expressway is .02 miles wide. Multiply that by the number of miles of expressways, and then divide the product by the total square miles of inner city, neighborhoods, or residential areas. In every city I have looked at, the resulting figure is well under 5 percent. In New York and Philadelphia it is under 1 percent.

What, you say, less than 5 percent of our cities is in highways? No, in expressways. People who argue that expressways chop up our cities usually, perhaps deliberately, confuse the issue by citing the total percentage of land area devoted to all highways. They include parts of the city that are not expressways, that were dedicated as streets before the development began. Indeed, these streets made possible the development. It is not that the highway is devouring the city, but that the highway creates the city. All of our cities grew up around streets and roads. The road patterns of all of our major inner cities—in Manhattan, Washington, Philadelphia, Detroit, Chicago—were laid out and the streets were dedicated before anybody even thought of the automobile.

The highway is "paving over" the countryside.

This is related to the preceding argument. A few simple figures can put this delusion to rest. According to Department of Transportation estimates, there are 3.8 million miles of highways in the United States. If we assume that they are on the average forty feet wide (most of them are city streets or rural roads ranging from twenty to thirty feet wide) the total highway area of the U.S. is about 30,000 square miles—or 1 percent of the national land area, excluding Alaska. Another 1 percent of the total would be taken up by areas reserved for parking, if there were thirty spaces for each of the 100 million cars—I suspect there are many fewer. In addition, there are unmeasured miles of private roads, mostly driveways. Most of the total highway area is now paved, but this was not always so. Over the past fifty years, what has been "paved over" is not the countryside, but previously existing roads. Before being "paved over," the country was covered by dirt roads. We have actually added surprisingly little highway mileage in the last half century—in 1921 the country had just under 3.2 million miles.

The automobile has destroyed our cities.

According to this hypothesis, the advents of the automobile and highway have caused our cities to suffer "urban sprawl" and the destruction of city life, resulting in the current urban problems, slums, fiscal difficulties, and the devouring of the countryside by ticky-tacky housing. This is a grave charge against the automobile, and to be candid, it cannot be objectively refuted. I can only present an alternative view of the situation, and allow the reader to decide whether the car is a hero or a villain.

The automobile unquestionably contributed to the destruction of our cities—if you mean what have passed for cities through most of history. Until the automobile appeared, there was a clear distinction between city and country. The city could be identified by its high concentration of population and buildings. The area was small and the density high because the transportation systems were inadequate. For most of urban history, city size was limited by the distances that people could walk, and for the last century by the limits of collective transit lines.

However, with the availability of the automobile and the much greater range thus permitted almost everyone, the cities began to spread out rapidly, and the density of buildings and people per unit of land area dropped precipitously. The automobile did not cause these changes, but its availability made them possible. With improved transportation, people had wider choices of where to live and work. Beginning with the very rich, and eventually extending down to the prosperous working classes, most opted for what we call "suburbia." Remember, the automobile did not require that people move from high-density tenements and row houses to lower-density garden apartments and single-family homes; it only offered them the opportunity to do so, and given that chance they selected suburbia.

Most people who comment on urban design and structure have a deep-seated prejudice against suburbia. They see it as an abomination, a pathological form of development. But the great majority of Americans, and people in most countries of the world, prefer it. The history of our nation and culture predisposes people toward rural life and low-density development. All manner of poll data and observation of economic choices indicates that an overwhelming majority prefer low-density single-family housing—which is found in suburbia. Almost everyone wants single-family homes on big lots in open, green communities. The automobile made this preference practical. I would argue that suburban development is not a cost to be charged to the automobile, but a benefit to be assigned to it. The car has made a better quality of life possible for most Americans.

Nonetheless, a significant and vocal minority is nostalgic for the old-style city. Urbanologists such as Jane Jacobs have glorified the traditional high-density walking city. This is certainly a legitimate preference, but one wonders if they have the right to impose it on the rest of us. Most would probably agree that those who want the traditional kind of urban life should have a right to keep it, and that certain parts of our country should be maintained as "urban museums" of that style of existence. It would be a crime to destroy the French Quarter of New Orleans, old Charleston, Newport, Center City Philadelphia,

Georgetown, Greenwich Village, and other interesting pockets of archaic urban living that still survive. But it would be a worse crime to impose this nostalgic existence on the rest of the country, which clearly does not want it.

Most of our so-called urban problems are evidence rather of the desirability of suburbanization. For the very simple reason that they have less money, the poor tend to be concentrated in the older inner cities. A capitalist economy assigns goods on the basis of ability to pay, and the poor thus get the worst of the lot. High-density urban areas are less desirable than other parts of the metropolitan regions, so their property values and rents are lower than in the suburbs. It is not unreasonable that the poor have these areas equipped with the most effective mass transportation facilities simply because they are desired least by the society at large. With a few important exceptions, the general rule in America is that the more money you have the farther you live from the central city, the larger the house and lot you have, and the more likely you are to drive a car.

Furthermore, it is not the automobile that begat suburbanization, which goes back centuries. Those of you who saw the film *A Man for All Seasons* may recall Sir Thomas More commuting to work in the City of London by boat from Chelsea. Chelsea has long been swallowed up in metropolitan London, and practically nobody lives in the old City of London any more.

Automobile-induced suburbanization is devouring the countryside.

According to the 1970 U.S. census, 1.15 percent of the land area of the continental United States was in "urbanized areas," and about another .5 percent in small towns. Thus less than 2 percent of the land area is "urbanized" by the Census Bureau's definition. And the Census Bureau counts an area as urbanized if it has a population density of more than 1,000 people per square mile—which is about 1.5 people per acre, or about one house for every two acres. As you know from looking at the fringes of any of our cities, the countryside is being "devoured" by what A. C. Spectorsky called "exurbia"—single-family houses set down in fields and woods, or more concentrated developments surrounded by fields and parks. It is difficult to think of a more harmonious integration of man and nature, which should by no means be confused with the asphalt and concrete image we have of the older high-density preautomobile city. The automobile makes the garden city possible.

Cities should be for people, not cars.

Well, of course—who would deny it? No one is claiming that cities should be for cars. The debate is whether cities should be primarily for people who use cars, or primarily for people who use other means of transportation. Since almost all people prefer to use cars, keeping automobiles out of the city really means reserving it for the use of only a few people.

The automobile requires that people spend an inordinate amount of time commuting.

This contention is absolutely wrong. Everyone has to make a complicated choice concerning where he is going to work and live. He can take a job close to his residence or one far away. If the distance is too great to commute in a reasonable time or cost, he can move. He must also make a trade-off between the cost of his house and the cost of commuting; for example, many employees of the City of New York commute from northern Westchester and Rockland Counties. They endure a long and expensive daily trip, but can get good single-family houses at a much lower price than they could in the city. As in so many other things, the automobile has thus expanded the choices available to them.

A substantial number of Americans still walk to their jobs. A few, particularly in rural areas, travel what seems to be incredible distances to get to work. But the average American family, according to poll data, appears to regard about twenty minutes as a reasonable time to get to work, and the great majority do reach work within that period. It is often forgotten that the average American, even the average urban American, does not live in a great metropolis. As Messrs. Scanlon and Wattenberg have reminded us, the typical American family lives in a city about the size of Dayton—around 600,000 people. You can live anywhere and work anywhere in metropolitan Dayton and travel the distance in twenty minutes. For most residents of Dayton the time to work is less than ten minutes. Great numbers of long-distance commuters exist only in our very largest metropolitan centers—New York, Los Angeles, and Chicago.

But what of these very big cities? It is true that if you live on eastern Long Island, it takes several hours to get to work in New Jersey, or if you live in the San Fernando valley it takes several hours to reach work in Orange County. So very few people make such trips, and they do so only temporarily, or because something very special about their circumstances makes the commute worthwhile.

Very few people consider such long-distance commuting necessary or desirable—merely a preference among conflicting choices. For several years, by way of example, I lived in Philadelphia and commuted to work by foot—total door-to-door time, three minutes. Under different conditions, I lived in Philadelphia and worked in Westchester County, New York—total door-to-door time, three hours.

But surely, people need not waste forty minutes a day commuting? Apparently it does not bother them very much. Scattered data from around the world suggest that in all urban settings, regardless of the transportation system available, people are willing to spend twenty minutes going to work, whether they travel by foot, bicycle, trolley, rapid transit, or automobile. Substituting the car for the other modes really means that they can go farther within the same twenty minutes, and therefore have greater choice of jobs and/or residences.

The automobile has created congestion.

On the contrary, the automobile has relieved congestion. People who talk about auto congestion cannot have seen a photograph of a major U.S. city before there were cars. The streets were jammed with pedestrians, bicycles, trolley cars, and all manner of horse-drawn vehicles. They were a mess. What people really mean when they complain about congestion is that in certain places there is more traffic now than before. But they do not look at the entire system.

Let me give an example: It is often said that it takes longer to cross Manhattan today than fifty years ago.* Okay—but Manhattan is a much smaller part of metropolitan New York than it was fifty years ago. When we compare the average speed of everybody in the metropolitan area, there is more speed and less congestion.

Furthermore, complaints about congestion are largely the result of heightened standards. When the best we could do was about ten miles an hour on a horse, twenty miles an hour in an automobile seemed like a blazing speed. Now when we expect sixty miles an hour in a car, twenty miles an hour, bumper-to-bumper, is a maddening crawl. What I call "Bruce-Briggs law of traffic" applies: At any level of traffic speed, any delay is intolerable. To someone accustomed to the traffic in New York it is amusing to hear the residents of Houston and Atlanta complain about the highway congestion: imagine, in rush-hour bottlenecks they have to slow down to thirty-five miles an hour!

The conventional cures for congestion are twofold: increased traffic capacity, usually by building more highways; or reduced traffic, usually by shifting commuters to other forms of transpor-

* Notice that the comparison is made with Manhattan fifty years ago, not seventy-five years ago. Seventy-five years ago was preautomotive, unquestionably more congested and slower; fifty years ago was probably faster, because only the prosperous owned cars or could afford taxis, and the bulk of the populace was jammed into subways.

tation. As we shall see, each of these raises very difficult problems. Better solutions can be derived from a more fundamental
understanding of the phenomena. Congestion is caused by an
inadequate ratio of highway capacity to "traffic generators"—
that is, by too many people having too few thoroughfares for
them to go where they wish. Merely building more roads is not
enough if the construction is simultaneously accompanied by
development and more traffic generators. This is what has been
happening in Los Angeles. The 1950s saw a major investment
in freeway development, but also the removal of the height
limitation on buildings in Los Angeles, which pushed up densities, and therefore created more traffic, which required still
more freeways. Fortunately, most American cities have not gone
the way of Los Angeles. As highways have been built, the population has dispersed along them, so that densities and therefore
potential congestion have decreased. The entire system of the
automobile must be taken into account: with cars, people spread
out, populations drop, businesses follow their clients and workers to the suburbs, traffic generators decentralize, traffic diffuses.
This process is often seen as the cause of congestion; in fact, it
is the solution.

But, in a considerable sense, complaining about congestion is
rather like complaining about having to wait in line to buy tickets
to a hit Broadway show. Congestion is an excess of success.
Congestion really means that people so prefer driving that they
are willing to tolerate crawling bumper-to-bumper.

The automobile has ruined the mass transit system.

Yes, the introduction of the automobile-highway system permitted people to abandon other modes. Because collective transportation systems require significant volumes of traffic to be
economic, the loss of part of their ridership increased the unit
cost of operation thus requiring higher fares, which prompted
more people to switch to the cars, creating a downward spiral.
People selected the superior system; that goes without saying.

There would be something wrong with the automobile if it had not substituted for the inferior systems. One might just as reasonably say that the refrigerator ruined the ice box, or that shoes ruined bare feet.

The automobile is subsidized.

In common usage, a subsidy means that the government is giving you money. To anybody who drives a car and pays license and registration fees, tolls, and gasoline taxes, the idea that the automobile is subsidized seems ridiculous. But "subsidy" has the broader meaning to economists, social scientists, and politicians that some activity is not paying its full cost to society. Presumably what is intended by this is not that the automobile is subsidized, but that *users* of cars and highways are. Critics will cite the enormous outlays of public funds for building and maintaining highways. Their case would be a little more credible if they also mentioned the enormous direct levies laid on highway users. At the time of writing, there is a four-cents-a-gallon federal gasoline tax, which means that someone who drives 10,000 miles a year and gets 15 miles to the gallon pays about $27 a year. He also pays state gasoline taxes, on the average of eleven cents a gallon, or about $70 a year. He is also subject to a fee for the renewal of his license, as well as an annual registration fee. Tolls are common in the eastern states; some states also levy a personal property tax on cars. Trucks pay similar taxes, but at much higher levels because they are heavier and create more wear and tear on the roads. (Perhaps you have seen signs on big trailers on the road reading "this vehicle pays $5,000 in road taxes.")

From 1920 to about 1970 highway-user levies were approximately equal to highway expenditures. The gap has widened since then, because the federal excise taxes on automobiles and parts were dropped in 1971 and because inflation has pushed up highway costs faster than the politicians have been willing to raise taxes. Nevertheless, in 1974, total government highway-user revenues were $18.8 billion while total expenditures were $24.5 billion. Since there are 135 million vehicles, the subsidy per vehicle was $42. If we cared, this could easily have been made up by raising registration fees or gasoline taxes or by some other direct levy on motorists. In fact, nobody really cares if the highways as a whole balance their books.

Now, it can be claimed that this form of accounting is inadequate. There are many costs of the highway that do not appear in the government budget. For example, I have heard it said that we should charge to the highways what the rights-of-way would be worth if they were devoted to some other purpose. What would Main Street be worth if it was developed? That would be an interesting calculation, although a very difficult one. But if you make that estimate you should make the other relevant calculation—what would the nonhighway property in the United States be worth if it had no highway access? Without access, property is worthless, and therefore cannot generate tax or other revenue. But this is a game for academic economists, not for the real world.

A more valid objection is that even if the total revenue from highway users has been nearly equal to the total expenditures, the distribution among governments has been inequitable. Most revenues are realized by federal and state governments, and even substantial subventions do not entirely make up for county and local expenditures. Few cities have the means to levy directly on the automobile, but do have large expenditures for street maintenance, cleaning, snow clearance, lighting, and traffic control. Moreover, the pattern of state expenditures, especially for new highway construction and the paving of dirt and gravel roads, favors rural areas over urban areas, whose needs are more likely to be reconstruction and maintenance. Study after study of urban highway costs and expenditures has shown that municipal costs of servicing cars are not entirely supported by levies on highway users, and that other revenue sources must be tapped to make up the difference.

This can be said to be inequitable. But we forget that until the early 1960s, it was considered proper that the prosperous cities be taxed to support impecunious rural areas. The paving of rural highways with urban money was regarded as—and was in fact —an income transfer to the poor. While it is still the case that most rural areas are less prosperous than even the shabbiest cities, today's polity prefers to view "central cities" as more deserving of largess. How ironic that the present heightened concern with the equity of public spending leads many to the *ex post facto* application of today's standards. It is not the first time that the previous generation's "social justice" is seen as today's "rip-off."

Another argument holds that merely counting direct government costs of the automobile is grossly inadequate. The automobile has large indirect costs, imposed on the government and the public at large—so-called neighborhood or spillover effects, or externalities. Some of these are obvious and accurate—pollution, safety—and will be discussed at length in later chapters, but pursuing "externalities" much beyond the most direct rapidly leads to absurdity. It is simply not possible to even estimate all the costs of the automobile.

Take police as an example. Even if there were no cars there would have to be policemen. Most police on patrol try to prevent all manner of crimes, not just traffic offenses. Calculating the costs of policing the automobile is as impossible and unproductive as attempting to estimate how much rape prevention or the apprehension of fugitives cost. Street lighting presents a similar analytical problem. In addition to aiding traffic, most street lights also help pedestrians, merchants, and homeowners, and assist in crime prevention. How can we say how much should be assessed to which function?

Even the highways themselves cannot entirely be charged to motor vehicle users. Most highways are also used by pedestrians. In cities and suburbs, streets and roads also serve as rights-of-way for water, sewer, and gas mains. The air space over highways is used for electric and telephone lines, whose standards are usually placed in the rights-of-way. In highly developed areas, highway rights-of-way (remember that sidewalks are technically parts of streets) are used for fire alarm boxes, fire hydrants, police call boxes, telephone booths, mail boxes, and litter baskets. These are relatively trivial uses, but they add up.

Moreover, the highway itself serves as an open space for the abutting properties. Unless our cities are to be rabbit warrens like the preindustrial cities of the Orient, this function is necessary for light and air.

On a broader perspective, if we are to charge "external" costs to the highway, we must also credit it with the external *benefits*. How can we calculate what roads and automobiles are worth to our people? The economic benefits are obviously incredible, amounting to a major chunk of our gross national product—several hundreds of billions of dollars a year. Highways and motor vehicles permit a more efficient distribution of goods and services throughout the country. How do we know that the auto-highway system is more efficient? Because businessmen calculate its benefits in choosing it over other modes of transportation. If widgets can be shipped by truck more rapidly, more reliably, and more economically than by any other means, that much additional speed, reliability, and economy, calculated in dollars, is added to our gross national product and therefore to our national wealth, standard of living, and quality of life.

Similarly, the increased utility of the auto-highway system permits the more efficient allocation of labor, with the effect of reducing unemployment. People have many more job choices. And there are many other benefits that are difficult to count in money and therefore not normally considered by economists. How much is it worth to enable people to visit their relatives more often? What is the value of getting people to the hospital faster? Can the value of meeting faraway friends be assessed? Or the value of being able to visit parks once reserved for the rich?

The reader must pardon me for going on at such length concerning this subsidy argument, but it is taken seriously by all too many politicians, transportation planners, professors, and journalists. It is even used in fights between different highway users. For example, the American Automobile Association claims trucks are not bearing their fair share of user taxes because the cost of building and maintaining highways to support the extra burden of trucks far exceeds the taxes on trucks. Yet the whole economy and therefore the total tax revenues depend on the transportation of goods by truck.

The subsidy arguments sometimes approach the rococo. It has been written that off-peak-hour drivers "subsidize" rush-hour drivers because highways must be constructed for peak loads at enormous additional expense. But most of the off-peak-hour users also drive in rush hours, too—so they are "subsidizing" themselves. In most cities, almost everyone drives at peak hours, or has a member of the family who does, or in some way benefits from the goods and services produced by those who drive at those times—so everybody is "subsidizing" everybody else.

If we were to estimate the total costs and benefits of the automobile, we must compare the existing system with an automobileless America; that would be not an analysis but science fiction. In calculating the cost of the car, like anything else, we should stick as closely as possible to hard, measurable, out-of-pocket expenditures. The automobile is such a boon to the entire society that we should be pleased that these costs can be paid directly by users.

To illustrate some of the difficulties in many anti-automobile analyses, let me apply some of the same reasoning to another form of mass transportation—walking. If we assume 1.5 miles of walking per day per person, total annual "passenger miles" is about 100 billion miles, roughly a tenth of automobile use. Walking is the most widely available transportation system in the world; almost everyone has the necessary equipment and the skills. All structures are provided with walking facilities. Some portions of thoroughfares—not more than 5 percent—are provided with sidewalks reserved for walking. Streets are also used for walking. So to calculate the costs of walking we would have to count all of the capital costs of providing all of those corridors, paths, sidewalks, and some parts of the streets.

But walking has some severe drawbacks. It is wasteful of energy, the mechanism being very inefficient in turning solar energy and hydrocarbons into motion. This system produces a particularly noxious and potentially dangerous emission that costs the public billions to keep from polluting waterways.* Although walking is obviously very popular, its limited consumer acceptance is evident from the fact that, given a choice, a traveler normally opts for alternative modes. Walking is also unsafe. No hard data are available, but several tens of thousands are killed walking every year. Moreover, there is congestion where too many people walk at the same time. Now, if we apply to walking the type of economic analysis widely applied to driving, we must conclude that since it is not taxed, walking is heavily subsidized by the government! The labor expended in training people to walk is also not taxed, and is therefore subsidized (not to mention its "exploitation" of women). Compelling the use of pedometers to tax walking would doubtless cut down the activity; however, there is not yet any interest in this solution to the "problem."

THE SPECIAL SINS OF
DETROIT

In the demonology of the anti-auto forces, the American automobile manufacturing industry plays a leading role. While the car is a general evil, "Detroit" is an especially malevolent institution producing a particularly abominable form of motor vehicle. Most of the alleged sins of Detroit are as absurd as the general objections to the automobile.

---

* An anti-auto picket in Los Angeles is reported to have waved a sign reading "People don't pollute"—a triumph of ideological sloganeering over the most ordinary experience of humanity.

The highway lobby is responsible for highways.

This argument holds that we build highways only because the highway lobby—the contractors, asphalt producers, oil companies, and especially the automobile companies—have willed them. The presumed evidence is that all of these organizations have advocated highways, have lobbied for it, and have profited from their construction. How can one respond to this absurdity? Highways were built before anybody ever thought of automobiles. Moreover, before government became very active, private interests were providing highways—early turnpikes, some toll roads, and many bridges. For instance, the Ashley River Bridge in Charleston was originally a private venture. Even in the early 1960s the Atlantic City Expressway was financed as a private investment.

It happens that government has built most highways because the problems of land assembly and assigning of costs have been so difficult that market solutions would be impractical. Politicians have merely been responding to public desire for roads. Rural dwellers in the 1920s and 1930s demanded more and better roads and elected "populist" candidates who promised to build them. Now that major expressways have been constructed they are taken for granted, but those of us who can remember fighting from Washington to New York up old U.S. Route 1, wandering through the streets of Baltimore, and waiting for the ferry over the Delaware River, can appreciate the public investment. Saying that highways have been built because the highway lobby wanted them is rather like saying that social security is the result of agitation by the geriatric lobby, or that medicare came about because the doctors wanted it.

Highways have been built in response to public demands. The only unwanted roads that have been built are a few local thoroughfares. Almost everybody wants roads, but they would prefer to have them somewhere else; in many cases local opposition has been overcome by the general interest. But roads in general and most roads in particular are merely a rational response by politicians to national need and public demand.

We buy cars only because Detroit wants us to.

This is known as the "institutionalist" theory of consumption. It is a necessary part of a certain kind of contemporary elitist theory. Since we Americans have a democratic faith that the people are fundamentally good, and since people often do things we do not like, we must contrive a theory that they have been misled by malevolent and sinister forces. This is a typically American explanation of why things go wrong in America. (As you shall see later on, I am going to argue very much the same thing in this book.)

The anti-automobile forces cannot openly blame the all-good and all-wise American people, so they blame Detroit. The argument is similar to the "proof" of the power of the highway lobby—because GM, Ford, and Chrysler are pushing cars and making money selling them, the conclusion is that we have cars only because Detroit has willed that we must.

Of course, the opposite is true. Detroit profits because people want cars and are willing to buy them. Arguing that people buy cars because Detroit wants them to is rather like saying that people have babies so that Gerber Products can sell baby food, or that people indulge in sex so that Trojan can sell prophylactics.

Detroit "plans" the auto market and manipulates the consumer with advertising.

This contention presupposes that people are dumb. But people do not buy cars because of advertising; it merely tends to affect marginal choices among cars that are basically the same. Underneath the chrome, big Chevrolets, Pontiacs, Oldsmobiles, and Buicks differ little, a Plymouth is the same as a Dodge or a Chrysler, a Ford is the same as a Mercury, and all of them are very similar to one another. The reason for this homogeneity is that the automobile industry is highly competitive and relies on mass production, so manufacturers try to move toward the center of the market.

There are too many examples of the failure of advertising to make a credible case that marketing can force an unwanted product on the American people. The Edsel had massive advertising, but it appeared at a time when the middle-price auto market was collapsing, and it failed utterly. British cars had the lead in the foreign car market and tried to extend their advantage with massive advertising. In the early 1960s Triumph tried to push their small sedan with a big campaign that "the British are coming"—but the car was a piece of junk, and quickly went. Renault sold few cars with its cute ads featuring little balloons. Conversely, Volkswagen initially built its market with no advertising at all. Cars sell because people want them—which one they choose is largely a function of engineering, styling, past experience, knowledge of the dealer, and word of mouth. Once the word gets out that a certain car is a dog, the manufacturer or importer is in big trouble, and no amount of advertising can save him.

Still, I do not suppose I will convince anybody of the powerlessness of marketing—the advertising industry has done too good a job of selling itself.

As for "planning," recent fluctuations in automobile demand have driven the manufacturers crazy. They were unprepared for the oil boycott and were left with huge stocks of large cars. They tore out their assembly lines at enormous costs to produce smaller cars, but by that time the market had slackened and the demand for big cars increased again, and they were stuck with yards full of subcompacts.

Detroit builds big gas-guzzling dinosaurs.

Yes, Detroit builds mostly big cars that get lower gas mileage than European cars. The gas mileage issue has been considerably exaggerated; gasoline has been very inexpensive in the United

States. With all the talk of enormous profits of those bad oil companies, it is interesting to note that throughout the 1950s and 1960s, oil increased in price less quickly than most other consumer goods—so that compared with incomes the price of gasoline was dropping. With gas at thirty cents a gallon, less than half the European price, it is understandable that gasoline mileage was not a major concern to car buyers and therefore car manufacturers. Some simple numbers make this point: if you drive 10,000 miles a year and gas is thirty cents a gallon and you get 10 miles per gallon, then gasoline costs you $300 a year. If you get 20 miles per gallon, the cost is $150 a year. But 25 miles per gallon cuts your annual expenditure only to $120, 30 miles per gallon reduces it only to $100, and 40 miles to the gallon only to $75. In other words, in gasoline consumption costs, the point of diminishing returns is quickly reached. With cheap gasoline, good gas mileage is a trivial consideration in selecting a car. People are willing to pay a bit more for a large, comfortable, fast car.

As for the complaints about auto size, most people prefer big cars, which are simply more spacious, comfortable, powerful, and convenient. I happen to like small cars—I drive a Honda—but that is not a general taste, and I can understand why Detroit has not concentrated on building cars for me. A commercial enterprise makes money by producing what most people want.

But it is incorrect that Detroit builds only big cars and that the models have been growing over the years. Yes, the top lines have been; the largest of the Chevrolets and Fords have steadily grown in size and weight over the last forty years. But that is misleading. Look at the accompanying chart (Figure 1). As the "standard" car has gotten bigger, the auto companies have been sandwiching other lines under it. In fact, it is archaic to think of the standard "full-size" Chevrolet as typical of the brand.

Let's trace this development. In the early 1950s American cars started growing, but some of the minor companies tried to squeeze in under the Big Three. Crosley, Willys, Hudson, and Nash came out with smaller models. All of them flopped, except

Figure 1: THE GROWTH OF CARS?

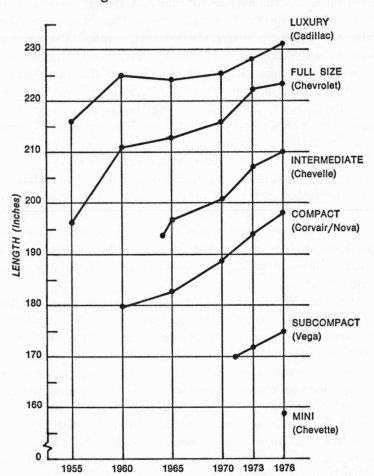

Nash's Rambler. But in the late 1950s, the regular lines were becoming so massive that the Rambler and foreign cars began to penetrate the market. The big American manufacturers fought the trend, first by bringing in their "captive imports," Opel, Vauxhall, Simca, and English Ford. In 1959 they countered with the first line of domestic compacts—Falcon, Corvair, Valiant, and Studebaker Lark. This was not sufficient, so in the mid-1960s the "intermediate" lines—Fairlane, Chevelle, and Fury—between the compact and the "standard" models were introduced. All of these cars tended to become bloated, and again foreign car sales grew, this time particularly the Japanese imports. So Detroit again countered with its subcompacts—Vega, Pinto, Bobcat, and Astre. But that still wasn't enough, and now Chrysler is importing Mitsubishi cars under its own trade names, GM is producing the minicompact Chevette, and Ford's Fiesta has just appeared.

Detroit wants to make money by selling cars. It will sell you any kind you want. But like most other institutions, carmakers tend to be conservative. A particular problem is with the merchandizing and sales force, who are conditioned to like and sell the big car. The whole organization of the industry has a midwestern cast to it, and it has some trouble adapting to alternative products and emerging life-styles.*

The accusation that Detroit builds "dinosaurs" implies it is making machines that are obsolete, both socially and technologically. The social arguments rest heavily on the assessment of material and energy supplies, which I will consider in detail in a later chapter. But I think Detroit deserves a defense on the technological issue. Compared with some European cars, American cars are mechanically retarded. Although the detail engineering is superb, the basic design—front engine, wishbone front suspension, solid rear axle, and drum brakes—is forty years old. It is hard for us to realize now that Detroit was once the leader in technological innovations. It was the great General Motors engineers—such as Leland, Kettering, and Olley—who introduced quality mass production, the self-starter, and independent front suspension to the world. A little later GM also led with important detail improvements—automatic transmission, power steering, air conditioning. Cadillac's overhead valve V-8

---

* GM's much vaunted reduction of the size of its big cars in 1977 need not be taken too seriously. The "full-size" Chevrolet was cut back to its early 1960s dimensions.

of 1949 set a worldwide standard—even Rolls-Royce copied it.

But for the last twenty years, General Motors—though the leader of the industry—has suffered an almost continuous run of humiliating failures whenever it tried to introduce some major new device or product. In the mid-1950s electric eye headlight dipping was tried and failed. In the late 1950s air suspension was introduced and flopped. Fuel injection in the Corvette was a dead end. In the early 1960s GM tried a major innovation in car design—a relatively large air-cooled rear engine car, the Corvair, which took several years to debug. At the same time GM tried a tricky flexible drive shaft and a 4-cylinder engine, cut off a V-8, in the Pontiac Tempest—which failed commercially. A small aluminum V-8 for Buick did not succeed nor did a V-6, which flopped and was sold to Jeep. Turbo-charging on the Corvair Monza and Olds F-85 found few buyers. In the mid-1960s the front-drive Olds Toronado was a remarkable technical achievement, but the system was not imitated. In 1970 the Vega was introduced with an aluminum block, without conventional iron cylinder linings. It has had so much trouble that Chevrolet has been obliged to provide a five-year guarantee to assure potential buyers that the difficulties have been straightened out. During the same period, Chrysler and Ford made conventional machines and profited from GM's mistakes. Small wonder that Detroit has the idea that innovation does not pay, preferring to invest its best brains in cost reduction—that is, until the last decade, when the devilish job of meeting ever-changing federal safety, emissions, and fuel economy standards diverted most of the intellectual energy of the auto industry.

Detroit cars have terrible handling and brakes.

This is the "Detroit Iron" complaint, particularly widespread among the sports car set on the East and West Coasts. The accusation seems credible, unless you know Detroit. In the Detroit metropolitan area, as in most of the American heartland, the terrain is almost absolutely flat, the roads are laid out in a straight grid, and there are few turns or curves, only sharp right-angle corners. These conditions have determined the design of the American car. It needs good acceleration, but not the capability to negotiate winding roads. Driving in Detroit requires following a straight line, occasionally braking for a sharp corner, and accelerating out of that corner. A car does not need very good brakes because the sight lines are so long. The narrow roads and greatly varying terrain of Europe and Japan put more of a premium on handling and brakes. It is understandable why many drivers on both coasts of the U.S. have found European and Japanese cars more suitable.

But this increased interest in handling did not go unnoticed in Detroit, and the capability of American cars has been greatly improved over the last generation. Today they are at least roughly comparable to equivalent European models, especially if ordered with the very inexpensive optional packages of stiffer springs, shocks, and other suspension parts that improve handling—though somewhat to the detriment of the riding comfort which is a primary concern of most American drivers.

Detroit has suppressed other engine systems.

It has been argued that because of the huge investment required to produce internal combustion engines, along with its bull-headed obstinacy and its generally antisocial attitude, Detroit has deliberately crippled research into other types of power sources. Critics are not much impressed by the industry's repeated experiments over the last twenty-five years with gas turbines, sterling engines, steam engines, electric cars, and fuel cells. They claim that the point of these was merely to produce specious evidence that such systems would not work. Why then did General Motors ballyhoo its gas turbine and sterling-powered "dream cars" as automobiles of the future? Why did Chrysler build an entire series of experimental gas turbine cars in the early 1960s? Why has Ford been a leader in fuel cell technology? Why have GM and Ford built a long series of electric and steam prototypes? Why did Mr. William Lear, the promoter of the most serious steam car project, testify thus before the Congress:

> He (Ed Cole, President of General Motors) said, "What do you want?" I said, I want a bus, I want cars and transmissions and generators and so forth.
>
> He said, "We will consider it." Two weeks later he said, "We are willing to give you everything you want." They appointed Mr. Don Manning, whom I believe was chief engineer of their bus and truck division, as my liaison with the company.
>
> As a result all of these things were provided me without charge and without obligation except to show them what emissions we obtained.
>
> This, of course, will be public information in any case. So they really asked for nothing, and readily furnished the materials to me.
>
> As a matter of fact, Mr. Manning at one time said that "It normally takes a writ of habeas corpus to get anything out of this corporation."
>
> For Bill Lear, they got it out immediately. I did have that cooperation from General Motors. I've never asked them for money, although I did discuss with Mr. Cole a possibility that we would need money to go beyond making the engineering prototype to the production prototype.
>
> I estimated that we would need $35 million. He corrected me by saying it would be nearer $50 million. However, he said, "When the time comes General Motors will be standing in line with their money in their hand."

Not that GM was being overly generous. When Lear abandoned his steam car quest, he reported there was only "one chance in five hundred thousand" of replacing the internal combustion engine. Detroit knew that already.

The annual model change is wasteful.

Perhaps somebody still does believe in advertising, because the whole idea of an annual model change is fallacious. The

usual "annual model change" is the substitution of some strips
of chrome with some minor mechanical changes that would
have had to be made anyway. A major retooling of the body
occurs every three, four, or five years at most. The compact
Chevy II, now called the Nova, is on its third body style since
being introduced in 1962. Retooling is enormously expensive,
but would have to be done in any event; the tools that make the
cars wear out and must be replaced. Also, the tooling has to be
changed to make possible improvements.

The car most often cited as a paragon of virtue by those who
advocate dispensing with the annual model change is the basic
Volkswagen, the so-called Beetle. But if you compare the Beetle
today with the Beetle of twenty years ago, you will notice that
although the general shape and layout is the same, practically
every part in the car has changed. And have you priced the
Beetle lately? It's not cheap. The reason is that German labor is
very expensive. Tooling requires a lot of capital, but tooling costs
for mass production are spread over millions of vehicles and
amount to very little compared with labor costs. And how many
Beetles are being sold these days? The car was very advanced
when it was first introduced, but modern technology has passed
it by. Progress requires changes; it does not matter very much
whether they are made gradually in the course of production, or
as annual model changes, or as entirely new models.

Cars wear out too soon.

It would be better if cars lasted longer. During the energy
crisis, the Harris Poll asked if people thought it would be a
good idea if cars went 100,000 miles before being junked.
Seventy-nine percent of the sample said yes. That was a reasonable answer, because the average car *does* last 100,000 miles
before it is junked. The reason cars do not last longer is that
few people want them to. Any car can be kept running forever;
the only problem is the cost. Normally, a ten-year-old car is so
beat up that nobody wants to go to the expense of fixing it.

Auto repairs are custom hand labor, which is inordinately expensive in an economic democracy compared with capital-intensive mass production. Building five new cars is cheaper than completely reconstructing one old one. The very high prices for auto repair parts result from the cost of handling individual pieces. Shipping a whole lot of parts together as an assembled automobile is very cheap. Packaging, handling, and keeping track of individual pieces runs the price of any single item way up.

Actually, American cars last as long as cars anywhere else in the world—indeed, longer than most. In fact, most autos last about a year. Because the American car is used only for about two hours a day, that year of use is spread out over ten years of ownership. Of course, it is possible to make cars last much longer just by maintaining them better. Change the oil more often, grease it, perform the maintenance religiously according to the schedule. Do you? No, that's too much trouble—and you are going to trade it in anyway.

Manufacturing cars to last longer than a year would not be difficult. Always remembering that a chain lasts only as long as its weakest link, it would merely be necessary to do some upgrading to improve resistance to wear, redesign some parts to function effectively when heavily worn, uprate the quality of undercoating and rocker panels, substitute stainless steel and nonferrous alloys for parts that rust, and the like. Not difficult, but expensive—although it is reasonable to assume that a car could last twice as long without costing twice as much.

But would you buy it? Suppose you had a choice of two identical cars in the showroom. Model M would last twice as long as model N, and cost 50 percent more. But all this would mean is that you would own a car that lasts twenty years on the road instead of the normal ten. How many people do you think are interested in buying an auto and keeping it for twenty years? Think back to what was available in 1957. Chevy and Ford had pretty good cars. The Chevy V-8 installed then is still in use—one of the great triumphs of engine design. But since that time there have been twenty years of detail improvement, and I suspect that a twenty-year-old car would not now be satisfactory to most Americans. In 1957, for example, air conditioning was a luxury for only the very rich, now it is nearly ubiquitous. The worldwide consensus seems to be that an automobile should last for a hundred thousand miles.

And while we are talking about longevity, it is surprising how few people keep a car even ten years. A good part of the reason for trading in a car before it has worn out is simple boredom. People get tired of otherwise satisfactory clothes, furniture, houses—and even wives and husbands. The American ideal seems to be to buy a new car and trade it in every three or four years. This system provides a great benefit to the working people of this country, which is not properly appreciated. The main cost of operating an automobile is depreciation, the difference between what it costs new and used. This is absorbed by the relatively prosperous initial buyer. The less prosperous driver then buys the same car second-hand at a considerable markdown. At this stage in its life, the car requires more maintenance, but the second owner is likely to be a working man who is more apt to have the skills necessary to repair it.

This system of an annual model change which has the effect of selling new cars to the well-to-do and providing the less prosperous with high quality second-hand cars was evolved by General Motors during the 1920s. Before then automobile distribution in the U.S. was very much like that in Europe today. One bought a car designed for a given price range and social class. The famous Model T Ford was extremely primitive, but it was cheap and sold in incredible numbers—until people found that they could buy a used Buick for the same price. Europe continues this old system today. A very prosperous German buys a Mercedes-Benz, keeps it for ten years, and then gets a new one. A somewhat less well-off German buys an Opel or a Ford. A white collar or skilled worker buys a Volkswagen. An ordinary semiskilled or unskilled worker cannot afford a car at all. There is a very little trickle down of the better cars to the less prosperous segment of the market.

The European distribution system very nicely reflects a class system where the different life-styles are clearly delineated. The American system reflects the ebb and flow of the fluid American society. It is certainly understandable that would-be elites in America dislike our manner of distribution. Imagine: The working man buys the same sort of car they do. No wonder that significant numbers of the better sort seek to differentiate themselves by obtaining exotic foreign cars.

The automobile embodies irrational and adolescent tendencies.

The assumption is that all devices should be entirely utilitarian. People who have taken this view of the automobile have always bought very plain basic transportation. American Motors and its predecessor, Nash, have long catered to this taste. However, most people like a few additions for aesthetic reasons, or whatever. For a few, perhaps the irrational aspects of the automobile dominate. I do not quite understand why this should bother anybody. If they are willing to pay for irrationality, why not? I think Herman Kahn put it very nicely when he said that buying virility and status for a few extra hundred dollars is a bargain.

The automobile is a status symbol.

Almost every consumer item is a status symbol. Possession of goods is a method of distinguishing one's self from the world, and improving one's self-esteem and presumably one's standing in the eyes of one's neighbors. This is true in all societies—the Bedouin on the desert accumulates camels and decorates his women with jewelry. What is particularly fascinating is that opposition to the automobile on this ground is most prevalent among people who themselves buy automobiles as status symbols. Buyers of Volvos, Mercedes, and Porsches see themselves as high-minded, aesthetic, and sensible—superior in their taste, judgment, and world view to the great unwashed masses in their Buicks, Dodges, and Cadillacs.

Detroit makes a lot of money.

The auto manufacturers are among the largest companies in the country, so it is understandable that they have among the largest absolute profits. But the profit margin per unit of sales and the return on capital are comparable to those of other large manufacturing companies.

The automobile is a monopoly.

There is a long history of the combination of automobile companies. At one time or another in this country, there have been approximately 2,500 manufacturers of automobiles. Almost all of them went broke, and the remainder were absorbed into the surviving companies.

Economies of scale are apparently crucial in making cars. Europe today is going through the same weeding out of companies that the United States went through in the 1920s and 1930s. Most of the smaller makers trying for a mass market are in serious danger of being eaten up by their large neighbors. Lancia has been swallowed by Fiat, Peugeot is just beginning to digest Citroen, Volkswagen has absorbed Audi, Volvo has annexed the Dutch Daf, and the Leyland organization is itself a merger of several previously merged British firms. Apart from some small specialists like Lotus and Avanti, the great names in automobiles are in serious difficulty. Ferrari sold out to Fiat, Maserati and Aston Martin went broke and had to be reorganized, Lamborghini is subsidized by its parent tractor company. Of the remaining independents, only BMW, Porsche, and Rolls-Royce are prospering at building excellent high-quality and very expensive automobiles in relatively large numbers.

No industry has perfect textbook competition, and the auto industry is no exception. The limits on pure competition in building cars are for the most part unobjectionable. First, no one who knows the business doubts that General Motors has the capability to crush its competitors if it so desired. With half of the domestic market, extremely competent management, and the highest profits per unit of production in the industry, General Motors could slash prices by hundreds of dollars a car, and destroy American Motors and Chrysler within a few years. Ford might be able to hold out longer, but if General Motors was willing to engage in selective "predatory pricing" or selling cars below cost, it could also squeeze Ford to death. Since we must assume that a corporation does not operate according to benevolent sentiments, the reason that General Motors does not push a policy of maximum aggressive competition is that it fears government sanctions. Should General Motors exceed its present 50 percent of the market, political pressures would build to break it up and restore a measure of competition. GM obviously does not wish this to happen, considers the existing situation desirable, and therefore competes only enough to maintain its present market share.

However, it would probably be an oversimplification to suggest that a conscious policy toward that end is fixed in GM corporate headquarters. There is fierce competition among the divisions of General Motors; the market shares of Chevrolet, Pontiac, Oldsmobile, and Buick fluctuate considerably. The overall market share of the corporation is apparently maintained by eschewing price cutting strategies that might maximize sales.

Another limit on competition is one that most readers probably find agreeable. The great auto manufacturers take positive steps to keep their smaller competitors alive. The principal aid that GM, Ford, and Chrysler offer competitors is providing them with technology (especially by publicizing research results and sharing patents in the automotive field) and by selling them components. For example, General Motors was first with a workable automatic transmission, Hydramatic, in its luxury cars, which gave it a formidable advantage.

Nevertheless, GM sold Hydramatic components to Lincoln and Packard until they developed their own automatic transmissions. In the early 1950s Lincolns were equipped with GM Saginaw power steering units. At present, American Motors Corporation buys several important components from the Big Three, who consider its survival good for the industry.

The major automakers also keep minor competitors alive by selling components to specialized manufacturers of limited-production cars for enthusiasts. Chrysler sells engines to the English Bristol and Swiss Monteverdi luxury cars, and sold them as well for the late, lamented Jensen Interceptor. Chevrolet engines are sold to Avanti, Checker, and Excalibur. Ford is perhaps the most important purveyor of proprietary engines, selling V-8's to Italia, AC, and many other makes. English Ford engines are fitted to many models, particularly Morgan and TVR. The abortive Bricklin sports car first had AMC and then Ford engines. Similarly, transmissions, rear ends, suspension components, and other bits and pieces of automobiles are sold by major manufacturers to minor manufacturers. The Jensen-Healey sports car had engines from Lotus, transmissions from Chrysler, and suspension units from General Motors. The little guys could not survive without access to these benefits of mass production.

We should not think that the big auto manufacturers are being especially generous. There is considerable evidence that they could not monopolize the market even if they wanted to. A minority of people will always desire a vehicle distinct from their neighbors. The best example of this is seen in Italy, where the giant Fiat company manufactures more than 80 percent of the cars, with most of the rest made by Alfa Romeo. Since almost everyone has a Fiat, some people want something different, so a limited-production car market flourishes in Italy. Fiat has capitalized on this phenomenon by selling platform chasses to specialty manufacturers who fit individualized bodies, giving the customer a distinctive car with the additional attraction of readily available Fiat parts, the expertise that every Italian mechanic has of Fiats, and the cost benefits of mass production. Since a minority will demand specialized cars in any event, it makes sense for the big manufacturers to make a little money on the side by providing components.

The most obvious block to competition in the automobile industry is caused not directly by the companies themselves, but by the government. Present mandated "safety" and "emission" standards have reduced the variety of models produced in the U.S. and prevent Americans from buying more than half of the automobiles in the world. If you have any complaints about the selection of automobiles available, do not gripe to Detroit—take it up with Washington.

All Detroit cars are the same.

Since all manufacturers are trying to sell to a mass market, it stands to reason that they would produce a similar product, so there is really little difference among big Fords, Chevys, and Plymouths. That this is the result of market forces is apparent from the evolution of innovative designs. An early example was Detroit's attempt to bring out sports cars in the mid-1950s. Nash, Kaiser, Ford, and Chevrolet each tried; the first two flopped, Ford converted its Thunderbird to an up-market "personal" small luxury car, and after considerable development and market experimentation, Corvette finally achieved the unique status of a super-hotrod. When compact cars were introduced in the late 1950s, each of the manufacturers took a somewhat different approach, ranging from the stark Ford Falcon to the sporty Corvair to the pudgy Studebaker Lark to the European-style Valiant. It took about five years for the compact market to sort out; it then became apparent that the second series Valiant was the winning design, quickly imitated by the Chevy Nova and Ford Maverick. A similar process is going on today with subcompact and minicars.

Actually, the reality is less that all Detroit cars are the same, than that all American cars are the same—because all national cars are the same. English, German, French, Italian, and Japanese cars are more like one another than they are like their foreign counterparts or competitors. Each nation has its own style of automobile, determined by its road conditions, social organization, and tax laws. The cars made by Ford in England and Germany are more like GM's German Opel or English Vauxhall than any of them are like the American products of the same organizations. Every nation has particular tastes in consumer products: take beer as a useful analogy. American beers are all more like one another than any of them are like English or German beers.

Detroit deliberately murdered mass transportation.

The evidence in support of this charge is the involvement of the General Motors Corporation in an antitrust case involving National City Lines and other transit holding companies during the 1930s and 1940s. GM put up equity capital in a few cities, thus permitting the conversion of trolley systems to buses. The subsequent conviction of General Motors on an antitrust violation is on the record, and this gives some substance to the theory—except that it exaggerates both the power of General Motors and the paltry sums involved.

GM was involved only to a very limited degree with a very few companies. Even had the corporation plotted to destroy those particular transit lines, that would have had no effect on most of the interurban and urban trolley lines in the United States. Furthermore, the companies tied to GM began to convert to buses before GM's involvement and completed their conversions long after GM dropped out. The fact of the matter is that buses were more economical to operate than trolleys. There were strong civic pressures against trolleys because of the overhead wires and the safety problem faced by passengers who were forced to dash to the curb after being dropped in the middle of the street. During the 1930s transit companies had trouble raising capital for converting to buses, and GM put up some money and thus ran afoul of the antitrust laws. I have read the most detailed exposition of the thesis that "GM murdered mass transit," written by a somewhat incompetent staff member of the Senate Judiciary Committee, and have also read General Motors' rejoinder; neither is very convincing. What is clear is that the staffer is afflicted with a manic hatred of General Motors—he accuses it of collaborating with the Nazis and manipulating World War II to its advantage. It also appears to me that General Motors was suffering like everybody else during the Depression, so GM decided to cash in not only on the sale of buses to companies that were converting, but also on the more profitable operations of the companies that converted, and in addition to assure that they would convert to General Motors equipment. This was difficult to achieve without running afoul of the complex and arbitrary antitrust laws; GM did not quite slip through, and was nailed on a technical violation. It was not the last time, as we shall see, that General Motors has been ill-served by its legal talent.

You can believe what you want on this particular issue, but how does substituting buses for trolleys kill mass transit? Buses are also mass transit; indeed, they are a more efficient form of mass transit than trolleys.

The automobile is much too noisy.

This is really the only legitimate complaint on this list. Operating automobiles on highways does generate a good deal of noise, and steps should be taken to alleviate the problem. But in order to eliminate some part of our "noise pollution" we must understand the nature of the phenomenon. For a long time, engineers and legislators have been attempting to cut the amount of noise generated by motor vehicles. The muffler already eliminates most of the noise—the sound of the explosion in the engines coming through the exhaust pipe. Mufflers can be marginally improved, but at some expense in efficiency—because, as racing cars demonstrate, the most efficient performance is achieved with no muffling at all.

Most states have laws requiring mufflers, and a few states are beginning to enact laws limiting the amount of sound, measured in decibels, that a vehicle can produce. Unfortunately, a great deal of noise pollution results from the failure to enforce existing laws. I believe every state prohibits motorcyclists from removing their exhaust pipes, but kids with straight pipes are seen regularly. (To a few blithe spirits, the sound of an open exhaust pipe is not noise, but music. There is no reason they should be able to impose their tastes on others.) Many cities have laws prohibiting the use of horns, except in emergencies. But these laws are not enforced. That they are enforceable is evident from the achievement of Paris in the early 1960s. The French are even more individualistic and less law-abiding than the Americans, but horn blowing was stamped out altogether by the very simple expedient of slapping heavy fines on transgressors. No less could be done in North America.

Tires make a noise on the road, not noticeable at low speeds, which is perceived at high speed on expressways as a high-pitched hum. Most of the advances in reducing the noise made by tires have been achieved already. Within existing technology, there is no way to reduce significantly this noise without seriously cutting into the tire's primary function of providing safe traction. Tires also produce squeals made by hot-rodding kids during rapid acceleration or fast cornering. There seems to be little that can be done about this; fortunately these same people also tend to buy big fat tires, which make it harder to break traction.

Engine sound is the other major source of noise. This has been cut in recent years as a second order benefit of emissions requirements. Because air-cooled engines are less efficient in controlling the engine temperatures necessary to reduce emissions, the standards have effectively driven these noisier engines off the road. Water-cooled engines much better muffle engine noise. Two-stroke engines, as used to be fitted on DKW and Saab, have been wiped out for much the same reason.

But tightening emission controls may worsen the problem again because of the pending introduction of diesel engine cars. Diesels operate by igniting the gasoline-air mixture by high compression, which creates the same kind of sound perceived as "knock" in a spark ignition engine; it is noisy. But worse than the mere level is the quality of the noise. Diesels sound just plain ugly. Faced with the threat of federal standards, truck manufacturers in particular are working on reducing the diesel noise. It is possible to provide insulation of the whole engine compartment. The more insulation the less the noise, but the more the cost. This is merely a trade-off. Higher noise standards mean more insulation, which means higher truck prices, which means higher prices for all goods and services moved by trucks. But this is only an initial step toward noise abatement. In the longer run, it will be possible to modify engine design to reduce noise—sound dynamics is a tricky business, but it is quite likely that detailed changes can be designed into engines to prevent sound from resonating beyond the water jacket.

Although annoying, the noise problem is considerably exaggerated. Only a very few areas in the country have serious difficulties. These are the high-density parts of our country, which fortunately are losing population rapidly. Heavy traffic and therefore noise is worse during the day, when it is least objectionable, and lowest at night, when it is most annoying. More important, economics has dealt very nicely with most of the noise problem. Locations along busy highways with heavy traffic are noisy (not to mention smelly), so they are not the most attractive places for residences or other property uses that require quiet. Logically enough, people who do not like noise do not locate along highways. Conversely, factories and stores depend on heavy traffic and are willing to pay for accessibility with noise. The resulting pattern is called "strip development," which is a very efficient method of charging the costs of noise. But this is not a universal solution. Modern expressways do not permit strip development so that the natural economic buffer cannot operate. We are beginning to learn something about the noise dynamics of these roads. Elevated expressways are particularly nasty, while sunken expressways muffle and disperse the noise. For level areas, berms or dykes made from the excess dirt and materials of construction are useful.

Needless to say, people with the worse gripes are those who bought a very quiet place and then suffered when a road was put in later. The purchaser of a house near a noisy road has no legitimate complaint, since the adverse condition was reflected in the lower price of his house—if the location was noisy enough to bother people, the house was worth less. But a new road reduces the value of a house; this is another argument for putting in roads before development occurs.

Apart from noise, all of the other costs, disbenefits, and sins of the highway, the automobile, and the automobile business cited in this chapter are exaggerated or simply false. Yet they have been widely circulated. Why?

4.

Emissions

Let us now turn to the real costs of the automobile, beginning with one of the most exaggerated and misunderstood—emissions.

The discovery of the air-pollution effects of auto exhaust emissions is one of the great ironies and minor tragedies of history. Remember that the introduction of the automobile was supposed to alleviate the pollution problem caused by the effluents of draft animals and coal-burning trains. For fifty years the world labored under the delusion that vehicular air pollution was a thing of the past. Toward the middle of the century, however, people in Los Angeles began to notice something in the air, which later came to be labeled "smog," presumably a combination of smoke and fog. But the scientist Dr. Arlie Haagen-Smit learned that it really resulted from the action of sunlight and heat upon hydrocarbons and oxides of nitrogen in the air, particularly those emitted from automobile exhausts. The phenomenon is properly called "photochemical smog."

The process that results in smog is incredibly complicated and by no means perfectly understood, but its outlines are not disputed. Gasoline consists of complex compounds of carbon and hydrogen. In an automobile engine these are combined with air,

72

which is about 80 percent nitrogen and 20 percent oxygen; the mixture is ignited by a spark to produce an explosion, which results in heat and rapid expansion of the gases pushing on the piston and thus propelling the vehicle. If this combustion process were ideal, only water vapor (H_2O), carbon dioxide (CO_2), an inert and harmless gas, and nitrogen (N_2), also inert and harmless, would issue from the exhaust. Alas, the process is not perfect. Some of the hydrocarbons (HC) in the gasoline are unburned, and some of the nitrogen in the air combines with oxygen to form oxides of nitrogen (NO_x, pronounced *knocks*). Instead of carbon dioxide, the process produces some carbon monoxide (CO). If sufficient concentrations of the hydrocarbons and oxides of nitrogen result and are subjected to the right amounts of heat and sunlight, noticeable concentrations of ozone (O_3) and related oxidents collect in the atmosphere.

Keep in mind that this phenomenon was first noticed in Los Angeles—but not because the automobile was so popular there. When smog first appeared, Los Angeles still had substantial parts of its excellent collective transit system, Pacific Electric's "Red Car" trolleys and buses. Smog was first detected there because of the peculiar atmospheric conditions prevailing over L.A., which is in a basin between the sea and the mountains. The structure of the atmosphere above the city exhibits a layer of cold air above a layer of warm air; materials in the warm air layer are trapped at the lower levels, unable to rise because of the "inversion layer" above it, unable to escape eastward because of the mountains, and held in the basin by the prevailing winds from the west.

L.A. is certainly not alone in having smog, which now seems to be a normal condition in most southwestern cities having similar combinations of heat, light, and mountains. Smog can also appear on the desert, but is not a serious problem there because it blows away and is dispersed. Nevertheless, smog is not a universal problem, and is most severe in Los Angeles because of the special local conditions of temperature, humidity, and terrain.

Some people confuse photochemical smog with the famous industrial fog and smoke that used to hang over all of our great cities. The London fog is the most famous example. Industrial air pollution has practically nothing to do with photochemical smog. Industrial fog is mostly made up of particulate matters and oxides of sulfur issuing from industrial processes, especially the burning of coal. Much coal has sulfur, and almost all coal burning produces particulate matter, or tiny little bits of dirt. The resulting fog is a deadly killer in large doses; in serious outbreaks in many manufacturing towns, the death rate has gone up precipitously, particularly from respiratory ailments. In the early 1950s a particularly bad fog in London resulted in the death of several hundred people.

Happily, this type air pollution is almost a thing of the past. Controlling smokestack emissions has been one major solution. But the most important was merely the substitution of oil for coal; the former has far less particulate matter and usually much less sulfur than the latter. And it is largely because of the automobile that this change occurred. Large amounts of oil became available for industrial and heating use because of the production of petroleum to provide gasoline for cars. Only part of a barrel of crude oil can be refined into gasoline; the remainder is of too low a quality to fuel an automobile. However, these lower quality residual oils are eminently suited for industrial burning, power generation, and home heating. All of the advanced industrial countries have just about finished cleaning up this traditional type of air pollution.

The photochemical smog is another matter. Its adverse health effects have not yet been determined. Various ingenious attempts have been made to correlate the level of smog with the death rate from various diseases, particularly respiratory diseases—with no great success. The quality of the data on both sides of the correlation is inadequate for any strict determination. Both air pollution and health indicators are measured in very tiny fractions that are difficult to measure precisely. The scale of air pollution is "parts per million" (PPM). For example, the federal standard for oxidants is .08 PPM, or less than one unit of oxidant for one hundred million units of air. Obviously, measuring such tiny levels is extremely difficult and only recently has reasonably accurate equipment been widely installed in our metropolitan areas.

Health problems are equally tough to measure. Death rates are very low, and often result from compound causes. Suppose an old man is mowing his lawn, gets caught in a rainstorm, catches a cold, tries to treat it himself, and finally goes to the hospital, where it is learned that he has pneumonia; complications set in, and he dies of heart failure on a day when there is an air quality alert. Did he die of air pollution, heart disease, pneumonia, failure to seek proper treatment, exposure, law mowing, or old age?

It would be very convenient if we could say that so-and-so-much air pollution has such-and-such adverse health effects, but in practice, other factors, like the age distribution and ethnic background of the population, are far more important for health. There are differences among cities in the amount of photochemical smog and the death rates from respiratory diseases, but these differences do not seem to relate to one another very well. Still, I know of no one who claims that smog is good for you; the question is how bad it is for you.

However, there is no record of anybody ever dying of photochemical smog. What may be happening is that the addition of smog to the air may compound other difficulties. For example, if you already have some sort of a respiratory ailment, bronchitis or pneumonia or tuberculosis, the smog may worsen the condition. Fortunately, since smog is more likely to appear in semidesert climates than colder climates, it is worse in the very places where there is no cold weather to compound respiratory ailments. Thus because the effects of smog, whatever they are, do not even begin to match the normal climatic effects on health, Los Angeles still has a better health record than, say, Montana.

Moreover, nature itself does not provide us with clean air. There are natural background levels of oxidants produced by plants, which can, as in Washington, D. C., recently, produce air quality alerts under adverse climatic conditions.

Estimates made several years ago in a study for the Congress by the National Academy of Sciences and the National Academy of Engineering produced a range of estimates that smog may result in an additional 4,000 deaths a year. On the basis of this finding, it was often reported in the press that smog killed 4,000 people annually. Given the present state of knowledge, however, 4,000 must be considered to be an upper limit, and there is also an equally valid lower limit—zero. It is not so much that smog is killing people but that it is making the difference between life and death in marginal cases. To put this in perspective remember that every year about two million people die, and since we will all die anyway, even if smog is responsible in some way for 4,000 deaths annually, its toll represents at most .2 percent of those who die, and .01 percent of the population. Ten thousand people are murdered every year; fifteen thousand die from falls.

The other major pollutant from automobile emissions is potentially more dangerous. Because the combustion process is incomplete the internal-combustion engine produces some carbon monoxide (CO), a deadly gas. Your blood is a CO junkie—it likes CO so much that it will gobble it up instead of the oxygen you need for life. This danger has long been recognized; it is the reason that leaving the garage door open while running the car is a well-known safety precaution, and conversely the reason that neglecting to do so has long been a popular means of committing suicide. Although sufficient quantities of carbon monoxide will kill you, it is by no means clear what trivial amounts will do to you. Several years ago, Paris was concerned about the effects of CO concentrations on police performing traffic duty. It was learned that the traffic cops had better health than police on other assignments. Why? The traffic cops were not permitted to smoke while on duty. CO from smoking cigarettes is many times more concentrated than the worst traffic pollution. In fact, there is no evidence of adverse health effects of small amounts of carbon monoxide (which, by the way, also appears naturally in the atmosphere). But no one claims that CO, like smog, is good for you.

Since the reader has likely been inundated for years by misinformation on the subject of auto-related air pollution, let me quote at length from a National Academy of Sciences report to the Congress:

In the "Report of the Panel on Photochemical Oxidants and Ozone," the panel reached the following conclusions regarding the national preliminary standard for photochemical oxidants:

1. Adverse health effects from short-term exposure to photochemical oxidants and ozone at the standard concentrations have not been observed in man.

2. There are human and animal data that suggest that adverse health effects might be expected at concentrations near the standard, especially under conditions of long-term exposure or in the presence of copollutants.

Most importantly, the panel noted, "The technical base for the oxidant standard was inadequate at the time the standard was set (1971) and remains inadequate, considering the implications for public health and the economic impact."

With regard to carbon monoxide, there is only very limited evidence that this pollutant has adverse effects on morbidity [illness] at ambient levels typical of urban areas. The Cohen et al. (1969) analysis of hospital patients admitted with myocardial infarction suggested a possible association between such admissions and levels of carbon monoxide; however, the results of the study could not be replicated in a subsequent analysis for Baltimore by Kuller et al. (1974). In addition, although there is other evidence that carbon monoxide may aggravate certain symptoms in highly susceptible populations, it is widely held that such effects are reversible. Thus, it has not yet been demonstrated that reductions in ambient levels of carbon monoxide would have significant effects on morbidity. This same conclusion must be reiterated with respect to morbidity and hydrocarbons. Only one study, Burrows et al. (1968), evidenced a possible association between symptom severity in patients with chronic respiratory disease and levels of hydrocarbons. Numerous other studies could not detect similar results.

Very few studies implicate mobile-source pollutants [motor vehicles] as important determinants of mortality. The Lave and Seskin (1974) cross-section time-series analysis of 15 SMSAs [metropolitan cities] found that a 10 percent decrease in the ambient levels of nitrogen dioxide was associated with .25 percent decrease in the total mortality rate (other factors held constant). This estimate can be applied to an appropriate national population which is at risk from nitrogen dioxide exposure in order to derive a crude estimate of the benefits of nitrogen dioxide abatement in terms of reduced mortality. Since the relevant population at risk is not known, we have made several calculations:

1. Los Angeles and Chicago are the two areas for which the present nitrogen dioxide standard is exceeded. Using their combined population (approximately 18,600,000) as the relevant population at risk and assuming that a 45 percent reduction in nitrogen dioxide levels takes place as a result of proposed mobile-source abatement strategies we obtain a decrease in annual total deaths of approximately 2,100.

2. Using the actual data from the Lave and Seskin analysis we find that their estimate was based on a population at risk of approximately 20 million for the 15 SMSAs. Assuming that the mean level of nitrogen dioxide across these SMSAs was reduced to the national standard, a reduction of about 15 percent, we obtain a decrease in annual total deaths of approximately 800.

3. Finally, assuming that the entire urbanized population of the U.S. (about 118 million persons) is the relevant population at risk and that the mean level of nitrogen dioxide across all of these areas must also be reduced by 15 percent, we obtain a decrease in total deaths of approximately 4,400.

Thus, under various assumptions, abatement of nitrogen dioxide has a potential of reducing annual total deaths by between 800 and 4,400. Again, to put this estimate into perspective, both the Sprey and Hallock (1974) and the Sprey et al. (1973) studies found similar mortality effects from nitrogen dioxide exposure. On the other hand, McDonald and Schwing (1973) did not discover an association between dioxides of nitrogen and mortality rates, although their analysis used pollution potentials rather than actual ambient concentrations.

The only evidence that suggests increased mortality may be related to carbon monoxide levels was presented by Hexter and Goldsmith (1971). However, an earlier study undertaken by Hechter and Goldsmith (1961) failed to uncover a similar association. In addition, attempts to correlate daily deaths with daily pollution levels or other daily environmental measures are fraught with difficulty due to the inherent variability in the day-to-day death rate. Furthermore, Sprey and Hallock (1973) and Lave and Seskin (1974) were unable to detect associations between carbon monoxide levels and mortality. The mortality effects of carbon monoxide, like its morbidity effects, have not been demonstrated clearly enough to allow potential benefits to be assigned to reductions in ambient carbon monoxide concentrations.

No study can be cited which found that photochemical oxidants exhibited a significant and independent association with excess mortality. Sprey and Hallock (1974) related high ozone concentrations in conjunction with high nitrogen dioxide levels and warm weather with increased mortality, while Hexter and Goldsmith (1971) could not detect any significant associations between daily mortality and daily oxidant levels in Los Angeles. Thus, we must conclude that mortality effects of photochemical oxidants have not been adequately demonstrated; hence, at this time no potential benefits in this area can be assessed.

With regard to hydrocarbons, a similar conclusion must be reached. Neither McDonald and Schwing (1973) nor Lave and Seskin (1974), the only two relevant studies, discovered an association between mortality effects as potential direct benefits from reduction in the ambient levels of hydrocarbons.

So why is there so much agitation over automotive air pollution? To begin with, smog is ugly. Especially in a place like Los Angeles—which is and ought to be an earthly paradise—it is annoying to look toward the horizon and see a dirty line in the sky like a ring around the bathtub. And even if the health effects are trivial, most of us are bothered by a lot of crud in the air. Nobody likes to have his eyes smart from smog. Economists have calculated that air pollution (mostly not smog) costs us several billions of dollars each year. Air pollution also has adverse environmental consequences—but really not very much is known about them. To give some sense of the quality of the research, let's look at a careful study by NAS of the effects of air pollution on vegetation.

Weidensaul and Lacasse (1970) carried out a statewide survey of air pollution damage to vegetation in Pennsylvania during 1969. Ninety-two field investigations, generally undertaken by county agents, were made in 28 counties. Of these, 60 uncovered damage in 23 of the counties. Vegetables, fruits, and agronomic crops appeared to be most seriously affected by pollution, accounting for $3.2 million in direct losses. Direct losses associated with damage to lawns, shrubs, and woody ornamentals amounted to $200,000; damage to timber losses was estimated at $30,000; and damage to commercial flowers and foliage amounted to $56,000. These direct losses included only production costs. If the crop was not completely damaged, the loss reflected only that portion affected, e.g., the reduction in yield and/or quality, the cost of cleaning, etc. Eighty-three percent of direct losses to vegetable crop in the Delaware Valley (approximately $3 million) was attributed to oxidant pollution. The major source of this pollution is, of course, the automobile. The other pollutants, in decreasing order of importance, were: oxides of sulfur, lead, hydrogen chloride, particulates, herbicides, and ethylene.

In an attempt to make a more complete economic assessment, the authors also estimated indirect losses. These included $7 million for grower profit losses (arrived at by questioning the growers themselves); $0.5 million for reforestation of denuded land (based on area affected, topography, site preparation, cost of plant material and planting); and $0.5 million for grower relocation and crop substitution costs. Other indirect losses such as those associated with decreased aesthetic values, damage to home lawns, discontinuation of crops because of pollution (e.g., spinach), and actual farm abandonment were noted but not quantified. In addition, environmental losses due to erosion, stream silting, and damage to watershed retention capacity were not captured in the estimates. There are two weaknesses with this type of areawide survey. First, by its very nature, such a study is highly subjective in that field investigators must make value judgments as to the extent and cause of observed damage. Second, observed damages are not necessarily caused by injury occurring during the survey year. In most cases, however, attempts are made to isolate that portion of the damage applicable to the year in question. Because of these and other factors, Weidensaul and Lacasse (1970) concluded that a more realistic estimate of the *direct* annual losses attributable to air pollution in Pennsylvania is $2.5 million (no similar adjustment was made for indirect losses). Since some economic costs discussed above were not included in either the direct or the indirect loss estimates, such a downward adjustment may not be in order if one's goal is to assess the 'true' economic damages. However, what is particularly disturbing in this case are the results of the subsequent survey which was undertaken for 1970–71.

Lacasse (1971) replicated the earlier Pennsylvania survey in order to assess air pollution damage to vegetation for the period 1970–71. The results of 53 investigations, using the same methods which had been used in the previous survey, uncovered 44 incidents of direct air pollution injury. In this case, however, direct losses were valued at only $218,630. The most harmful pollutants were found to be heavy metals, molybdenum, oxides of sulfur, oxidants, and hydrogen chloride gas and acid mist. (Direct losses attributed to oxidants totaled only $6,040.) Total indirect losses, including known profit losses and reforestation costs were estimated at only $4,000.

These two studies were undertaken by many of the same personnel using consistent techniques, yet damages differed by orders of magnitude [ten times as much]. One cannot help but remain uneasy in evaluating these studies and their implications. . . .

When Los Angeles began to notice air-pollution problems, it began to do something about them. An air-quality board was established and began to prohibit various types of polluting activities. The oil refineries were found to be a major source of pollution and were required to clean up their processes. Outside incineration of trash was also prohibited. Then L.A. began to go after the automobiles. And the L.A. and California programs have generally been followed by the rest of the country.

The first step was easy—preventing the escape of hydrocarbons from the oil in the engine's crankcase. The fitting of positive crankcase ventilation valves (PCV) in the early 1960s accomplished this cheaply and very simply. It was also found that hydrocarbons entered the air by evaporation from gas tanks and carburetors, and evaporative controls were required in the late 1960s. These two steps alone reduced hydrocarbon emissions from automobiles by 45 percent.

Exhaust emissions have been a little tougher to control. Beginning in 1968, federal standards were mandated for automobiles, which were annoying to drivers because they cut into performance, reliability, "driveability," and economy. But by 1970 the redesigned cars were producing only 30 percent of an uncontrolled car's emissions. It wasn't very difficult to cut emissions once the problem was recognized. Remember that for seventy years automobile engines have been designed to maximize easy starting, performance, fuel economy, reliability, and smoothness, and to minimize weight and cost. Recognizing emissions as a new parameter merely complicated the design a little bit more. It took a while for the engineers to learn how to deal with emissions, but they have done so pretty well.

In 1970 the Congress (which I believe does not include any engineers) responded to environmental agitation by passing the Clean Air Act, which required that by 1976, auto emissions be reduced to 10 percent of existing levels. That doesn't sound very difficult, does it? The trouble was that Congress didn't require the reduction of the level of emissions to 10 percent of uncontrolled cars, but to 10 percent of 1970 cars—which were already

producing only 30 percent of the emissions of uncontrolled cars.*
Ten percent of 30 percent is 3 percent. That is tough. To squeeze
down to the last little bit of anything is incredibly difficult.
Maybe you can get 90 percent of the juice out of your orange,
but the remaining 10 percent is tough, and the last 1 percent
is impossible. In the real world the cost of achieving totality approaches infinity and increases exponentially. Typically, if it costs
a thousand dollars to achieve 90 percent of something, it will cost
ten thousand to get 99 percent, a hundred thousand to get 99.9
percent, one million to get 99.99 percent, and so forth. That last
bit is always a backbreaker.

But even that would not have been so bad if the Congress had
stuck to unburnt hydrocarbons and carbon monoxide, which both
result from incomplete combustion processes. So improving combustion by detailed modifications of major design changes reduces both, but the rub is the oxides of nitrogen. Decreasing the
hydrocarbons increases the NO_x.

Look at the chart (Figure 2). An auto engine runs on a mixture
of gasoline and air—the normal operating range is from 13.5 to
16.5 parts air to one part gasoline. Within normal operating
ranges, hydrocarbons and CO can be reduced by increasing the
ratio of air to fuel but NO_x goes up. This is simple to understand.
Reducing HC and CO requires better combustion to obtain more
combination with oxygen, producing harmless H_2O and CO_2.
But better combustion also results in more combination of nitrogen with oxygen, producing NO_x. The nature of operation of the
Otto-type internal-combustion engine, used in almost all cars in
the world, precludes eliminating both hydrocarbons and NO_x.
Now the reader may reasonably ask this question: If the smog is
caused by the *combination* of NO_x and hydrocarbons, why is it
necessary to get rid of both of them? That is an excellent ques-

* The father of smog, Professor Haagen-Smit, said "the Muskie bill
passed last December [1970] without Congress understanding that
emissions in 1970 vehicles had already been controlled 70 to 80 percent." He described the EPA air quality standards for hydrocarbons
as "absurd."

Figure 2: EMISSIONS AND AIR/FUEL RATIO

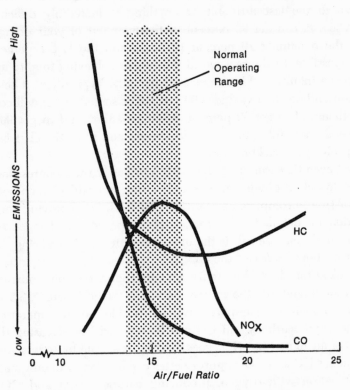

tion, and many serious air pollution control experts are beginning to ask it. Since the Clean Air Act of 1970 was written, a good deal more is known and the enthusiasm for eliminating NO_x has abated considerably. This does not mean that NO_x is not a problem or might not be a problem, but there is certainly less concern about it now than at the time of the Clean Air Act.

When the Clean Air Act was written in 1970 the automobile manufacturers maintained that it was impossible to meet the schedule. Congress took the position that in order to force them to clean up exhausts it was necessary "to hold their feet to the fire"—thus the NO_x standards were written into law. The technical problem is as severe now as it was in the late 1960s. There is simply no way that automobile manufacturers can meet the existing requirements of NO_x reduction. Clearly, the simplest solution is not to worry so much about NO_x, and modify the standards accordingly. But some of the more enthusiastic clean air types, for reasons that shall be discussed later, would certainly say then that the politicians have "sold out" to Detroit. To be absolutely candid we cannot be entirely sure that NO_x is not a problem; there may be things that we do not know about yet, which might still require action.

But take a look at Table 1. Automobile emissions have been cut so much that, compared with an uncontrolled car, 1977 models produce only 17 percent as many hydrocarbons, 17 percent as much carbon monoxide, and 57 percent as many nitro-

Table 1: FEDERAL EXHAUST EMISSION STANDARDS
(Grams/Mile According to Current EPA Test Procedure)

	HYDRO-CARBONS (HC)	CARBON MONOXIDE (CO)	NITROGEN OXIDES (NO_x)
Uncontrolled			
Pre-1968 Average	8.7	87	3.5
Existing (1976) Standards			
1968–69	6.2	51	—
1970–71	4.1	34	—
1972	3.0	28	—
1973–74	3.0	28	3.1
1975–76	1.5	15	3.1
1977 ·	1.5	15	2.0
1978	.41	3.4	.4
(1976) EPA Proposals			
1978–79	1.5	15	2.0
980–81	.9	9	2.0
1982	.41	3.4	*

* Final NO_x standard left to EPA administrator

gen oxides. This incredible progress was achieved by recognizing that the main difficulty was incomplete combustion. Now there is more complete combustion. The first thing that the engineers did was lean out the mixture a little bit.

A little less gas with the air costs power, fuel economy, and driveability, but allows the explosion to properly burn the gasoline. Another method that also costs money is an inelegant solution that engineers dislike—the air pump, a device that injects additional air into the exhaust manifold to continue burning gasoline after it clears the combustion chamber, thereby reducing the amount of unburned hydrocarbons and carbon monoxide. Another minor modification involved changing the ignition timing. It was also found that particularly severe emissions occurred when you took your foot off the accelerator. So engineers put a little gizmo in the carburetor that prevented the butterfly valve connected to the gas pedal from closing too rapidly; this device explains why contemporary cars do not have quite as good engine braking as they used to. The engineers also learned that the car continued to pump a little more gas into the engine when it was turned off, so they added a little solenoid valve to shut off the gasoline immediately when the car was stopped. Warm-up periods were also a cause of heavy air pollution, so various steps were taken to speed the warm-up of engines by modifying thermostats, providing warm air to the carburetor intake, and transferring heat from the exhaust manifold to the intake manifold. These steps also cost something in performance and economy, because the optimum design by traditional parameters is having cool air come into the engine.

Take a look far out on the right-hand side of the emissions chart. There is an area where the NO_x goes sharply down; unfortunately, this is beyond the normal range at which the air:gas mixture will fire with a conventional spark plug, so automobile designers look for means of providing a hotter spark. Improved ignition systems have been one solution; combined with more carefully metered carburetor design, this is basically Chrysler's "lean-burn" system.

Another widely publicized approach is the stratified charge. In the combustion chamber the mixture is kept so lean that it could not normally be fired, but there is also a richer mixture next to the spark plug. The spark plug ignites the rich mixture, which is hot enough to ignite the rest. In its simplest form, such as the Honda's CVCC configuration, there is a separate little combustion chamber next to the spark plug, with its own tiny valve and its own tiny carburetor; the main mixture of the engine is very lean. This system works very well, but it suffers from lower power and worsened fuel economy, not to mention some extra cost for the separate valve and carburetor.

There are several other methods of modifying the existing Otto-type internal-combustion engine. One solution, now used by some expensive cars but not beyond the reach of mass production, is fuel injection. Instead of the carburetor, for mixing the gasoline with the air, there is a much more complicated gadget that squirts a carefully measured amount of gasoline into each individual cylinder. Fuel injection permits much more careful metering of the amount of fuel used. The system can also be controlled electronically, so that the amount of gasoline can be much more perfectly adjusted to the power needs of that engine, while controlling emissions at the same time. A carburetor necessarily requires compromises: What provides the best performance at one engine speed will not necessarily be very good during acceleration or deceleration or idling or different engine speeds. Electronic fuel injection permits much more sensitive adjustments. The only problem is it is expensive.

Another conceivable modification is the supercharger, which does for air what fuel injection does for gasoline. It forces air into the engine under pressure. With supercharging it is possible to get much more exact and predictable concentrations of air into the engine. Supercharging also vastly increases engine output. Racing cars with supercharging can produce twice as much power as normally aspirated engines, though at considerable cost to gas economy and also emissions. But what can be done for power can also be done for other purposes. To my knowledge no one has yet gone to the trouble of putting all or most of these modifications together on the same engine. I suspect such an engine would be very impressive in terms of its low emission output—but extremely expensive.

But there are still other ways of reducing emissions from an internal combustion engine. You can also clean them up after they leave the engine through converters of various kinds. There is the thermal converter, used by the Mazda among others, which operates in much the same way as the air pump—additional heat burns off the emissions. But this system requires a very rich mixture, which is one reason why the Mazda has such notoriously bad gas mileage.

General Motors took another tack—the catalytic converter, a little cannister filled with pellets that help complete the combustion and cut emissions of HC and CO. The exhaust is run through a bed of noble metals that force the impurities in the exhaust to combine with oxygen in the air, thus reducing emissions. By adopting catalytic converters, 1975–1977 model-year cars managed to achieve lower emissions than earlier models with various engine modifications, and therefore had better performance, driveability, and fuel economy. The present systems handle hydrocarbons and carbon monoxide.

Down the pipe a little way is the "three-way catalyst," which can deal with oxides of nitrogen as well. This is not quite as simple as it sounds, because a three-way catalyst must "oxidize" (add oxygen to) the HC and CO as well as "reduce" (take oxygen from) the NO_x. Unfortunately, the materials, like platinum, required in converters are expensive and are found in only a few places in the world, particularly the Soviet Union and South Africa—and Americans have little sympathy for either. But the technology is rapidly advancing.

The catalytic converter has some other drawbacks, but these have been grossly exaggerated.* (The auto companies claim that

* The introduction of the catalyst led to another auto emission concern which turned out to be without substance. Gasoline contains a tiny bit of sulphur. When the catalyst oxidizes the hydrocarbons

these are foul lies spread by the oil companies; the "auto-industrial complex" is by no means monolithic.) Converters necessarily run hot because of their function of processing exhausts. In some cars, heat is certainly noticeable because of the location of the catalytic converter under the passenger seat, but reports that they were responsible for starting brush fires in California have been proven false. Converters can also be fouled and made inoperative by small amounts of lead, which has been used a long time to increase the octane of gasoline, thus permitting higher compression ratios, and greater performance. It is possible to blend high-octane gasoline without lead—Amoco has been doing so since World War II with converted aviation gasoline refineries—but it is much more expensive. GM led the catalyst business and put the muscle on the oil companies to re-equip stations and pumps with special nozzles to make sure that ordinary leaded gas could not get into the cars equipped with converters.

Other modifications of the internal-combustion engine are also possible. Small microprocessors will soon be introduced for automobile use. These are little bitty computers on a chip of silicon, very much like the components of a pocket calculator. With these microprocessors spark timing and fuel mixture can be carefully controlled from signals transmitted from the exhaust pipe, the outside atmosphere, the engine speed, and the accelerator pedal, permitting a very careful tailoring of engine operation and thus reducing emissions while improving economy, performance, and driveability.

Microprocessors might also be used to control the basic intake

---

and CO it also oxidizes the sulphur, producing sulphates—a particularly nasty form of pollution that is clearly carcinogenic. EPA produced a model which suggested that heavy traffic would produce unhealthy concentrations of sulphates along the edges of roadways. A multi-million dollar experiment involving hundreds of cars traveling thousands of hours at the GM Proving Ground was necessary to prove that the EPA model was incorrect. The amounts of sulphates produced are trivial and are rapidly diffused into the atmosphere. In any event, any sulphate problem could be easily eliminated by improving the refining of gasoline to cut out that little bit of sulphur.

and exhaust systems of the vehicle. A group of engineers in California has just designed an engine with hydraulic variable valves. The conventional valve system in use for nearly 100 years employs a camshaft to open and close the valves that allow the gas/air mixture into and the exhaust out of the combustion chamber. The variable valve engine operates the valves by hydraulic compression, allowing for example, a very mild tune for normal driving and more radical tuning for high speed. The capability of precisely controlling valve openings in this manner might have great benefits for dealing with emissions.

But there is still more than can be done with automotive engines. Remember that it is not the automobile per se that pollutes, but the internal-combustion engine. Well, even that is not quite right: it is not even the internal-combustion engine, but the internal-combustion engine burning gasoline. Yet a car need not burn gasoline. Let me reserve an extended discussion of alternative sources of energy to the next chapter, but merely point out that many of the emissions can be seriously modified and reduced to practically zero just by substituting other fuels. This is not a theoretical proposition. If you have the opportunity to visit Japan, watch closely while your luggage is being loaded into a taxicab at the Tokyo airport. You will note a large cylinder in the trunk—this is a propane tank. For emissions control purposes, all taxicabs in Tokyo are required to be fitted with propane, a liquefied gas that substitutes for gasoline. Any engine can be modified for almost any other bottled gas, merely by changing the carburetor jets. Other types of liquid and gaseous fuels are almost legion: among them are methane, methanol, and ethanol. (All of these will be discussed at length in the next chapter.)

In summary, existing technology can deal with hydrocarbons and carbon monoxide, although not yet with the NO_x problem. But assume that NO_x is bad—bad enough to warrant the maximum effort to get rid of it. Given the automobile we would seem to be stuck with NO_x—so we should get rid of the automobile, right? Yet people who say the automobile pollutes are making the grievous error of ignoring the fact that it is the existing type of internal-combustion engine that is responsible for emissions—not the whole car. If air pollution became a serious problem, we could switch to other means of powering autos. There are now many alternative power plants, but on balance they are all inferior to the spark-fired combustion engine.

The first of these is another type of internal-combustion engine, designed by the German engineer Rudolph Diesel. Instead of compressing the gas:air mixture and then igniting it with the spark plug, the mixture in a diesel engine is ignited by the pressure itself. Diesel engines are now in use; most big trucks and buses have them. You can buy a diesel car from your Mercedes-Benz dealer. But diesels have not yet been adopted in large numbers for automobiles because spark ignition is superior for most uses. Because of the greater pressures involved, the higher compression ratios, and the sudden bang of ignition, diesel engines must be built much stronger; they are much heavier in relation to their power output. To achieve good results, diesels also usually need expensive fuel injection.

The positive side of the diesel is found in two areas that are increasingly important—low emissions and high gas mileage. Another advantage is that it does not need high-quality fuel, and can burn just about anything. The diesel fuel sold to trucks is about the same low grade oil that your burn in your house, which is much less expensive than gasoline. Another advantage of the diesel is somewhat exaggerated—it does have longevity because of its heavy construction, but conventional engines would last just as long if they were built to the same standards and cost. The diesel has a few other trivial drawbacks that do not seem to present a serious bar to its use—if you follow along behind a bus you will see a little bit of smoke coming out. This looks like bad pollution, but the impression is misleading. The smoke is just a little bit of particulate matter that comes out—the other emissions are substantially lower than the spark ignition engine. The diesel is also relatively noisy. But if Herr Otto had not invented the spark ignition engine we know today, we all would probably be driving diesels and not really noticing the difference.

Another type of internal-combustion engine is the gas turbine. When you fly in an aircraft these days you are powered by a gas turbine, but a unit for automotive use does not rely upon a jet streaming out of the back end of the engine to push the vehicle along. Instead, the jet is passed through a big fan, or turbine, which is connected to the wheel and propels the car in a conventional manner. Gas turbines have been fitted for cars on the road—Chrysler is a leader in this type of technology—and give adequate service. The gas turbine is compact and can burn low-grade fuels, such as kerosene.

But the gas turbine has problems. It is a gas guzzler, and there is a real problem with throttle response. You cannot just step on the gas and get the kind of immediate reaction you do with a conventional engine. There is a lag of a few seconds, which can be annoying at best and dangerous at worst. The greatest problems of all for the gas turbine engine are the extremely high exhaust temperatures and the extremely high speeds at which the turbine spins, perhaps 50,000 rpm, requiring exceptionally high-quality and therefore expensive materials and machining. At the present time, the cost of the gas turbine bars it from widespread automotive use. But it is conceivable, especially with the progress being made in the scientific study of materials, that these problems can be licked within even a few years. It would be unwise to count on its use in mass production vehicles, but it cannot be counted out either. However, if we had not invented the spark ignition engine and the diesel, gas-turbine cars would probably be on the road today—at least for use by the rich.

Another candidate for replacing of the internal-combustion engine is one of its long-defeated rivals, the steam engine. This does not involve internal combustion but rather *external* combustion because the fuel is burned in a simple boiler, heating water to create steam, which is vented into the engine to push a piston or turn a turbine, thus driving the car. Steam power has long had its enthusiasts; it does indeed have many striking features. It is silent, potentially powerful, and needs no transmission. The steam engine has come a long way from the time of the Stanley brothers, but it still has a long way to go. Steam technology was kept alive in the 1920s and the 1930s by the great engineer Abner Doble, whose technological advances were the basis for building a steam car in the early 1950s—the aborted Paxton Phoenix. Just a few years ago there was the most ambitious steam car project ever. The inventor of the Lear automatic pilot and the Learjet executive aircraft, William Lear, who certainly cannot be considered a crackpot or a dilettante, mounted a major project to build a competitive steam car. He sank $5 million into the enterprise before abandoning it.

The steam car has several problems. Delivery of the correct amount of steam to the cylinders requires complex and expensive lines and controls. A fundamental fault in the design is the annoying delay in getting up a good head of steam before the vehicle can be started.

A steam engine can burn just about anything, and it does pollute, but it has a more regular flame, which is therefore much more easily controlled. A lesser problem is that unless the car is constantly refilled with water, the steam must be converted back to water by means of a condenser that would have to be three times as large as a conventional radiator—but that would not seem to be very difficult to design. The steam engine cycle is inherently inefficient, so it is a gas guzzler. Overall, steam cannot compete with the internal-combustion engine over the whole range of parameters. But in a pinch, we—or the rich among us—could drive steam cars.

Much like the steam engine is the sterling engine. This also operates by external combustion, but it uses hot air rather than steam to move the pistons that propel the car. Many European and American manufacturers have been experimenting with the sterling engine for some years. They all agree it has considerable promise, and all agree that it is not as good as the existing internal-combustion engine. But it too is a possibility and might fight it out with steam power somewhere down the pike.

Last, but certainly not least, is the other defeated rival of the spark-fired, internal-combustion engine—the electric motor, which might seem the ideal method of dealing with the pollution problem. It does not pollute at all. Well, not quite—electricity is not collected from the air; if it is stored in batteries, it must be produced somewhere else. So the burning of fuel is transferred from the engine itself to a power plant. However, this reduces emissions considerably, because the power plant can be equipped with much more stringent controls than an internal-combustion engine.

Unfortunately, the electric car has very serious drawbacks. Existing battery technology is such that a very heavy battery is required to store a limited amount of electricity. The amount of energy in a gallon of gasoline requires 1,400 pounds of batteries; stated another way: two of the heavy batteries in your car store only as much energy as a shot glass of gas. People have been experimenting with different types of batteries over the years, and have made several other designs that can store much more energy at lesser weight than the conventional lead-acid battery, but all of these are enormously expensive and unreliable. Doubtless much more can be done. However, while it is always dangerous to underestimate the possibilities of technology, we must remember that batteries have been with us over a century; despite great incentives to produce better batteries—as for instance in aircraft or space craft—improvements have been only marginal.

A potentially interesting method for storing electrical energy in the automobile sounds peculiar, but it may be more practical than batteries. It has been proposed that cars be fitted with a flywheel that would be spun by an electric motor at a "gas station" and the inertia tapped as needed to move the car, until the energy stored in the rotation was exhausted. With advanced materials this system can carry more energy in a lighter unit than existing batteries.

The drawback to the flywheel compared with the battery is cost—the new materials and necessary near-frictionless bearings would be very expensive. And compared with the conventional internal-combustion engine flywheel power has the same drawbacks as battery power.

Fortunately, there are other potential ways of powering an electric car. Still in its infancy is the technology for the "fuel cell," which converts liquid or gaseous fuels directly into electricity. This is very promising, but the existing designs are very expensive and unreliable. Ford has taken a lead in this technology, but nothing is feasible within the next generation.

Even further in the future is the solar-powered car. Solar power will presumably convert sunlight directly into electricity; we will never run out of the unlimited amounts of sunlight. Here too, technology is still very primitive. To generate a tiny amount of electricity a huge solar panel is required, much larger than a car could carry—and needless to say, solar power is seriously reduced during cloudy periods and is impossible at night.

Atomic power for cars was discussed some years ago, but it looks even more utopian than solar power. Unless some new technology is found to convert fission (or fusion) directly to electricity, atomic power would seem to be impossible. The existing nuclear electric power plants are really steam plants, where the reactor generates the heat for the boiler, which spins the turbines. Atomic power of this type has all the advantages and disadvantages of steam power, with considerable additional cost. While atomic power would be effectively nonpolluting, it would provide the slight risks of permitting fissionable materials on the highways—not a serious radiation hazard, but terrorists or other troublemakers could thus assemble a large amount of nuclear material and produce clandestine atomic weapons.

The most promising method of producing electricity in a vehicle is the so-called hybrid engine, in which a gasoline engine runs a generator that produces electricity to drive the motors. Compared with the existing system of mechanical and hydraulic transmissions, this is very expensive and inefficient because there are energy losses in the conversion from mechanical to electrical energy and back again. The compound engine is attractive because it is really a gasoline engine with an electric transmission, an infinitely valuable mechanism that permits the engine to run at almost a constant speed. Emission problems arise largely because the engine must turn at many different speeds, and must accelerate and decelerate. It is now within existing technology to achieve almost zero pollution if the engine can be kept turning at constant speed and load, adjusting the fuel-and-air mixture to operate accordingly. This technology is now in existence, but not produced because it would be extremely expensive compared with existing configurations.

Let me repeat: Most of the alternative systems described in this chapter are in existence, and they could be applied within a few years, if we wanted them. The problem is that all of them are inferior in many important ways to the existing internal-combustion engine. They are either less reliable, less fuel efficient, less powerful, less convenient, have less range, or suffer in some other serious way. More important, they all share the characteristic of being more expensive than the existing system. Always keep this in mind—people who advocate emission-free automobiles are advocating much more expensive vehicles. The significance of this will be noted later.

There has been a lot of loose talk about air pollution in America. Some enthusiasts maintain that it is continually getting worse and is about to choke us. The record is quite to the contrary. Some forms of pollution were worsening until we decided to do something about them. Since that time, although the capability for efficient monitoring is just beginning to tool up, existing data indicate that over the long term the levels remain the same or are improving. This progress has been made with the regulations that have already been applied, which will continue improvements until the last of the industrial pollution is cleaned up and until new emission-controlled cars replace older noncontrolled cars on the road. The Los Angeles air-pollution control agency confidently reports a timetable for achieving air standards. New York City has its own system of classifying overall daily air quality; Table 2 shows the measures of air quality progress made in only six years under present standards:

Table 2: NEW YORK CITY AIR QUALITY PROGRESS

	1969	1975
Good	0	107
Acceptable	38	204
Unsatisfactory	209	23
Unhealthy	114	19

And here is a recent report by the Environmental Protection Administrator to Congress:

Historical trends in air quality levels afford a convenient guide to determining progress in the control of air pollution. For some pollutants, lack of historical data on a national basis limits the inferences that may be made. However, the recent expansion of air pollution monitoring networks is providing data that will serve as a baseline for future trend assessment. Currently, a good historical data base on the national level is available for total suspended particulate [TSP] and sulfur dioxide primarily in urbanized areas. For oxidant, carbon monoxide, and nitrogen dioxide, historical data are limited and the geographical distribution is very sparse. Therefore, trends for these three pollutants are considered as a series of special cases. The present status of historical data reflects the evolution of air pollution monitoring efforts. For the most part, initial efforts were concentrated on the assessment of total suspended particulate and sulfur dioxide in center city areas. . . .

Carbon monoxide trends in the few cities having historical data suggest general improvement. This is consistent with the automobile emission reductions during this period. Data from the States of California, New Jersey, New York, and Washington show reductions in the percent of time the 8-hour CO standard is exceeded. The peak hourly values have been relatively stable, but in the majority of urban areas the 8-hour standard is the more serious problem and this is where improvement is being shown. Los Angeles and New Jersey monitoring data indicate that the percent of time the 8-hour CO standard was exceeded was reduced by approximately 50 percent from 1970–1971 to 1973–1974 (roughly 12 percent to 6 percent). The State of Washington showed consistent progress during the 1971–1973 period, and New York State and San Francisco data showed that less than .05 percent of the 8-hour values were above the standard. On a national basis, the number of CO monitoring sites increased consistently during 1970–1974, with more than 400 percent increase in 1974 over 1970 and a 25 percent increase in 1974 over 1973.

Oxidant trends in California continue to show long-term improvement. Data in the Los Angeles and San Francisco areas show 20 to 50 percent decreases in the number of times the 1-hour oxidant standard was exceeded. However, an important characteristic of the oxidant problem is the recognition of the wide spatial distribution of high oxidant levels. Recent studies have focused attention on oxidant as an area-wide phenomenon extending even to rural areas. The number of oxidant or ozone monitors has increased nationally by almost 600 percent between 1970 and 1974 with a 30 percent increase in 1974 over 1973. As these sites continue to report data, it will become possible to examine oxidant trends on a much broader basis.

Measurements of oxidants at rural stations from Ohio into Maryland and Pennsylvania through the summer of 1974 have confirmed earlier reports of high oxidant concentrations remote from urban areas. The history of air masses, plus the presence of distinctive man-made pollutants in the air masses, strongly suggests that the observed oxidant concentrations are the product of man-made ingredients received by the air masses in passing over an urban area. These ingredients continue to react, forming photochemical oxidants, as the air masses move across the countryside.

Nitrogen oxide emissions have increased nationally since 1970 and upward trends in NO_2 have been seen in Los Angeles and Philadelphia. Because of recent changes in measurement methodology for monitoring nitrogen dioxide, very few areas have sufficient historical data to assess NO_2 trends during the 1970–1974 period.* However, between 1973 and 1974, the number of stations reporting a complete year of acceptable NO_2 data increased by almost 800 percent so that future reports should be able to more accurately assess national trends in NO_2 levels.

Nationwide estimates of pollutant emissions from 1970 through 1974 show steady declines in the tonnages of particulates and carbon monoxide being dumped into our air. Emissions of sulfur oxides and hydrocarbons evidence only slight declines. Nitrogen oxides show a slight increase in total emissions.

All this means is that air quality is getting better, but it does not mean that the problem will be solved. It is not even entirely clear what is meant by "solved." Perfectly clean air is not possible, because nature itself pollutes. Particulate matter produced by dust storms, volcanic explosion, and the normal action of the wind on the land produce much more pollution than anything man is capable of. Many of the rabid environmentalists make a religion of nature, imagining it to be very pure and delicate, and man to be incredibly powerful and capable of disturbing its balance. On the contrary, life and nature are dirty. And man is still a rather trivial thing scratching around on the surface of the earth. His feeble efforts cannot do much to disturb nature.

There are now established in the United States what are called "ambiant air quality standards." As far as I can determine these were made up more or less arbitrarily by the Environmental Protection Agency on the basis of the best information available at the time. Unfortunately not very good information was available then. These standards are periodically reviewed by commit-

---

* "Judgments concerning the attainment of the NO_2 national standards have been complicated by the discovery in 1973 that the ambient sampling method for this pollutant was faulty. The method that had been in use generally showed higher than actual levels of NO_2. An analysis of available data in the spring of 1975 indicated that only 16 Air Quality Control Regions (6 percent) have NO_2 concentrations at or above National Ambient Air Quality Standards. It is important to note that this is a preliminary assessment which will be revised as more data become available."

tees of scientists, who usually recommended that they see no reason for changing them—the standards were arbitrary in the first place, so there really is no need to change them to any other arbitrary standards. If that sounds a little nutty to you, it is.

To achieve the ambiant air quality standards that it more or less invented, EPA is taking draconian measures. Localities have been required to draw up clean air plans with specific objectives by such and such a date. The favored means that EPA has used to achieve these standards is "Transportation Control Plans" (TCP)—i.e., reducing automobile usage. Communities have been urged, under the threat of banning cars, to prohibit new parking, to build mass transit facilities, to promote car pooling, to increase tolls on bridges, and even to require prior EPA approval of such facilities as shopping centers that would attract traffic, and presumably increase emissions and therefore air pollution. Clearly, this type of thinking is directed not toward improving air quality but toward reducing automobile use. Supposing their real interest was in reducing air pollution—which would be the more effective approach: reducing the amount of driving by half or reducing the amount of auto emissions by half? The first involves social engineering, the second physical engineering. It is always easier to modify equipment than people; this, as we shall see, is the logic behind the auto safety regulations. But the environmental issue allows the social-engineering tactic to be attempted. Yet the engineering route is really the way to go; enormous progress has already been made.

But not enough for the politicians. As I write this in Spring 1977, federal law effectively prohibits the production and importation of automobiles after 1977—since the Congress has required auto emissions standards that cannot be met by any car in the world—large or small, domestic or foreign. From the very beginning of air pollution control legislation, the auto engineers told the Congress that the .41 HC, 3.4 CO, and .4 NO_x standards were impossible to meet. The original timetable for achieving the Muskie standards was 1975; this was permitted to slip to 1976 and 1977—and the automakers have been accused of dragging their feet. This is rather like requiring people to run a three-minute mile next year, giving them several years grace, and then blaming them for stalling. The emission standards simply cannot be met. The HC and CO standards are within the realm of possibility, but the NO_x standard is unattainable given existing technology.

Even if the emissions standards could be achieved, the auto engineer is in a Catch-22 situation because he must also meet safety and bumper standards that increase weight, as well as fuel economy standards that require less weight and more pollution—and must design a car with the performance, comfort, reliability, and low cost that consumers want. It is difficult to escape the conclusion that the Congress is responding to a constituency that wants to drive the automobile off the American road, or at least run the price up so far that the average American cannot afford to own a car.

Let me summarize the argument: Most air pollution is not caused by automobiles. We do not know the effects of automobile emissions on public health; what little evidence is available suggests that the effects are at most trivial. Existing emission controls have reduced auto emissions to a fraction of their previous levels, and the air is getting cleaner. If the air were getting worse and bad air was a real problem we could always go to clean methods of auto propulsion that would be inferior in other ways to the existing internal-combustion engine. Yet we are told the opposite of all this, and the government is moving to shut down our cities and close off our driving opportunities. Why?

5.

Fuel

The most recent charge is that the automobile is devouring irreplaceable world resources, particularly fuel. This accusation has developed from the Arab oil boycott and the "energy crisis" of the winter of 1973–1974. If we are to believe many of our scientists, journalists, and politicians, the earth is rapidly running out of most raw materials, and the continued use of the automobile is a major contributor to bankrupting the whole world and leaving our grandchildren in penury.

This, of course, is the "limits-to-growth" or "neo-Malthusian" hypothesis that has been widely publicized over the last five years. I am happy to tell you that it is almost entirely spurious; it has no scientific basis. And I use the qualifying phrase "almost entirely" only because there are necessarily some uncertainties about the future. But in fact there is no reasonable theory that the world will run out of resources. Let me leave fuel aside for a moment because the point is made much more clearly by reference to other resources. The production of automobiles consumes large amounts of iron, aluminum, plastics, glass, copper, and rubber. Geologists and other scientists have made estimates of the known reserves of these materials and can calculate how rapidly they will be used up, given present rates of expenditure. If we continue at the current pace, the resources will be exhausted in, say, fifty years; if we accelerate our usage at the rate we have in the past, they will last, say, only another thirty years. This kind of calculation is the basis of neo-Malthusian arguments. The projections are fraudulent.

Various companies, private and public, are in the business of producing and selling iron, aluminum, etc. Keep in mind that their business is manufacturing and marketing, not exploration. Searching for new sources of materials—new mines—is expensive and laborious. Industries invest in only as much exploration as is necessary to guarantee their supplies for ten to twenty years ahead. Of course, we will run out of *known* reserves in twenty years—because nobody goes to the trouble of finding the resources for future use. In fact, there has been very little exploration of the world. Geology is still a very primitive science, and the existing mines have been found almost by chance, by sending a few men to the boondocks to chip at rocks. If you sent out serious teams to explore the world, God knows what you would find. Credible estimates have been made that the earth's crust is 6 percent iron ore and 8 percent aluminum; if they are anywhere near true, that is more than we could hope to use in millions of years.

The idea that we need to conserve iron and aluminum is ridiculous. Other materials are in even vaster supply. Glass is made from sand, and not even the most enthusiastic neo-Malthusian thinks that the world is going to run out of sand. Plastics can also be made from sand. Copper is probably not as common as aluminum or iron, but fortunately other products can easily be substituted for it.

Furthermore, only a small amount of the material in an automobile is actually expended. With the exception of a very few that are saved for historical or hobby purposes, every car is eventually junked. All useful parts go into some other car, which is itself eventually scrapped. The large aluminum parts are cut out and recycled, and the rest is compressed into a ball of iron and steel, which is used to make new steel when there is a market for scrap. In recent years the demand for the kinds of steel that use a lot of scrap has been very low, so presumably some of this material is wasted. In the real world, recent experience is just the opposite of the conception of the neo-Malthusians. Instead of any possibility that we are exhausting our resources, we have such a surplus of quality iron ore that there is no need for the somewhat cruddy scrap provided by recycling automobiles. Let us not worry about raw materials.

But gasoline is another matter. According to the generally accepted theory, petroleum results from geological pressures on large amounts of dead organic material from prehistoric ages; like coal, it is a "fossil fuel." Although the world has been around many million years, it seems reasonable to believe that there is some limit to the number of animals and plants which died and were subsequently squished by geological pressures to form coal and petroleum. Furthermore, world exploration for fossil fuels is far more sophisticated than for other resources. Oil geologists are the most skilled of all. They have good theories about what sort of ground formations produce petroleum (and natural gas), and their explorations are taking them into offshore areas, and even arctic waters. It appears that the easy oil has already been found, and it is probably true that any new oil will be much more expensive than the oil already found. Exploring, drilling, and extracting oil from places like the North Sea is much more costly in every way than taking it out of Texas or the Persian Gulf. So as we reach for more and more oil the price will rise higher and higher.

All this is true, but almost entirely misleading. Oil is cheaper now than it was in the past. Let us trace its history: In certain areas of the world, such as Mesopotamia, people long ago noticed smelly sticky liquid occasionally bubbling up through the ground, stuff which would burn when lighted although it was otherwise annoying, aggravating, and disregarded. During the same period it was also discovered that certain animal and vegetable oils could be used for lighting. The lamps mentioned in Scripture burned these sorts of oil. In more recent times, it was learned that whales produced a very important and useful type of oil, and a major industry was developed to fuel the homes of the early industrial revolution.

Fortunately, as the whale herds became depleted, we learned that the previously ignored sticky stuff called petroleum could be refined into an excellent lighting fuel called "kerosene." A large industry was built around this material in the late nineteenth century. An early promoter named John D. Rockefeller put all the oil companies together into the Standard Oil Company of New Jersey, an organization that has been regarded as the exemplar of a predatory monopoly. It has almost been forgotten that as a result of his operations the price of oil steadily dropped throughout the period that the trust was intact. Standard Oil was broken up in 1911, and World War I followed shortly thereafter, greatly increasing the demand for oil, so the price went up precipitously. In the early 1920s there was widespread speculation that the world would run out of oil, so prices increased, and the prospectors went out and found more petroleum in such places as the Oklahoma oil fields that created the famous Indian millionaires. From the 1920s through the late 1960s, the relative price of oil dropped—that is, although the nominal price increased slightly, it did not rise as rapidly as other prices, or as much as consumer income. In retrospect, it may seem strange that the period of that notorious international oil cartel was an era of declining prices. The big oil companies were able to maintain themselves only by continually holding the price line, and even then they were undercut by many large independents, such as the famous Mr. Paul Getty.

The current high prices and potential shortages do not result from the exhaustion of oil resources. The real problem is a formidable new cartel, not of companies, but of governments. The Organization of Petroleum Exporting Countries, formed in the early 1960s, did not become a serious force on the international scene until the early 1970s, when it took advantage of the unstable political conditions in the Middle East to pull itself together under Arab leadership and run up the price of oil. If OPEC should fall apart, prices would plummet back to low natural market levels. And there is indeed every reason to expect that OPEC will come undone. History indicates that cartels are very unstable. This requires a bit of explanation. A cartel is a very sensible organization; it is in each member's interest to co-operate with the cartel to keep the price up. But higher prices reduce demand, so production must be cut to maintain them. But every member of the cartel is seriously tempted to keep up full production to maximize his income—so everybody cheats. And since everybody knows that everybody cheats, the cartel falls apart. The principal reason that OPEC has not yet collapsed is the vital role played by a single country, Saudi Arabia, which keeps OPEC together by seriously restricting its own production. Unlike the other members of OPEC—such as Iran, Iraq, and Algeria, who have major commitments for economic development or defense—Saudi Arabia is a very small country with a feudal government having very few ambitions other than maintaining a traditional Moslem society under the Saudi dynasty. It can afford to make the necessary sacrifices to preserve the cartel.

In Saudi Arabia, oil can be extracted for less than twenty cents a barrel (42 gallons) and shipped to the United States by tanker for about $2.00 a barrel. The current OPEC monopoly price for oil is $12 a barrel, so the Saudis have plenty of room to play. But it is almost certain that OPEC will collapse, since cartels have only been possible when supported by the state. As OPEC is a cartel of governments and there is no international government, there is no one to maintain order. The OPEC countries are from diverse parts of the world, with different cultures and interests. They have in common only the fact that they export oil. Even the Arabs have nothing in common, save general resistance to what they regard as "Zionist" aggression against a part of the Arab nation; otherwise, they hate each other's guts. OPEC would probably have come undone by now, except that

powerful interests in the Western countries wish to keep it together for their own purposes.

But before going into that, let us complete the discussion of
the effects of OPEC. The problem is not that there is insufficient
oil in the world, but that the price is artificially kept very high.
If OPEC were not in operation, it would be easy for us to buy
almost all of our oil from the Persian Gulf. This is where it is
most efficient to extract petroleum, and the supply would not
run out until the next century, at least. (There is probably plenty
more oil there, but the Persian Gulf countries already have so
much that they see no reason for further exploration.) The only
problems now are that oil costs us something in foreign exchange,
and that the Middle East situation involves some political problems.

Foreign exchange is really a minor problem, because the OPEC
countries are for the most part industrializing and buying more
and more of our goods. They sell us oil, we sell them machine
tools and other manufactured goods as well as our own resources
—coal, grain, soy beans, tobacco, cotton, etc. Even at the current
monopoly price, the United States is not paying insufferable
amounts for oil. The current outlay for oil is about $35 billion,
of which $24 billion goes to OPEC countries. Most of those
"petrodollars" are "recycled" to buy U.S. goods. When the OPEC
price was first jacked up in 1973, many "experts" frantically told
us how "petrodollars" would upset the world markets and substantially damage our domestic economy. This has not happened;
the theory itself was a little ridiculous. The U.S. gross national
product of total goods and services is well over a trillion dollars
a year, and the increase in energy prices was well under one
percent of this. The higher oil price does hurt some of the developing countries who must rely on imported oil; their development will be slowed somewhat, but not necessarily halted. In
any event this hardly matters to the United States.

The second and real problem with OPEC is political. Most
OPEC countries are friendly with the United States, and we have

no particular objection to relying on their oil. Some Arab countries are another matter. They have already indicated their intention of using the "oil weapon" to force the industrial West to reduce its support of Israel. Since we wish to support Israel and we are generally averse to being pushed around by foreign countries—particularly by such sordid regimes as the Arabs, who unfortunately suffer from corrupt feudal rulers or equally corrupt but considerably more ambitious "socialist" gangsters—we wish to be free of this type of pressure.

Consider the magnitude of the problem. Currently we are importing about 40 percent of our oil, mostly from OPEC countries. However, oil produces just under half of the total energy expended in the U.S. (Thirty percent is from natural gas, 20 percent from coal, 4 percent from hydropower, and 2 percent from nuclear power.) Energy has to be considered as a total package. Many different sources are interchangeable. For example, over the last half century, oil has largely replaced coal for electric power generation, industrial use, and home heating because it was cheaper and easier to handle. But since the price of oil has gone up, the demand for coal has increased precipitously. Similarly, natural gas (which has been held below market levels by Federal Power Commision intervention) has been relatively cheap and therefore has been replacing coal and hydropower.

At the present time, automobile use amounts to about three quarters of all gasoline consumption, 50 percent of transportation energy use (the rest accounted for by aircraft, trucks, and diesel and electric rail vehicles), about 30 percent of oil consumption, and about 13 percent of total energy use. But remember that we are already importing 40 percent of our oil, so even if we stopped driving cars altogether, we would still have to import it. And, in addition, remember that gasoline is just one component of oil. While there is some margin of flexibility in refining a barrel of oil into different grade products, refining it for diesel or other uses would still produce some gasoline.

This perspective helps, but not very much. We are becoming increasingly dependent on foreign oil, particularly Arab oil. Are we to have our national well-being sacrificed just so that people can go joy riding? This outlook makes the widely advocated emphasis on conservation plausible—but the numbers make the strategy impossible. If 30 percent of our oil consumption can be charged to the automobile, merely cutting gas mileage by half (which no serious person believes can be done) will not achieve energy independence. At best we can only slow down the increasing reliance on the Arab oil.

Another option is to force the Arabs to lower the price. After all why are we paying enormous taxes to support a huge military establishment? What are our troops for? When the American republic was young, a group of Arab gangsters, the Barbary pirates, tried to hold us up. A Congressman said "Millions for defense, but not one penny for tribute," and we sent a fleet out to the Mediterranean, beat up on the Arabs, and had no more trouble with them. Alas, the Arabs have some powerful friends today, namely the Communist countries, and we do not want to risk a war over oil. Also, we do not seem to have the vigor and will of our forefathers; we would rather lie down and take whatever insults these various "third world" dictators prefer to dish out.

Another approach is the diplomatic one, whereby the energy-consuming states—the U.S., the Western European countries, and Japan—are trying to get together as a group to negotiate with OPEC. Unfortunately, a buyer's cartel is even more difficult to maintain than a seller's. Possibly the only thing that the International Energy Agency has done is help OPEC keep the prices up. In fact, this is exactly what it wants to do.

The principal reason we are not doing much about OPEC is that high energy prices are considered desirable by the people who matter most in America. High prices have the effect of discouraging energy use, which is considered a plus from the viewpoint of national security, as well as environmentalism. Limits-to-growth agitators favor energy conservation to discourage economic growth: "consumer advocates" favor it because they are fundamentally opposed to mass consumption of consumer goods. The oil interests favor it for obvious reasons: the high OPEC price forces a high domestic price. OPEC has created a windfall for domestic oil producers and for energy providers in general. Because of the high price of oil, there can be high prices for alternative forms of energy—coal, hydropower, nuclear power, natural gas, etc.

But most important of all, the high OPEC prices provide the opportunity for breaking the OPEC monopoly. The higher the price OPEC sets, the more attractive alternative sources of energy become. Our historical reliance on oil is purely a matter of economics. Oil was cheap and available. If it is no longer cheap and not so readily available, we will convert to other types of energy, which are marginally less cheap and slightly less available than oil used to be. So long as Arab oil could be landed on the United States at $3 a barrel it was impractical to consider such sources as coal liquefaction, oil shales, tar sands, and various forms of nuclear, wind, tidal, geothermal, and solar power. Now these look more promising. It is quite plausible that by the end of this century we will have energy coming out of our ears.

Furthermore, the high OPEC price makes it more attractive to perform otherwise more expensive and less efficient ways of producing oil in North America—"secondary" and "tertiary" extraction from oil wells. The easy kind of drilling draws about half the oil in a reservoir, but by investing more in pumping, the entire pocket can be cleaned out. A higher oil price also makes it attractive to drill in places where the pockets are perhaps a little smaller. Most drilling has concentrated on very large reservoirs that could be easily exploited, and the small independent companies have sniffed around the fringes of the fields. With the higher price, peripheral drilling becomes more economic. (Over the last few years the actual amount of oil recovered in the U.S. and Canada has been declining—but this is largely because the government has been holding down oil prices. No independent observer knowledgeable about the oil business doubts that oil and gas will magically begin to appear when the price controls are lifted.)

The high oil price is the real means of achieving the "Project Independence" advocated by the Nixon and Ford administrations. Maintenance of OPEC is a necessary condition to make that policy credible. While the chances of achieving anything near independence in the relatively short run—say in the next ten years—are so slim as to be effectively impossible, the long run prospects are much more credible. Remember that almost all types of energy are interchangeable, and the array of energy sources is enormous.

We already have the capability of producing gasoline from coal, oil shale, and tar sands. We do not simply because it is more expensive than making it from oil. But during World War II the German government, which had very little petroleum available, kept its planes and tanks running on artificially produced gasoline. It was expensive—about $10 a gallon—but it could be done again. It is just a question of cost.

Ten percent of our oil is currently being used to generate electric power. Some of this could be replaced with more effective hydropower, but a more interesting possibility is increasing the use of coal, of which we have at least 500 years of reserves. (These reserves are much larger than any other reserves because of intense exploration in the late nineteenth century when it was believed that coal usage would continue to expand at previous growth rates. But oil came into use, so coal was "over-discovered.") There really is no need to use oil to generate power. Many plants have reconverted to coal power, and others have delayed for such trivial reasons as the fact that many coal yards were replaced by parking lots. Other major bars to the use of coal are environmental considerations, which are partially justified because of the high sulfur content of some coal, which increases sulfur dioxide, stuff better not put in the air. But some reasons are just frivolous, such as the resistance of big-city environmentalists to chewing up the western mountains to extract coal. It is a little difficult to understand why people are concerned about mountains they will never see—especially since the terrain can be restored to almost its natural contour once the coal is extracted.

Another possibility is nuclear energy. Fission reactors are now producing 2 percent of our natural energy; the amount produced can be expanded almost ad infinitum. But nuclear energy is also being held up by frivolous environmentalist objections. The safety record of atomic power plants is perfect, and the chances of any damage to anyone are so slim as to be effectively zero. There is no possibility whatever of a reactor blowing up, because a nuclear power plant is nothing like a nuclear bomb. The risks, such as they are, are the potential leakage of radiation to the local areas and the potential theft of nuclear materials by foreign powers or terrorists. Both of these can be almost nullified by building reactors underground, at slight additional construction costs. (Lest the reader think me blind to these issues, I lived for two years within a half mile of one of the largest nuclear reactors. Neither I nor my neighbors worried—nor should we have.)

Some people—including some in the nuclear business, who should know better—have projected that we will soon run out of the uranium necessary to run these reactors. Based on known reserves, we are indeed going to run out of *high-grade* uranium, but there seem to be limitless supplies of *low-grade* uranium. Enough uranium to keep reactors going thousands of years can easily be obtained merely by raising the price, which will happen anyway as the high-grade resources run out. The cost of uranium is a tiny cost of producing electric power from a nuclear plant; paying ten times as much for the uranium would only increase the per kilowatt-hour cost of electricity by a fraction of a cent.

The reason that the people in the nuclear business exaggerate the possibility of running out of fuels is that they want to push for more advanced technology. In the short run they are working on the so-called breeder reactor, which as a by-product of making electricity generates more fuel that can then be used to produce even more electricity. This looks like something for nothing, but is merely a more efficient means of using nuclear energy. Many people object to breeder reactors on the grounds that the by-product bred is plutonium—the raw material for atomic weapons. While there is no chance that the plutonium will explode in the reactor, it might be seized by foreign agents or domestic terrorists; the spread of nuclear technology throughout the world would give any country with a breeder reactor the capacity to make nuclear bombs. Any physicist now has the knowledge necessary to make a primitive nuclear weapon, so all that holds up universal manufacturing is the scarcity of the necessary plutonium or uranium 235. Increase the amount of these nuclear raw materials and atom bombs will be everywhere. This is such a grave threat to the world that I support very strongly the efforts of those who would halt the further development of the breeder reactor technology—but on political, not safety or environmental grounds.

Beyond the breeder reactor is nuclear fusion, which now exists only as a theoretical possibility in the minds of scientists. The idea is to harness for peaceful use the type of energy created by a hydrogen bomb. A recent major breakthrough in another form of technology may provide the key to fusion power. The laser provides the capability of creating the great heat necessary to fuse hydrogen and produce power. Most people who have been working on the subject expect controlled fusion to be achieved by the end of this century; if this comes about, it would provide an absolutely limitless source of energy. The fuel would be hydrogen, the principal component of water, one of the most common components in the world. Not even the most ferocious neo-Malthusian imagines that the world is going to run out of water in the foreseeable future.

We have by no means exhausted the variety of potential power sources. Many people have spoken of the possibilities provided by wind, at least in local applications. Geothermal power has incredible potential. The center of the earth is extremely hot; by digging a deep hole (perhaps in the future with a laser) and allowing a fluid to be heated, energy is produced, either directly as heat or through a turbine to generate electricity. Even the tides can be harnessed in certain areas of the world; by means of dams and channels, the incoming and ebbing tides are passed through turbines that produce power.

But the potentially most interesting source of all is the sun, which dwarfs any alternate source of energy. We sometimes forget that most of our light and heat now comes directly from rays of the sun. It is a real problem to convert solar energy into other forms.* But low-grade solar heaters are already used in homes, especially in places like Israel and Japan where oil is particularly expensive, and primitive devices already exist even for converting solar energy to electric power for use in automobiles and elsewhere. A lot of money is now being invested, and some of the best brains in the world are working on solar energy. NASA has made some major contributions by providing the solar technology for powering satellites and space stations. How much more development there will be is largely a function of how much is invested.

One major problem with many of the energy sources mentioned above is that they are not suited for automobile uses. By definition, something that is "auto-mobile" must carry its own power sources. We still do not have any serious idea of how a long-range, high-performance electric vehicle might be constructed; so the alternative forms of energy that produce electricity will help solve the gasoline problem by substituting for oil in the production of power, but not as fuel for the automobile itself. So let us look at the kinds of energy that can go into a car as we know it today. We now use gasoline from crude oil to power an automobile for the very same reason that we use the internal-combustion engine—it is the most efficient source of

---

* One of the problems with existing solar power technology is that the very large panels required to collect the energy would occupy an immense amount of space. Since everybody has his own crackpot schemes, let me contribute mine—drive on the panels. Let the highways themselves collect the sun's rays.

energy. Gasoline has a very high BTU content; that is, it produces more energy per gallon than other potential types of fuel.
But if we had not discovered gasoline, we would be happily
making do with other fuels—alcohol, for example, which can be
used very easily in automobiles. Brazil's national oil company
regularly dilutes its products with methanol, depending on
fluctuations in the world market price. Wood and grain alcohols
are a fine fuel, although they have a lower BTU content than
gasoline. But alcohol has another advantage—it is a renewable
resource; you can grow it.

This does not exhaust the list of fuels for cars. Another possibility is liquefied gases. At normal temperatures they are gaseous,
so for use in an automobile, they must be pressurized and re-
leased slowly for vaporization in the engine. This is how propane
is used in your home, or in a portable heater. I mentioned earlier
that Japanese taxicabs use propane. Propane production could
be upgraded enormously. Instead of having a tank filled up with
liquid gasoline at a station, you might eventually have a tank
charged with gas in the same way that air is put in tires, or
perhaps a new tank would be put in. Such a system would
currently be more expensive than gasoline and would provide
inferior performance, but it could be an adequate substitute if
no gasoline were available. As I mentioned earlier, some of the
alternatives to the internal-combustion engine need no gasoline
at all. The gas turbine, sterling, and steam engines run perfectly
well on kerosene and residual oils.

And there are still other possibilities. William Brown of the
Hudson Institute has recently published a paper pointing out
that down around 10,000 feet under the oil fields in the Gulf
of Mexico are vast reservoirs of hot water mixed under high
pressure with methane. The technology is already available to
release this energy; the only problem is how best to harness the
power that could be generated by the pressure, the heat, and
the gas. The amount of reserves in this one field alone are *more
than all of the oil in the Middle East.* And we have no idea how
many reservoirs like this exist worldwide. What is the drawback?

Simple, oil is currently cheaper. If we start running out of oil, which is unlikely, we can tap the methane.

But, you may reasonably ask, what good are all these for the car I have now? Well, two sources of energy could be made available in the future, one for the older cars and one for the new nongasoline cars. A more likely possibility is simply that conversion kits will be produced. It is a very easy matter to re-jet a carburetor—the part costs a dollar. Even adapting the present car to propane or some other type of liquefied gas is not difficult. During World War II in Europe, cars were converted to coal power by putting a coal-gas generator in the trunk and piping the gas forward to the motor.

But that is not all, because I have not yet discussed the most likely source of energy in the future—ordinary oil from wells. Only a relatively small part of the world has been seriously explored for petroleum. It is quite likely many other places besides the Middle East have vast reservoirs of oil. Who would have thought that the North Sea could contain oil, or the Labrador coast, or the China Sea? It is highly possible that the gap between the time when known reserves are exhausted and new energy sources become available will be filled by—more oil.

Once again, I fear the reader has been buried in options. Which of these will provide us with fuel in the future? It is certainly an open question. Obviously, many of these will have serious problems, probably to the point of impracticality. But can anyone really claim that all of these alternatives to Arab oil are going to fail? I think not. Nevertheless, as the reader is well aware, shrill voices are advising us that we are about to run out of fuel and that we must curtail our driving. Why?

6.

Safety

Now, let us examine a real cost of the automobile that has been recognized all along—safety. Each year highway use results in the killing of several hundred thousand people worldwide, and the injury and crippling of many hundreds of thousands more. The auto-highway system is one of the most significant killers in an advanced society. In 1975, 46,000 Americans were killed in road accidents, and although this rate has dropped from that of previous years, we have come to expect approximately 50,000 deaths annually from driving.*

Paradoxically, one reason that this carnage continues is that the automobile is almost perfectly safe—so safe that we cannot

* Not all of these fatalities are accidents. There are suspiciously large numbers of single vehicle collisions involving a fixed object such as a bridge abutment. It is reasonable to conclude that cars are a favorite tool for committing suicide in America. Disguising a suicide as an automobile accident is an excellent way of guaranteeing double indemnity for one's heirs; researchers have guessed that this is the cause of perhaps one in seven single vehicle "accident" fatalities. It is also quite probable that faked automobile accidents are used for murder.

take the notion of being hurt or killed seriously. Few people are killed roller skating on airport runways because that activity is so obviously perilous. Conversely, driving an automobile is not at all dangerous, so we do it casually—which leads to fatalities.

Let me make the point clear with some numbers. Annually more than 1 trillion (1,000 billion) motor vehicle miles are traveled in the United States. Approximately 45,000 drivers were killed last year. The average car is driven 10,000 miles a year, and the average trip in a car is about 5 miles. So the odds against being killed in an average car in an average year are about 5,000 to 1, and the odds against being killed on an average trip are about 10 million to 1. In fact, in urban driving, the chances are even smaller—20 million to 1 for a 5-mile trip.

Look at these odds expressed as probabilities. The probability of being killed on the average 5-mile trip is less than .0000002—which is effectively zero. Now let us suppose that a safety device or technique could cut the numbers of deaths in half, saving over 15,000 lives a year. That would reduce the probability of being killed on any given trip from less than .0000002 to .0000001. But both figures are effectively variations of zero; the individual driver cannot experience the difference. That we care so little about safety is obvious because we do not even bother to institute the two personal safety measures that could each independently bring about that 50 percent reduction—wearing seat belts, or not drinking while we drive.*

However, the policymaker and politician look only at the aggregate figure, not the probabilities. They see the projected 50,000 deaths. There is thus a distinct difference in perceptions of the individual driver and the policymaker, which cannot be reconciled in any rational way. But the notion of "carnage on the highways" has to be put into perspective. First of all, there

---

* Of course, we all take certain ordinary safety precautions, not so much against being killed as against making contact with another car —which we know is likely to be expensive and time consuming, as well as likely to get us in trouble with the law and with the insurance company.

is a long-term decrease in the rate of highway fatalities, almost independent of any government intervention. (See Figure 3.) Early cars were dangerous toys, but the death rate per registered vehicle and per vehicle mile traveled has steadily dropped ever since accurate figures have been kept. This decline was brought about by many different factors. Safety can be best understood

Figure 3: TRAFFIC DEATH RATES

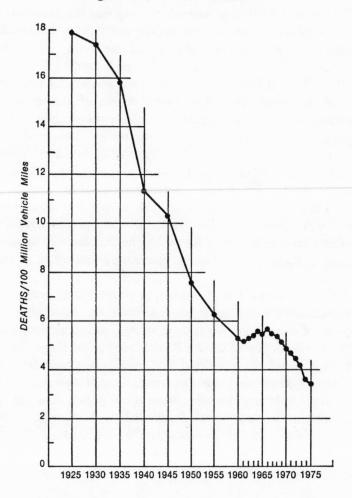

in terms of the three main elements of the American mass transportation system: the highway, the vehicle, and the driver.

Over the years, improving highways has rapidly cut down the opportunities for accidents. Merely paving roads made more effective braking possible and eliminated the dust that once so severely limited visibility. Building sidewalks removed pedestrians from the thoroughfare. General road widening reduced the potential for collision, as did four-lane and later divided highways. Better street lighting was a big help in urban areas. And one of the major gains in promoting safety was the invention of the limited-access parkway and expressway that, with carefully designed sight lines and carefully plotted curves, have incredibly low accident rates. The latest figure for such roads is 1.3 deaths per 100 million vehicle miles—less than half the overall rate. The massive chain-collision accident with dozens of victims is the exception, not the rule. Expressways are impressively safe.

The sheer success of the auto-highway system in overwhelming other transportation systems also resulted in improved safety. The elimination of horses and the near disappearance of bicycles from the road reduced opportunities for casualties from both. Liquidation of trolleys did away with accidents caused when wheels were caught in trolley tracks, or when people were hurt crossing from the trolley to the curb. The shrinkage of railroads eliminated many grade crossings, places very productive of accidents.

The second element in the American auto-highway system has also contributed to cutting down casualties. The automobile has a history of steady improvements in safety innovations and modifications. The notion of Daniel Patrick Moynihan, Ralph Nader, and other misinformed critics that the carmakers have been indifferent to safety is quite erroneous. Detroit has not talked much about safety, to be sure, because safety talk does not sell cars, but their engineers and designers have been continuously improving the safety of their products. Merely making cars run more reliably constitutes a safety measure—it is very scary to have your engine falter just when you need some power for passing or getting out of a hazardous situation. The windshield improved visibility, as did the windshield wiper and washer. Headlights are an obvious safety device, as are running lights, brake lights, and turn signals. So are effective suspension systems that permit the driver to retain control in emergency conditions, and brakes, which have also been steadily improved (largely as a result of auto-racing experience, not safety testing). The best safety devices are those that *prevent* accidents, but for reasons I shall discuss later, most safety "experts" have concentrated on reducing injury *after* an accident has occurred.

The last element in the great American mass transportation system has probably improved safety the most. The quality of American driving is at an all-time high, certainly the highest in the world. It is amazing that so many people, a majority of the population, have learned to operate automobiles so well. This was not always the case. Driving was an innovation that took people a while to learn to manage. Happily, most of our population learn to drive in adolescence and have vast experience. The average American will drive a half million miles in his lifetime.

Being in effect born behind the wheel is probably the most important promoter of safety. This is evident from the experience of foreign nations, where accident rates are very high, particularly in times of rapidly expanding automobile ownership, for a very simple reason: people without experience in driving cars, and especially those who learn to drive as adults, do not master the skills as well as those who were bred to it.

Table 3: FATILITIES/100 MILLION VEHICLE MILES (1973)

U.S.	4.2
U.K.	5.2
Australia	6.6
Canada	6.7
Italy	8.8
W. Germany	9.9
Japan	11.2
Belgium	17.4

We see evidence of this in our own country. Ordinary observation reveals that those unaccustomed to driving are the most erratic and therefore potentially the most dangerous drivers on the road. For example, it has long been folk wisdom that Jews were rotten drivers. Well, Jews have tended to concentrate in urban centers with mass transit facilities. Only in the post–World War II period did they begin to suburbanize and auto-mobilize seriously. In California today they drive as well as anyone else.

One can learn a number of useful skills growing up on concrete, but driving a car is not one of them. Learning to drive in your late 20s will make you a less-skilled driver than someone who learned when he was young. This problem is compounded if you learn from someone who himself learned at an older age.

There is a more recent example of the effects of experience on driving skills. Common observation reveals that the worst drivers in America today are black, particularly black women. During the 1960s, black America achieved very rapid economic gains, and vastly increased its relative and absolute ownership of automobiles. Millions of black people learned to drive for the first time as adults, and as with any people learning something new, their skills are still not entirely polished.*

Overall, the best safety program is simply letting people drive. But that is not quite enough, so let us also consider the effects of government action. From the beginning, cars have been regulated by the state—but originally not with safety in mind. Early speed laws were meant to prevent cars from bothering horses

---

* By the way, the anti-auto bias of our academics and government researchers led the sociologists to disregard this remarkable trend of "auto-mobilization" by black America. Nearly 60 percent of black families now own cars. There was an even more rapid expansion in the number of black auto mechanics. A glance around the working-class urban neighborhoods that now house the bulk of the black population of the United States will reveal dozens of people casually working on their cars in the garages, driveways, and even the streets. The uglier aspect of this same phenomenon—car stripping—also indicates a high level of mechanical ability and orientation toward the automobile.

and pedestrians, and licensing was intended to raise revenues. The first primitive safety legislation was passed during the 1930s when some minimum equipment was compelled for automobiles, particularly headlights. Later came the requirement of annual auto inspections for lights, brakes, and sometimes wheel alignment and shocks. It seems reasonable to believe that inspections probably had some effect in keeping equipment on the road in better condition, but there seems to be no hard evidence whatever, one way or the other.

Certainly much more significant was state action to improve road controls. Traffic lights, stop signs, and enforcement of laws against drunken driving surely have some effect—but interestingly, not speeding laws. The oft-repeated slogan, "speed kills," is of doubtful validity. Most accidents occur at legal speeds, and changes in the speed limit have little or no effect on the accident rate. The principal effect of high speed driving is that errors of judgment are more likely to lead to accidents, and accidents to fatalities. The relatively large number of accidents at high rates of speed—that is, illegal rates of speed—reflect less the effects of driving at those speeds than the fact that the most risk-prone and lawless driver is most likely to be breaking the speed laws. Aggressive motorists drive fast and have accidents; they have accidents because they are risk-takers, not because they drive fast. With a few exceptions maximum speed limits could probably be raised 15–20 miles an hour without any noticeable effect on the accident rate.

Concentrating on speed was a major part of the first great traffic safety campaign during the 1950s. This was a period of increased prosperity when the number of cars on the road probably expanded more rapidly than at any other time in history. The pent-up demand for cars during the Great Depression and World War II was satisfied, the percentage of households in America owning them increased from 55 to 80 percent, and the bulk of the urban working class became auto-mobile. During a period when large numbers of new drivers were appearing on the roads, accidents should certainly be expected to increase.

Nevertheless, during this period the number of fatalities rose only slightly. There were 33,000 traffic deaths in 1930, 34,500 in 1940 followed by a drop during the war, and 35,000 in 1950. The total crept up only very slowly to 38,000 in 1960. A major reason for this was the demographic profile of the country. Because of the low birth rate during the 1930s, the driver population in the 1950s had only a relatively small percentage of accident-prone adolescent males.

Nevertheless, the supply of safety features and programs was not increasing as rapidly as the demand for safety. In the mid-1950s, for reasons that I shall try to explain later, the first great auto safety campaigns began. When I was a boy, Connecticut was labeled "the police state." When you entered the state on the Merritt Parkway, your first sight was a huge statue of a state trooper with a sign reading, "Speeders Lose Licenses." Governor Abraham Ribicoff responded to the great perceived plague of traffic deaths in his state (less than 300 per year) by decreeing that anyone given a traffic ticket for speeding would lose his license. During Ribicoff's tenure as Governor more than 10,000 residents lost their licenses and were immobilized, to their great annoyance. Ribicoff proudly announced later that the traffic death rate had gone down. Unfortunately, the rate had gone down even more in adjoining states that did not employ his draconian measures against motorists.*

Those familiar with the mentality of politicians will never admit to making a mistake; if they appear foolish it must be somebody else's fault. So having failed to cleanse his state's roads of highway carnage by purifying the driver, Ribicoff turned against the automobile. He had read a magazine piece by one Daniel Patrick Moynihan that blamed all on the car. He also found a useful aide in a peripatetic young lawyer from his state, Ralph Nader.

Nader had been interested in auto safety for some time. While

* As this is written, Connecticut is trying another antispeeding crusade. The State Police Commissioner has declared "we're going to save lives, whether people like it or not."

he was drifting around trying to find employment, he fell in with Moynihan who had come under the influence of William Haddon, a public health specialist who had decided to make a career of auto safety. Haddon was part of an emerging school that regarded minimizing the effects of the "secondary collision" as the proper way of dealing with accidents. This thinking is elegant in its simplicity. Instead of preventing accidents by modifying highway design or driver behavior, adherents of this school of thought seek a technological solution to reduce the chances that an occupant of a car will get hurt *after* the vehicle crashes. The secondary collision, which does the human damage, results not from the car hitting the tree, but from the occupant being thrown against the interior of the car and impaling himself on the steering wheel, gouging his jugular on the windshield, or flying out onto the concrete, there to bounce around with the traffic.

Concentrating on the secondary collision is an excellent idea. But it is somewhat odd that it has been urged by people who consider themselves politically "liberal." Liberalism in America and worldwide has great faith in modifying human behavior by adjusting "underlying social conditions" to make people desire the right thing instead of the wrong thing. In its clearest form, this is the response to crime control by liberals, who are not much interested in tougher sentences, improved security devices, better-armed and equipped police, more escape-proof prisons— they seek to change society or the malefactors, so that people will not want to commit crime. This is also the form of the liberal solution to most foreign policy problems—we should behave in a better manner and reorder the world so that the urge to war will be reduced, and mankind will live in better harmony. This faith in sociological solutions is characteristic of most aspects of liberal policy—except regarding the automobile, where a technological solution is desired, backed up by harsh sanctions against car manufacturers. Muggers require sympathy and understanding, but auto executives and engineers deserve fines and jail sentences—very odd, very illiberal.

Nader was brought by Moynihan to Washington as a con-

sultant to the U.S. Department of Labor and was engaged by
Ribicoff for the U.S. Senate Commerce Committee. He produced a report for the committee that laid the entire blame
for accidents in America on the automobile manufacturers.
Nader claimed they had designed cars without regard for their
potential to cause accidents and deaths. He did not explain why
they should want to kill off their customers—but that was irrel-
evant. The thesis was enthusiastically received by Mr. Ribicoff
and his Senate colleagues.

Nader then began to turn his government report into a book
(incidentally beating out his former patron, Moynihan, who was
also planning a book on the subject). His opus, *Unsafe at Any
Speed*, appeared in late 1965. Certainly, not even its most devoted apologist would describe it as a serious work. It is a polemic
against the automobile expressed in demogogic language. The
style and intent are apparent from the beginning. Nader quoted
a statement by the then president of General Motors attacking
self-appointed amateur safety experts, and followed it with a
description of a woman who lost her arm in a Corvair accident.
Any serious reader would stop in disgust after page two; anyone
who knows the first thing about safety, or indeed any human
activity, knows that everything has some danger and some costs.
The important question concerns the level of danger compared
with the cost of reducing it. Nader never went into this. He gave
a lot of anecdotal information about what happened to cars
in various types of crashes and claimed that the automobile
manufacturers were not doing enough about safety and were
emphasizing styling and performance too much. The bias of
Nader's book is apparent from his omission of obviously important facts—that the fatality rate had been steadily declining
and that several auto manufacturers had attempted safety campaigns to sell cars (Kaiser in 1952 and Ford in 1956),* and these

---

* Nader tried to dismiss the Ford experience by asserting that its
sales had suffered in 1956 only because its competitors came out with
new models while it did not. This is simply not true—*all* 1956 model
cars were only slightly modified ("face-lifted") from 1955 models.

efforts had flopped. Detroit had learned that safety didn't sell. Perhaps these issues were misunderstood, but an impartial book would have made some attempt to discuss them.

Nader displayed some other tricks—misquoting, for one. In *Unsafe at Any Speed* he writes:

> Styling's precedence over engineering safety is well illustrated by this statement in a General Motors' engineering journal: "The choice of latching means and actuating means, or handles, is dictated by styling requirements. Changes in body style will continue to force redesign of door locks and handles."

The real text was as follows:

> The choice of latching means or handles, is *also* dictated by styling requirements.

Nader later claimed this was a typographical error and changed the passage in later printings. But he still failed to include the key sentence in the GM journal:

> Throughout the design and testing stages, the most important considerations are safety, reliability, operating ease and reasonable cost.

The major part of Nader's book was an attack on the Chevrolet Corvair. This compact car had been introduced in 1960, and its configuration imitated the layout of the extremely successful Volkswagen—an air-cooled horizontally opposed rear engine and independent swing axle rear suspension. Nader claimed the Corvair was inherently unsafe because it had excessive "oversteer," a technical term that Nader curiously cannot understand. When a car loses traction in a turn and the rear end slides out faster, that is "oversteer." If the front end goes out first, that is "understeer." Most American cars "understeer," not as a result of extreme road conditions, but because an understeering car has better directional stability under normal conditions and is therefore more comfortable to drive at highway speeds, particularly in crosswinds. People who have driven Volkswagens in high winds know the annoyance of having constantly to correct the steering to maintain a straight line.

Nader seized upon one design element of the Corvair as leading to oversteer—the swing axle rear suspension. Its technical aspects are difficult to describe in words, so Nader used a small diagram that grossly exaggerated and therefore incorrectly characterized its effects. Today, no automobile has the swing axle rear suspension. It has been supplanted by superior designs, but when the Corvair was designed in 1957–58, it was the preferred method of laying out an independent rear suspension. Nader's claim that the rear engine swing axle cars were inherently unstable was extremely odd. The Volkswagen was designed by the German engineer Ferdinand Porsche, and the car that bore his name was in production when Nader began acting as an auto safety expert. The Porsche 356 had exactly the same configuration as the Volkswagen and the Corvair, yet it was well known that the Porsche was the best-handling, safest automobile in the world. Nader never mentioned it in his book.

Perhaps the most revealing aspect of Nader's approach to automobile safety was his claim that the Corvair was more dangerous than other cars. Yet he did not present one scrap of comparative data indicating this was so. There is absolutely nothing in *Unsafe at Any Speed* to prove that the likelihood of being injured or killed was higher in a Corvair than in any other car. Moreover, throughout the entire book, and indeed throughout Nader's whole approach to auto safety ever since, there is a curious lack of evidence concerning what effects the modifications he proposes would have on the injury or death rates. And he seems utterly indifferent to the legitimate engineering and consumer concern for "reliability, operating ease and reasonable cost."

Indeed, it sometimes seems as if he thought the only function of the automobile was to crash. A car designed according to Naderite standards must be characterized as a "tank"—it would have to be large, heavy, strictly utilitarian, and incredibly expensive. This is not a very attractive prospect for most people, especially considering that the average driver correctly assumes that his car is not going to be in a serious accident. But, as we shall see, the idea of making cars more expensive is extremely attractive to those social elements whom Nader represents.

The best part of *Unsafe at Any Speed* was an attack on the existing traffic safety establishment, which Nader quite properly characterized as inept and operating under false pretenses—for example, in its emphasis on highway traffic code enforcement and the phony "speed kills" campaigns. Anyone who knows anything about state governments will recognize in the safety field the typical pattern of bureaucrats of modest abilities trying to get along until they can collect their pensions. But Nader, characteristically, saw these feeble bureaucrats as manipulated by sinister forces in Detroit. *Unsafe at Any Speed* was a silly and antisocial book, and would have sunk without a trace but for the fact that General Motors made a *cause célèbre* out of Nader.

Exactly what occurred is disputable, but some things are clear. While Nader was working for the Senate Commerce Committee and preparing *Unsafe at Any Speed* for publication, a group of ambulance-chasing lawyers—apparently independently—had found the Corvair to be a very useful means of attempting to extract money from General Motors. Several people who claimed that their Corvairs suddenly went out of control took GM to court. These cases were enormously expensive for General Motors and potentially highly profitable to the trial lawyers—who typically collect as much as half of the damages in such suits and who were pleased at the prospect of putting little people on the stand against big General Motors, expecting juries to be more than sympathetic toward milking the great auto giant.* Defending against these suits became one of the major activities of the General Motors legal department. At this time GM began to

* The journal of the American Trial Lawyers Association raved about *Unsafe at Any Speed*. Understandably, it opened the door to potentially lucrative suits against the auto companies.

investigate Nader's background claiming that the purpose was not to discredit his testimony before the Senate Committee, but to discover what connection, if any, Nader had with the Corvair suits and to gather information to refute his testimony in the event he appeared as expert witness in any of those cases. Checking into the background of witnesses in this manner is a perfectly legal and ethical procedure. If Nader were to testify at a trial that the Corvair was not safe, it was appropriate that General Motors have information concerning the credentials he possessed for making such assertions.

Unfortunately for General Motors and for the nation, the investigators went beyond his *bona fides* as a safety expert, and checked into his personal background. And the investigation was conducted in such a sloppy manner that it soon came to the attention of Nader and his friends. The word got back to the Senate, which was incensed at the company's attempt to meddle with one of its witnesses and staffers and demanded a dramatic confrontation in which the president of GM, John Roche, apologized to Nader for setting private detectives on him. In retrospect, this was an incredibly stupid thing for Roche to have done, for it established Nader's reputation as the "giant killer." The outcome would have been different had Roche said something to this effect: "This fellow Nader was circulating a lot of lies about our products, so we naturally assumed that he was hired by one of our competitors. We still have not found out who he is working for, but we suspect Ford." Ford would have denied it vigorously, General Motors would have claimed it still did not have enough evidence, and the public debate would have looked like a feud between auto companies. In order to resolve the dispute, the information uncovered by the detectives would then have been publicized.

It is a sorry commentary on American politics that this little squabble should have been the impetus for the Highway Safety and Traffic Safety Acts of 1966. Of such is legislation made in America. Because General Motors sent private detectives to investigate an inconsequential lawyer, Congress passed with overwhelming majorities a bill that gave the federal bureaucracy almost unlimited powers over the design of automobiles in America. The Traffic Safety Act effectively empowered what is now the National Highway Traffic Safety Administration to prohibit (by punitive fines) the sale of any car that did not meet its standards of "unreasonable risk" of injury. "Unreasonable risk" is such a loose concept that the NHTSA can require almost anything—and sometimes has. The Highway Safety Act gave the bureaucrats power to bribe state governments into passing legislation against the motorist by threatening to withhold federal highway subsidy funds. It is illegal for individuals to bribe public officials; only politicians are permitted to do so.

In accordance with the terms of the Traffic Safety Act, a traffic safety agency was born in the Department of Commerce (and later transferred to the newly created Department of Transportation). The initial administrator was William Haddon, the mentor of Moynihan and Nader. Haddon was slightly handicapped in writing the regulations because he knew practically nothing about automobile safety—since nobody knew very much. There was very little information available concerning modifications to prevent or lower the risk of accidents and reduce the damage after accidents. Haddon was also handicapped in the most fundamental way: he knew practically nothing about the manufacture of automobiles—apparently he did not even know about "lead time," or the obvious fact that it takes several years to design a car and organize its production. The design of a 1978 car must be firmed up in 1976 so that the manufacturer can arrange the purchase of components from the tens of thousands of subcontractors, order the machine tools, design the production lines, and hire the workers. But ignorance could not stop Haddon; he had no choice—the law demanded that regulations be prepared. Here is the timetable he had to operate by:

15 Oct 1966—Haddon appointed traffic safety czar.
30 Nov 1966—Preliminary standards issued for comment.
31 Dec 1966—Final date for comments on standards.
31 Jan 1967—First motor vehicle safety standards issued.

He began with no staff at all. The law required that the safety standards "consider relevant available motor vehicle safety data" —there were hardly any such data. Since the preliminary standards had to be written in six weeks, he made up a list working by the seat of his pants. Actually, considering the terrible constraints he had to work under, he did not do a bad job. Most of the initial regulations appeared to be commonsensible.

The Feds required some equipment—such as windshield defrosters, windshield wipers, headlights, rearview mirrors, shatterproof glass, door locks, and seat belts—that was already fitted to all vehicles because of state law, previous federal regulations, or ordinary industry practice. More interesting were the new standards for brakes and interior impact, which seem reasonable but cannot be demonstrated to have any significant safety effects. Another apparently reasonable requirement was that fuel tanks not leak after a front-end crash at 30 miles an hour.

The original standards also led to the so-called Nader knobs, which replaced dashboard switches because of the notion that a passenger might get hurt in a crash if he struck a switch. This obviously stupid standard has long since been modified. Another annoyance that resulted from the original federal standards was the lock, which keeps one from easily flipping the front seat forward to get into the rear of the car or, a more frustrating experience, to put packages back there. It is hard to find convincing evidence that this device is of any value whatever. The oddest requirement was the prohibiting of "winged projections" from wheel nuts; the requirement outlawed the knockoff hubcaps that had been in common use by sports cars for decades with no record that any individual had ever been harmed by their use. It was also required that the parking brake hold a car on a 30 percent grade; again, it is difficult to see why this was necessary. Federal standards also mandated a universal pattern of gear selection for automatic transmissions—something that Nader had been agitating for, although how this regulation could prevent serious accidents is difficult to imagine.

It is necessary to bear in mind that there was no evidence at the time and still no credible evidence today that these features improve the safety of automobiles. And worse, there has been no serious attempt to compare the life-saving or injury-reducing benefits of these features with the costs of putting them in automobiles. Nevertheless, you cannot buy any automobile in the United States that fails to meet these and other requirements. Most of them necessitated the redesign of some part of a car, for which the consumer had to pay. Many of the smaller auto importers merely dropped out of the U.S. market. As the regulations escalated, the U.S. manufacturers reduced the number of models that they had to "certify" as "safe" to the Feds. Thus, as always, "consumerism" pushed up prices and reduced consumer choice.

But even all this was not enough for Nader. He immediately turned on Haddon, accusing him in effect of having sold out to the automobile companies. Nader had long since alienated Moynihan; Nader then began a vigorous attack on the traffic safety agency,* and soon turned on Ribicoff.

After much hemming and hawing and negotiating, GM decided the better part of valor was to pay off Nader rather than fight him in court; it forked over $250,000 to him. Immediately thereafter, Nader began attacking the Volkswagen. (Nader and General Motors deny any connections in the rapid sequence of paying off Nader, Nader's attacking the Volkswagen, and GM

---

* Under heavy pressure, Haddon bailed out of NTHSA and took a job as the safety director for the Insurance Institute for Highway Safety, an instrument of the automobile insurance companies. His approach to safety was modified somewhat. Largely at the prompting of the insurance companies, Congress required new cars to have bumpers that could take a five-mile-per-hour crash without injury to safety systems. These bumpers do reduce damage in low-speed crashes, but increase the cost of damage in high-speed crashes, add to the cost of the car, by making it heavier and thereby reducing gas mileage, and have no overall financial benefit to the owners, only to the insurance companies. Moreover, the bumpers are ugly, add to the length of the car, making it more difficult to park; and their requirement has driven many low-volume specialty automobiles off the U.S. market.

introducing the Vega subcompact in competition to the Volkswagen in 1970.) Nader's anti-Volkswagen campaign is an odd
story. Early on, he had solicited money to set up a Center for
Auto Safety, which was manned by a group of young lawyers
who, if possible, knew even less about auto safety than he did.
"Nader's Raiders" are known for an enthusiasm that outstrips
their abilities. Nader has had difficulty in recruiting experienced,
careful, and prudent people in his organization. They tended
to produce, not serious investigations of auto safety, but press
releases meant to gain headlines. But in the case of the Volkswagen study, the draft report was not virulent enough for Nader's
taste. According to one account Nader made the final report
more hostile to Volkswagen than it originally had been.

Although the sophistication of the Nader operation had improved to the extent that "Small on Safety," the VW study, was
able to draw upon some of the serious safety research done by
the Cornell Aeronautical Lab and others, "Nader's Raiders"
seemed singularly ill equipped to understand the results or use
them properly. The fallacies and misconceptions in "Small on
Safety" were nicely exposed by John Tomerlin in *Road and
Track*. The Naderites did not respond with detailed answers
to the specific criticisms, but by claiming that Tomerlin and
Road and Track were tools of Volkswagen. Attacking the motives
of his critics rather than refuting criticisms is a standard Nader
tactic—which, as the liberal commentator Murray Kempton
pointed out, used to be called "McCarthyism."

In the meantime, while this foolishness was going on, the
safety rate in the United States was fluctuating completely independently of what Nader or the government was doing. In the
early 1960s, for the first time in memory, the fatality rate began
to go up. This was almost certainly the result of increased affluent and demographic factors. In the early 1960s the baby boom
generation began to come of age, and the country was so prosperous that millions of aggressive young men began to buy high-
powered cars and kill themselves and others at unprecedented
rates. Between 1958 and 1968 the highway deaths of fifteen- to

twenty-five-year-olds doubled, from 8,000 to 16,000. But this was merely a slight jump in an otherwise downward curve; the auto fatality rate began to decline soon thereafter—long before the government safety regulations began to take effect. I do not know why this happened, but I suspect it was partially an un-expected by-product of the Vietnam War. Shipping a half million of the most aggressive young men in the conntry off to Southeast Asia was bound to have a positive effect on the accident rate. (In fact, it has been calculated that young men were statistically safer in Vietnam than in the United States, not having fast cars to amuse themselves.)

Surely other factors are improved hospital emergency care, particularly in rural areas, which has reduced the chance that an injury will be a fatality; better ambulance service (promoted as part of civil defense preparedness), which has had the same effect; and the construction of over 40,000 miles of super-safe interstate expressways, which has "saved" five thousand lives a year.

Since about 1964 (i.e., *before* federal regulation of auto safety) the highway fatality rate has declined, and since 1972 it has dropped markedly. It might be argued that the de facto case argues for the success of the auto safety regulations. But this is by no means certain, because there are so many other factors involved. Since the winter of 1973–74, the United States has been in a serious recession and a national fifty-five-mile speed limit has been imposed. Public statements concerning the recent de-cline in highway death rates lead one to doubt that the com-petence of safety experts is any greater today than in the early 1960s. For example, some experts claim that the fifty-five-mile-an-hour speed limit is responsible for the decline. But those places where the new limit could have no effect—because the speed limit was *already* fifty-five miles an hour or lower—evi-denced the same drop as the rest of the country. The principal reasons for the decline in deaths are economic and demographic. It has long been known, but rarely publicized, that auto fatality rates are strongly affected by economic conditions. Death rates decline during recessions. One reason is that people have less money and probably drive less. Recessions particularly hit young workers, who are laid off first; they are characteristically the most aggressive drivers. I also suspect that there is a psychological effect involved—good times mean good feelings, ebullience, optimism, and a tendency to put your foot on the gas and go. In hard times people are pessimistic and cautious, and are not risk-takers.

It is pretty clear that the federal traffic safety business has not attracted many competent people; let me give some examples of their blatant blundering. Doubtless you have seen photographs of cars being crashed with dummies in them, graphically showing what happens when the dummy is thrown against the instrument panel or the windshield. Look closely at such pictures. In every one the dummy's arms will be by its side. Human beings approaching a crash do not have their arms by their sides—they put them over their faces or up against the instrument panel (or at least they did when instrument panels were closer to the passenger seat—as a result of experience with crashing dummies, the dashboard has been pushed away so that passengers cannot easily brace themselves against it).

Even more absurd experiments, costing taxpayers several tens of thousands of dollars, were conducted with motorcycles a couple of years ago. Dummies on motorcycles were crashed into barriers to determine what effect the instruments and switches located between the handlebars would have on a rider's chest in an accident. If the experimenters had taken a few minutes to interview a single motorcyclist who had survived a head-on crash, they would have learned that at the moment of collision a motorcyclist braces his arms strongly against the handlebars and somersaults, as a result, over the handlebars, never coming near the instruments and switches.

Some other aspects of automobile safety have also been seriously disregarded. I was startled to learn from NHTSA that it knew of no research on the effects of age and experience on driving skills. We know that younger drivers have very high accident rates. It seems possible, however, that people who begin to drive young may have high accident rates when young, but may be safer drivers in later life, given their early experience with cars. But there is no information whatever on this subject.

An apparently more plausible federal safety policy is the law requiring the compulsory recall of cars with safety defects. This sounds like a fine idea, until one looks at the record. In early 1977, Jaguar was ordered to recall 4,468 cars because the brake warning light was labeled "brake warning" instead of the required "brake." Each is to be brought in so the dealer can block out "warning." (Meanwhile NHTSA is proposing entirely new standards for labeling of instruments and controls with symbols to replace labels like "light" or "wiper" or "fuel" which doubtless have led to carnage on the highways.)

Among its original requirements, the federal safety agency required states to have annual motor vehicle safety inspections. Some states had them already, but many more did not. California has been dragging its feet because it prefers to have continuing on-the-spot checking by the State Highway Patrol; NHTSA is leaning on California by threatening to withhold 90 percent of its federal highway aid funds. Here is an extract from a NHTSA memo in early 1975, eight years after it first promulgated the inspections requirement.

> NHTSA knows of no study that has been conducted which definitely proved that inspections prevent accidents. The cost of such an undertaking would be formidable. NHTSA has taken the less costly route of determining that mechanical defects cause six percent of all motor vehicle accidents and contribute to an additional eleven percent. That inspection can detect mechanical defects as an accepted preventive practice is prima facie.

Who says the cost of such an undertaking would be formidable? All that would be necessary would be to compare the fatality rate in states before and after inspection were imposed and compare the change, if any, with the rates of states that did not modify inspections requirements during the same period. And it certainly is not obvious that because inspection can detect mechanical defects, and defects can contribute to accidents, inspections thereby reduce accidents. Having a local mechanic look at your car once a year is a terribly poor way of sampling its total condition—providing that is, if he actually looks at it; the inspection procedure is notoriously corrupt. It also will not pick up important things like failure of materials in the wheels, steering, or suspension. Basically all an inspection does is make sure that your lights work, that you do not have cracked glass (there is no evidence anyway that cracked glass causes accidents), that your tires are not bald, and that the brake pedal is not too soft. Almost everybody already does this kind of inspection himself. The procedure can really affect only a tiny number of motorists.

The same memo from NHTSA claims that the "cost [of inspections] to the motorist is not available and impractical if not impossible to obtain." Well, it is not difficult to add up the cost of an average inspection and the cost of the repairs, and to make some rough estimate of the value of the motorist's time and the cost of driving to the inspection station. If the average annual cost is $10 an inspection, the total national cost is over a billion dollars a year. That might seem a bit steep for a program with no demonstrated benefits, but NHTSA does not care about the cost or annoyance to the bulk of Americans.

Haddon's Insurance Institute for Highway Safety recently published a paper claiming that the safety of new cars is appreciably greater than those of unregulated cars. This report was widely publicized; it is such an excellent example of a misleading study that I will devote some space to refuting it. To begin with, its display of graphic material is a tip-off that the report is slanted. When IIHS wants to exaggerate a difference, as it did in this study, it will show a full-page graph giving only a portion of the spectrum of variation. Conversely, when it wishes to minimize a distinction, it will show the full spectrum, but on a tiny graph so that the difference looks very small. According to the IIHS data, cars meeting the federal motor vehicle safety standards have lower occupant fatalities than do unregulated cars. However, IIHS does *not* emphasize that half of this difference is entirely due to the fitting of seat belts, which had been put in cars before the Feds required them. Moreover, the study failed to take proper account of the fact that older cars may be inherently less safe than newer cars simply because of their age, or the ages of their drivers. The report claims that fewer young drivers were in the older cars than in the newer cars (which I find hard to believe), but does not mention whether the older cars were more likely to have older drivers, which would also be of considerable interest. IIHS brushes aside the idea that older cars may be more dangerous than newer cars simply on account of their age by comparing the 1972–1975 Maryland data with national data for the early years. The claim is that the fatality rates for the unregulated pre-1964 cars in 1972–75 were about the same as the national rates in 1962–64. Well, the data do not show that. There was a precipitous drop in fatality rates for *all* cars in 1974 and 1975, reflecting the recession and gasoline shortage, and so the most recent and presumably safest cars also showed approximately the same accident rate as cars produced immediately before the federal safety regulations went into effect.

And in any event, even if the IIHS is correct, the difference between old and new cars matters little. Except for the fitting of seat belts, which strikes me as an absolutely reasonable regulation (and which automobile manufacturers were doing before anybody ever heard of Ralph Nader or the National Highway Traffic Safety Administration or the Insurance Institute for Highway Safety), vehicles meeting the safety standards had approximately 24.5 fatalities per 100,000 registered cars, while non-federally regulated vehicles had 28 fatalities per 100,000 registered cars. The odds against getting killed in Maryland in 1975 in a car with federally mandated safety equipment were 4,100 to 1, and in those without it, 3,600 to 1. Since there are 2 million registered cars in Maryland, the difference between the two standards would be 50 people per year.

Applying the IIHS data nationally would suggest that the federal standards "save"—i.e., delay the dying of—approximately 3,500 lives a year. Even if it was true, it would not be much of a return on an annual investment of $2 billion of the consumer's money. I have no idea what an average American life is worth, but I doubt if many people would support any other investment which costs $6 million a year to prolong it a few months.

And buried away in the same report is a remarkable admission —that the federal safety regulations have had no effect whatever on pedestrian fatalities. Many safety standards, particularly for brakes, tires, visibility, and lighting should reduce pedestrian death rates. In effect, they have not done so.*

The lack of effect of U.S. auto safety standards is perhaps best demonstrated by comparison with other countries (see Table 4). During the period 1968–72 (selected because the energy crisis of 1973–74 hit countries differently) every industrial nation had a sharp decline in highway fatality rates quite independent of auto safety regulation.

This suggests to me that the real change is either that worldwide drivers are getting better or that industrial civilization is

---

* However, I must caution the reader against an equally fallacious study on the other side. The economist Sam Peltzman in his "The Effect of Safety Regulation," *Journal of Political Economy* (July/ August 1975) and "Regulation of Automobile Safety," *American Enterprise Institute Comparative Studies*, No. 26 (1975) claims to demonstrate that the federal safety regulations have had no effect. His argument is that drivers have a certain more or less fixed demand for safety, so with safer cars they will drive more aggressively and their overall safety record will be the same. Peltzman's analysis is bizarre, even ludicrous. His complex calculations assume, for example, that people drive faster as their income goes up because their time is worth more. Of course, lower income groups actually tend to be more aggressive drivers. What is really the case is that federal regulations have made such a trivial difference in safety that they are unnoticed by the driver. Aggressiveness and other driving habits are a function of cultural background, personality, training, and age—not of safety equipment, income, or economic calculation of any sort.

Table 4: DECLINE IN TRAFFIC FATALITY RATES 1968–72 (*In percent*)

U.S.	−19
U.K.	− 9
Australia	−27
Canada	−11
Italy	−35
W. Germany	− 5
Japan	−36
France	−10

becoming more safety conscious. Even auto racers, by definition the most risk-prone drivers, are insisting on improved safety equipment in racing cars and at race tracks. In 1976, Niki Lauda, the 1975 world racing champion, threw away his chance to retain his title by dropping out of the Japanese Grand Prix because of a heavy rain. Ten years ago, such a "cowardly" act by a racing driver would have been unthinkable.

But for whatever reasons, auto safety is currently at an all-time high. Will it get better? Probably, but not very much. The latest brouhaha is the air-bag controversy. The Naderites and other auto safety enthusiasts want the government to mandate compulsory fitting of air bags that will, in a collision, inflate inside the car and protect the occupants from the effects of the "secondary collision." The auto companies intensely dislike the contraption, claiming that it will cost an enormous amount of money and that making the use of seat belts compulsory would work better.

Nobody questions the fact that the most effective auto safety measure anywhere at any time is the use of seat belts. Any individual seriously concerned about safety should insist that his family wear them. However, a majority of the population rarely if ever uses seat belts, correctly estimating, to my mind, that the chances of needing them are so slight as not to warrant the time and trouble of buckling up. The public's resistance to a compulsory seat belt law is evident from the reaction to the notorious seat belt interlock system. You will remember that three years ago the NHTSA in its wisdom ordered that no car could operate unless the seat belts were fastened. A tide of protest broke over the Congress and swept this requirement into oblivion. Congress and the legislative bodies in general are loath to meddle with motorists in this fashion. Although other countries are passing compulsory seat belt laws, it is doubtful that any jurisdiction in the United States could or would do so. Indeed, the current revulsion against "big government" is pushing matters the other way.*

The air bag has considerable potential for protecting passengers in frontal accidents, but not much in rollovers or collisions from the side or rear. Its advantage is that its effectiveness does not require any action by the occupant—it is labeled a "passive restraint" system. If the slobs will not go to the trouble of buckling up to protect themselves, by God, the government will come up with some gizmo to do the job for them. General Motors has offered air bags for sale as an option on their top-line cars for several years. They sold these devices at a loss, yet there were few takers. People do not want air bags, but the Naderites are trying to force them on the public.

The automobile companies are fighting this proposed regulation tooth and nail, claiming the air bag will add $200 to the cost of the car. Advocates say it will cost more like $60, and even $200 extra added to a $6,000 car does not sound like very much money. Actually, it is not the cost of the air bag that worries the automobile companies. What scares them to death is their liability if it fails. Consider the configuration of this device: an air bag has a trigger to inflate it when a car crashes at a certain minimum speed, say thirty miles an hour. If it fails to inflate in a crash at that speed, the occupant is likely to get hurt, and the manufacturer of the automobile is certain to get sued. Conversely, should it be triggered when you are not crashing—if it

* One of the first acts of the NHTSA was to have the states require motorcyclists to wear protective helmets. A recent counterattack against this law has been successful. The federal bureaucracy has even been defeated by the weakly organized motorcyclists.

should inflate during ordinary driving—a giant balloon blows up in your face and you are liable to crash, get hurt, and again the automobile manufacturer will get sued. This means that an air bag in a car has to be highly reliable, but with a very sensitive trigger. Imagine a super-reliable air bag system—99.99 percent reliable, as good as the ejection seat mechanism in a jet fighter plane. With 130 million cars on the road, that .01 percent means that 13,000 air bags are *not* reliable. Assuming that the unreliability is all on the side of inflating at inopportune times, the result is that 13,000 times a year somebody driving along will hit a bump and have a balloon blow up in his face—with wholly unknown effects. Assuming the unreliability is all on the other side means that there could be as many as 13,000 crashes at high speeds in which the air bag does not deploy properly. One way or another, 13,000 times a year, there will be an equipment failure, with the automobile manufacturers liable.

Why cannot the automobile makers make more reliable bags? Simple. Remember the rule that costs go up exponentially as you try to approach perfection? An air bag 99.99 percent effective is already expensive; trying to do better would push the cost into thousands of dollars. Isn't it clear why Detroit is scared to death of compulsory air bag laws? But surely the potential life saving is worth the cost—alas, the calculations assume that the occupants are wearing seat belts—the current air bag system is not really "passive restraint" at all.

The auto safety crusade has been a political and bureaucratic nightmare. With little or no research available, the American people have been burdened with safety equipment of marginal, dubious, or no value. They have had to go to the trouble of disconnecting ("deNaderizing") annoying devices like buzzers, seat-back locks, and ignition interlock systems. The total financial cost to the motorist is incalculable. Depending on whose numbers you believe, mandated safety equipment has cost up to $200 per car, or $2 billion a year, or $10 billion so far. That does not include the expense of maintaining the equipment, or the cost in gasoline of the weight added to cars.

Consumer choice has been reduced. Detroit has produced fewer models, and fewer foreign manufacturers will go to the trouble of adapting their cars to the arbitrary and ever-changing standards of the U.S. federal bureaucracy. Not only are Americans denied the choice of cars, but distinguished automobiles have been destroyed. It was not worth the trouble to the manufacturers to modify the Sunbeam Alpine and Tiger or the Austin-Healey sports car to meet the federal regulations, so production was halted. Aston Martin and Maserati, who relied on the American market, went broke. Ferrari had to be taken over by Fiat to survive. Most ironic of all, the Jensen FF with its four-wheel drive and Maxaret nonskid braking, was removed from the market. Here are the reasons, quoting the head of Jensen Motors:

> It was a requirement of legislation that each model had to be certified independently, which meant that we would have to go through the whole costly process both for the Interceptor and the "FF." Consequently, we had to assess the cost in respect to the "FF" in relation to our small production capacity for this model and bear in mind that even at retail price of £7,000 the car was only a marginal profit-earner for Jensen. It simply didn't make sense to put the car through the certification process which would have absorbed the profit of some 30 cars a year.

Jensen had always been a leader in auto safety, being one of the first cars in the world to install seat belts as standard equipment. The FF might have provided the prototype for a higher level of traction and braking, but it was destroyed by the federal safety regulations. (And at the same time, NHTSA was pumping millions of dollars into building "safety prototypes" produced by opportunistic contractors who had no interest in or possibility of eventually producing cars.)

Automobile accidents cause many personal tragedies, but we are willing to bear the cost. We are willing to pay with a slight risk of life and limb and a considerable risk of damage in order to have mobility. This is easy to demonstrate: Donald Brennan of the Hudson Institute has proposed a simple and effective method of reducing deaths and injuries to almost zero—simply imposing and enforcing a universal twenty-mile-per-hour speed limit. This would still make automobile travel as fast or faster than any other intercity transit mode, yet the idea is crazy. We are more than willing to pay for time with tragedy.

Yet, despite the continuing decrease in highway fatalities, the increase in highway safety, and the independence of death rates from safety equipment requirements, we are advised that the automobile manufacturers have been indifferent to safety, that "carnage on the highways" is increasing, that we must pay increasing amounts of money for "safety" equipment; and we must tolerate the interference of federal, state, and local bureaucracies in our personal mobility. Why?

7.

The Transportation Counterrevolution

Throughout most of this century, government policy reflected the public's desire to move up from inferior forms of transportation to the auto-highway system. Once the initial resistance to the automobile was overcome early in the century, public policy was highway oriented. Federal, state, and local governments kept controls on railroads and collective transit facilities, because they were monopolies. Interstate trucking has been regulated since 1935. The automobile industry needed no such regulation. It was highly fragmented and competitive. All the automobile-highway mass transportation system needed from government was investment in highways.

Government's role in providing roads was made politically expedient by the widespread demand for highways by all segments of the population. Cities demanded paving of previous dirt and gravel streets, and farmers wanted better roads to improve their access to markets and their general integration into urban society.

Regulation of the automobile itself was not a major issue. Very early it was considered useful that automobiles have some form of identification for the enforcement of traffic laws, for locating stolen cars, and for general law enforcement against criminals, who had also become auto-mobile. The licensing of drivers was soon adopted for safety purposes. But the primary purpose of driver licenses and auto registration was to provide revenue to support the highways.

In the early 1920s, someone hit upon the bright idea of raising money to build and maintain highways by levying a tax on motor vehicle fuels. This was an excellent tax because it was almost directly proportional to the use of the highway. The more you drove, the more gas you burned, and the higher the tax you paid. A gasoline tax was even slightly progressive: it burdened the rich more than the poor, because the more expensive, high-powered cars usually consumed more gas per mile than cheaper cars. This also was equitable because the heavier cars tended to subject roads to more wear and tear. Since the gasoline tax was originated as a means to pay for highways, organized auto-mobile owners, particularly those auto clubs assembled into the American Automobile Association, continuously lobbied to prevent the diversion of highway use taxes to general revenue purposes. They were not always successful, but usually so.

Federal aid to highways began in 1916 when Congress appropriated funds for half the construction costs of "rural post roads," presumably intended to carry mail. Aid was rapidly extended over the years to include "federal-aid primary highways," which for the most part are the "U.S." numbered routes. However, these are not federal highways. Except on military bases, there are no federal highways in the United States; there are only state highways partially supported by federal funds.

The federal gasoline tax began in 1932 at a cent a gallon, went to one and a half cents in 1941, and to two cents in 1951, and was pushed up to its present four cents per gallon in 1959. (It is important to mention that, because of inflation, the *real* cost of the gasoline tax has been cut in half since 1959.)

The peak of public support for the automobile can probably be dated precisely with the passage by the Congress of the

Defense Highway Act of 1956,* which created the highway trust
fund intended for the construction of a 42,000-mile system of
interstate expressways, 90 percent of which would be paid by
the Feds from a four-cent-a-gallon tax on gasoline, as well as
miscellaneous levies on tires, trucks, and other excises on motor
vehicle parts. The Highway Act was the result of lobbying by
various interested parties, and represented compromise between
a series of alternatives. It would not, however, have passed the
Congress by such overwhelming majorities had it not been for
the widespread public demand. The 1950s were a period of
rapidly expanding automobile ownership and suburbanization.
The importance of the latter in shaping the national highway
program is shown by the decision that the interstate system
would not merely connect cities but would provide freeways into
the center of cities, as well as bypasses, that would be a great
benefit to suburbanites.

Nineteen fifty-six saw the high-water mark of the public policy
in favor of the automobile. Immediately thereafter, while the
interstate highways were being built, while all highways were
being used by more and more Americans, elite opinion and
therefore the political scene began to turn against the car. The
complaints against the automobile that I have already listed
began to be heard—the highway was ruining cities, safety was
getting worse, emissions were getting out of hand, and so on
down the line. Hardly was the ink dry on the federal Defense
Highway Act when public policy began looking for alternatives
to the automobile. Almost all of these were technologically and
socially reactionary; the twenty years of searching for ways to
"fix" the American personal transportation system by attacking
the automobile and promoting inferior alternatives is a sad epic
of blunder and waste.

---

* Identifying the interstate highway system with defense merely
reflects the values of the 1950s. The highway system had practically
nothing to do with national security, but in the 1950s defense was
the way to label desired programs, just as "fighting poverty" or
"whipping inflation" were in the 1960s and 1970s.

We have already discussed the safety foolishness, which has cost the motorist billions of dollars with no perceptible benefits. The emissions campaign has been somewhat less disastrous, but clearly not as efficient as could be expected. But the worst federal disaster was the attempted transportation "counterrevolution."

Beginning in the early 1960s, the national government began a serious effort to reverse the verdict of fifty years of transit history by actually attempting to get people out of their private personal transportation system and back into collective "public" transportation. The government is still trying, but with considerably less enthusiasm today.

As might be expected by those who know how the political system operates, the attempt to revive mass transit was initially prompted by a cry from an aggrieved interest group. After generations of steady profits despite steadily declining ridership (see Figure 4), the private transit companies were slipping into the red in the late 1950s and early 1960s. Many of them could no longer endure the losses and began to liquidate operations. Cities considered local transit companies necessary, so most of them were taken over by municipal authorities of one sort or another. Commuter railroads were also losing money and began to get state subsidies for rolling stock and then for actual operations.

The first federal contribution to urban mass transportation was incorporated into the Housing Act of 1961, and the major thrust began with the Urban Mass Transportation Act of 1964. In 1968, federal support was established in the Urban Mass Transportation Administration (UMTA, pronounced "um-tah"), which has been pushing "mass transportation" ever since—supported, as highways once were, by huge majorities in the House and the Senate, indicating broad political support.

Federal aid to urban mass transportation has gone through the usual progression from a program for "demonstration grants," through subsidies for capital equipment, to direct operating subsidies. It has also exhibited the characteristic Washington

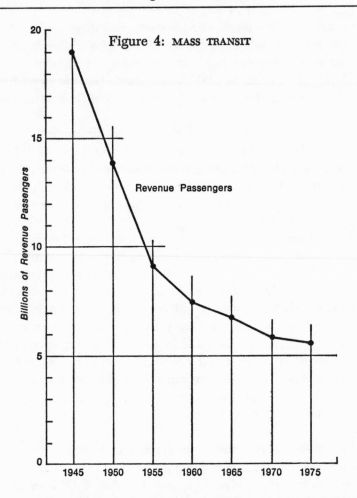

Figure 4: MASS TRANSIT

Billions of Revenue Passengers

Revenue Passengers

tendency of following erratic fashions, as the inexperienced and untrained young bureaucrats flounder desperately for short-term solutions to long-term systemic conditions. However, in the case of urban mass transit, the actual intellectual and administrative ability of the bureaucracy and its consultants was of little importance. Even had they been the most creative and competent analysts and managers, their efforts were doomed to failure. By undertaking to get the public out of cars and back into com-

Figure 5: AUTOMOBILE REGISTRATIONS

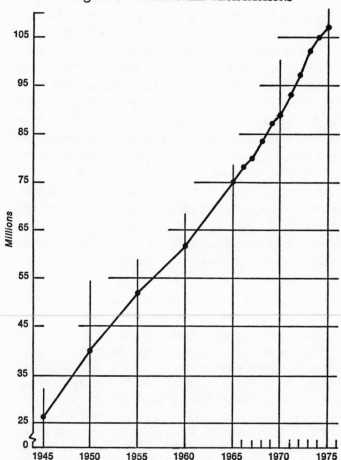

muter railroads, subways, buses, and even trolleys, they sought
to turn back history (see Figure 5).

Heavily influenced by the sorts of anti-automobile ideological
thinking that has been refuted in this book, the mass transit
promoters took the position that the car had won by default,
that the collapse of mass transit ridership did not reflect auto-

mobile superiority, but merely resulted from public investment in highways instead of mass transit and from technological and managerial inadequacies of mass transit operators. Infusing federal money, new ideas, and scientific management into its operation would result in such excellent service that people would flock back to mass transit. But such zealots could not cure the automobile "disease" because they had misdiagnosed it.

UMTA's operations have recently been relentlessly dissected by the distinguished transit economist and historian, George W. Hilton. His research makes shocking reading, except to those utterly inured to government waste and bureaucratic ineptitude. Almost all UMTA experimental programs were mere failures, and quite predictably so, but some were incredibly bizarre flops —enough to raise grave doubts about what has been going on in UMTA.

Hilton lists dozens of unsuccessful efforts. Let me quote from his evaluations of individual programs:

"A computerized system for changing routes and schedules of the principal operator in Washington, D. C. metropolitan area was unsuccessful, partly because the data on which the effort was based were obsolete, partly because the proposed modifications were politically unpopular." ". . . A computerized method of assigning drivers . . . is not known to have been adopted." "This was not continued when a public authority took over the bus system." "The design has not known to have been adopted as yet." "UMTA considers this project to be among its worst failures. [A research director] referred to it as a 'million dollar failure.'" "The project was reported abandoned in 1972." "The service proved a failure." "When the Peoria demonstration concluded in February 1966, the service was not continued." "The entire project was reported abandoned in 1972." "This project was also reported abandoned in 1972." "The project was reported abandoned in 1973 because the potential of the steam engine was inferior to a 'cleaned-up diesel' proposed for its prototype transit bus." "Unfortunately, the service was poorly patronized." "Under the circumstances, the line was abandoned

late in 1969." "Other projects of this kind failed as poorly."
"The financial performance was also poor."

And so on.

To my mind, the most incredible failure has been the West
Virginia personal rapid transit system intended to connect
downtown Morgantown to two university campuses, a run of
little over two miles and to replace buses and cars—at a cost of
over $40 million. All it is is a fancy bus. It never ran right and
at last report the good people of Morgantown are trying to get
rid of it.

A lesser but even more revealing failure was in West Hempstead, Long Island. The idea was to provide bus service from
homes to the Long Island Rail Road station so that it would not
have to provide parking and the commuter would not need a
second car. But as any commuter could have told UMTA, the
second car is not just a "station car" but also a weekend car, a
kid's car, and a backup car in the event that the primary car is
in the shop or otherwise out of service. Many collective transit
advocates forget that the commuter is not just a commuter. For
these other functions he is quite willing to bear the fixed costs
of a second car, which in any event are not severe because it is
usually an older used auto depreciated to a very low price.
Furthermore, the "problem" that the West Hempstead experiment was meant to solve was in itself an advance. As late as the
1950s the typical West Hempstead housewife had to drag her-
self out of bed and maybe pack the kids into the car to chauffeur
her husband to the train. The second car liberated her so much
that she got a job, requiring her to have a car and providing
more than enough money to pay for it. And finally, for everybody
who did not want to drive to the train, there was already taxi
service available, which could deliver the commuter to the
station and back for less than $500 a year.

The UMTA projects were not all unmitigated failures; some
of them are still in service. However, all of the successful "innovations" prompted by UMTA were quite within the intellec-

tual, technical, and financial competence of local transit operators. They sought UMTA's support only because UMTA funding was available. For example, Santa Monica, California, had the idea of fitting ramps to adapt a freeway for special bus use and applied for an UMTA grant. Santa Monica could have afforded to do this by itself. But if there is federal money available, why not take it—even if it means a delay in implementing the plan and increased costs resulting from filing federal applications?

To show the problems of the mass transit approach, let us look at the most vaunted attempts at a new system. In 1962, residents of the San Francisco area voted to establish the Bay Area Rapid Transit (BART), which finally went into operation in 1972. BART was a response to growing congestion in the city of San Francisco, especially in entering via the water crossings from the north and east. The original plan was to have all of the municipalities around the San Francisco Bay participate in the system, but Marin County to the north across the Golden Gate Bridge and San Mateo County to the south quickly dropped out, leaving only the city of San Francisco and Alameda and Contra Costa Counties on the east side of the bay to participate.

The BART system was designed to fit its constituency. Basically BART is a giant X with its crossing point at Oakland. From the junction a line runs north to Richmond, another one south to Fremont, and another east through the mountains to Concord. From the Oakland junction, the mainline of BART goes under the bay through downtown San Francisco, surfaces to the southwest, and terminates at Daly City just beyond the San Francisco city line. Except in downtown Oakland and San Francisco and the tunnels under the bay and through the mountains, the BART lines are at grade or elevated. In one spot the track goes down the median strip of a freeway.

Given the distribution of jobs and residences within the three-county area, the alignment of the route is unexceptionable. Unfortunately, almost every other aspect of BART has been a dismal failure. BART's designers deliberately decided to indulge in a frenzy of untested technological innovation. For over a hundred years, railroads in most of the world had been operating on a standard gauge, or width between tracks, of four feet two and a half inches. BART's designers went to a gauge of five feet, claiming that this design would give better stability at high speeds, particularly in high winds. But rail lines in Europe, Japan, and the United States have been running in high winds at very high speeds, far in excess of BART's top speed of eighty miles an hour, for decades. By going to a wider gauge, BART threw away generations of experience and vastly increased its cost by requiring custom-built equipment.

Worse, BART ordered newly designed cars that would be entirely automated and integrated by a control system operating from a central computer at the headquarters in Oakland. According to theory, the entire operation would be totally automatic. This was desirable because it has long been recognized that the principal cost of operating a mass transit system is labor. San Francisco has always been a very tough labor town with ferocious and demanding unions; anything that could reduce labor costs would certainly be desirable. In theory a BART train was to run untouched by human hands. It would stop, the doors would open and close, and it would start to the next station without any one at the controls. Well, it does not take a lot of thought to recognize that no system can be reliable enough to risk hundreds of riders hurtling along at eighty miles an hour with no human being to oversee it. So the design allowed for an operator in the cab to monitor the instruments and take over in case of failure. This raises a rather obvious question—if you have a man in the cab anyway, why not have him run the train, instead of investing in a hugely complex and redundant automatic system?

Similarly, the idea of having the doors open and shut automatically was entirely irrational. A casual rider of the New York, Philadelphia, Boston, or Cleveland subways would recognize that the amount of time required to load and unload the subway cars varies from train to train, even at the same time of day.

In practice, the BART system is controlled by a manual override operated by the motorman. The doors open automatically only during off-rush hours, and the existing program usually requires the doors to be open too long, thus delaying the train. The automatic doors cost BART a formidable amount of trouble. During test runs they had the disconcerting habit of flying open in the middle of the tunnel under the San Francisco bay, thus putting off the opening of the entire system. Automatic doors were an entirely unnecessary feature.

A key parameter in the design of any rail transportation system is "headway," or the time or distance between trains. In order to maximize the use of rails during rush hours, it is desirable to reduce the headway. So the BART system had a very complex system whereby trains could follow one another safely at as close an interval as possible. A train occupying a length of track would send signals into the computer, which would deny power to the section of track behind it so the next train could not get too close. Needless to say, this complicated design isn't working very well, so in practice the headway is controlled by individuals in booths in each station, who signal the motormen.

In other words, all of the vaunted technological advance of BART was wasted. The optimum system for controlling a rapid transit line was worked out before World War I. A motorman in the train controls the speed and braking and maintains the headway by watching signals triggered by preceding trains on the same track. Doors are opened and closed by a switch operated by a man who looks to see when loading is completed.

The BART designers also had some bright ideas about collecting fares. It is very expensive to have clerks in booths selling tokens. And another problem is how much fare is to be charged —like a commuter railroad, where fares are proportionate to distance, or like a city subway system, where a flat rate will take you any distance? Like most contemporary systems, BART decided to split the difference by establishing a low flat fare for short city trips, and adjusted fares for the longer suburban runs on the branch lines and the bay crossing.

A BART patron enters a station, puts money in a machine that gives him a magnetized card that electronically records how much money he has paid. Entering the turnstile, he inserts the card into a machine that opens the gate and spits the card back. On completing the trip, he uses the card again to exit the station, and in the process the machine calculates what the trip cost and deducts that amount from the value imprinted on the card. When the money has been deducted to zero the card does not work any more. Fine—except that the San Francisco Bay Area is full of electronic wise guys, and many are forging these magnetic cards. BART also made the socially motivated mistake of providing special cut-rate fares for older people. So aged or aged-appearing folk buy discount cards which are then used by younger people.

The scheme of automatic fare collection was intended to reduce labor costs. But the San Francisco Bay Area, like other American cities, is afflicted by urban crime. Policemen are necessary in the stations anyway. Also needed are people to give directions, not to mention watching for people who jump over the turnstile. So the stations are manned anyway by guards in nice progressive blazers who are probably paid more than the token collectors.

BART has been a fiscal disaster. It was sold to the voters on the basis of costing $900 million. The final tab will come in at close to $2 billion, an overrun far in excess of inflation during the period of its construction. BART was finished eight years later than scheduled. The original idea was that public money would be used to subsidize the capital construction, but the operations would be supported out of the fare box. Well, the initial capital money ran out fast, and was augmented by state and federal funds. Charges for fares have not begun to cover operating costs. At the time of writing, the fares are only covering 40 percent of operating costs; they are not even covering the salaries of the employees. BART is losing so much money on its weekday runs that it dare not extend service to the even less profitable weekend and night hours.

Has BART succeeded in winning people away from the automobile? Of course not. Like any rapid transit system, it can only
service part of a metropolitan area directly. BART is basically
a commuter railroad. Most of its users drive to the suburban
stations and park. It was originally planned for 258,000 trips a
day in 1975. The latest actual ridership is 131,000 trips per day.*
BART was intended to relieve pressure on the water crossing
from Oakland to San Francisco. But its usage amounts to three
months of the normal increase of auto-crossage of the Bay
Bridge. And even that small reduction in growth is attributable
not so much to the attractiveness of BART as to the increase in
the bridge toll, levied to help pay for BART. And most interesting of all, the promoters of BART deliberately put pressure on
the express buses that were previously providing the cross-bay
service. What BART has done is to substitute an incredibly
expensive and inefficient rail transportation system for a relatively cheap and efficient bus transit system. The primary result
of this transit experiment is that the citizens of the San Francisco
bay area, the state of California, and the United States of America have paid $2 billion down and $300 million a year—just to
transfer 100,000 prosperous commuters from buses to BART.
Think of what could have been done for $2 billion in the San
Francisco–Oakland bay area! One hundred thousand housing
units could have been built, or half a million automobiles could
have been *given* to the poor.

Other new rapid transit systems look as if they are going to
be just as disastrous. Washington, D.C. is putting in a system
that was originally budgeted at $2 billion though it will prob-
ably cost more than $6 billion. It suffers from the same dreams
of high technology and reducing the congestion in the city.
Baltimore is talking about such a system, so is Atlanta, and others

* Not all of this is transportation. BART does a respectable "excur-
sion" or joy-riding business. A whole generation has grown up who
have never ridden a train, and rapid transit is exotic to the 100 million Americans living west of the Mississippi. BART is an important
tourist attraction for San Francisco.

had been advocated elsewhere in the country. We should not suffer any illusions that they are being developed to benefit the rider. The main impetus behind them is that there is federal money available. A city like Baltimore is desperate for every cent it can get. Understandably, the construction unions who will build these systems are enthusiastic as well.

Given these failures, it is refreshing to be able to turn to a fairly successful new rapid transit system. The Delaware River Port Authority has long been operating bridges across the Delaware River at Philadelphia. The first of these, the Benjamin Franklin Bridge between Camden and Philadelphia, had a rail line slung under it, providing simple service between downtown Philadelphia and downtown Camden. The subsidiary of the Delaware Port Authority, the Port Authority Transportation Company (PATCO) made a very clever adaptation of this system merely by connecting it to an unused Pennsylvania Railroad commuter line extending out into the Jersey suburbs of Philadelphia to Lindenwald. A new roadbed and track were laid, automatic fare collection at new stations was installed, and thus was the "Hi-Speed Line" born. There was an attempt at automatic train operation, which works intermittently (bad weather is particularly harmful to the control system, so the operator always has to be ready to override the system manually). The doors are operated manually. PATCO carries only a few tens of thousands of commuters, but it does this well—and it is actually making money on operations. This strongly suggests that the way to go in rapid transit combines a few simple items: adaptation of existing systems and rights-of-way, straightforward technology, and no expectations of changing the world. This reflects stodgy Philadelphia's way of looking at problems—which is not a bad one, at that.

But perhaps the most grievous error of UMTA was to promote the unification of transportation systems. To the bureaucratic mind, words like "coordination" and "planning" have a magical quality. It seems "irrational" to have a lot of different transportation companies operating separate lines; they should all be put together under single management so that the entire system can be run more "efficiently." Skeptics might point out that large systems have much more room at the top for high-paid bureaucrats, planners, systems analysts, and consultants of various stripes. That may be debatable, but what is not is that a single operating transportation authority has a single union. A strike that previously knocked out just part of the network could immobilize the entire system. This gives unions much more leverage, and as might be expected, the period of federal intervention in transportation has seen a sharp increase in wage settlements. The principal effect of UMTA operations in mass transportation has been to transfer money from taxpayers to the employees of transit systems. In almost all cases, ridership has declined, and service has further deteriorated.

Even UMTA is becoming disillusioned with "rapid transit" (its young director bailed out and joined BART) and is looking for other transit fish to fry. These come and go in waves of fashion, so I may be already out of date, but let me briefly describe some current fantasies.* One of the new bright ideas afflicting mass transportation advocates for the last few years is "personal rapid transit" or "PRT." This sounds like a neat idea: instead of having to wait for a collective vehicle to come along, the prospective rider will go to a station where a little car will be waiting for him, or where one will come when he pushes a button; the rider gets into the car, and it takes him where he wants to go. Sounds great, doesn't it? It seems to combine the advantages of the automobile with the advantages of a transit system. But it really combines the disadvantages of an automobile with the disadvantages of a rapid transit system. The capital expense in building a PRT system would be enormous. It is expensive enough

* Fortunately, the once-vaunted monorail has been almost completely forgotten. It was nothing more than a gimmick, the system merely combining on a single large rail the two rails of a conventional train. Apart from the fact that an elevated monorail would not be quite as ugly, a two-rail system is superior in safety and cost. The monorail is a nice toy suitable for Disneyland; for utilitarian purposes the two-rail system is the way to go.

providing stations every mile in rapid transit systems, but to put
in the number of stations required in a PRT complex staggers
the imagination. There would be obvious crime, vandalism, and
joy-riding problems.

The most telling argument against PRT is that it literally will
not be able to work. Consider a type of PRT currently in use.
Many of the readers work or have worked in office buildings
with automatic elevators. This is the simplest form of PRT—the
elevator works in a single up and down track. The system is very
straightforward—all it has to do is come to your floor when you
push the hallway button, open the door, close the door, and go
to the floor you want. Elevators have been in operation since the
late nineteenth century, and automatic elevators have been in
use for over a generation. Have you ever noticed how often the
elevators in your office building do not work? The downtime on
these relatively simple devices is enormous. Yet they have the
great advantage of having only one elevator in one shaft. If there
was a single shaft with six elevators in it, knocking one out would
block the whole system. In a PRT system, multiple units on
tracks would also require switches, and acceleration and deceleration controls. A PRT is necessarily a complicated system impossible to keep operating reliably.

The latest fashion discussed by the rapid transit advocates is
what they call "light rail transit"—jargon for "trolley." Compared
with rapid transit, trolleys are far superior for most usages, but
we have already had trolley cars in America. They were abandoned and torn out because they could not compete with the
bus or the automobile.

Another often discussed technological pipe dream is "moving
sidewalks" or "people movers." These sound like a great idea:
the sidewalk you walk along will also move, thus greatly extending the range of walking. Well, look around the streets of your
downtown and get some sense of the necessary size of an effective system. Then look at the pedestrian and vehicular traffic
patterns and note how infrequently sidewalks are used by large
numbers of people. Then observe the nearest parallel to moving

sidewalks—moving staircases, or escalators. Notice how often they are under maintenance or repair. And escalators are usually enclosed, not outside subject to the elements as sidewalks are. Moving sidewalks also have some technical difficulties—if they are fast, there are problems of ingress and egress; if they are slow, like the ones in some airports, what point is there to them? There are also safety problems. (In fact, safety standards have increased so much since the turn of the century that it is quite likely that introducing the subway or the escalator today would be impossible—they are too obviously unsafe, because someone might fall off the platform or be caught in the steps. Of course, people are smart enough hardly ever to fall off platforms or get caught in steps—but our safety experts assume that the average citizen is a spastic cretin.)

Some other schemes are very strange. Many thoughtful transportation analysts are trying to revive the jitney, a system intermediate between the taxicab and the bus. In a jitney system, a marked car or a minibus cruises on regular routes. The rider flags down the vehicle and is either taken elsewhere on the route for one fare, or directly to his door for a higher fare. Jitneys flourished in the United States around the time of World War I, and are still very successful in third world cities such as Mexico City and Teheran. Unfortunately, although the jitney may have some limited use in some places, it is an archaic transportation system. It is appropriate to a country where the standard of living is such that there are many working men with just barely enough money to buy cars, who augment their income by using them as jitneys on the way to and from work, as well as moonlighting after work. The perfect analogy is the marginal home owner who takes in roomers to help pay the mortgage. With a higher standard of living, jitney operations collapse. Auto owners do not need to supplement their income, and most people have cars.

An even stranger concept is the so-called dial-a-ride. According to this idea, an individual calls up a central headquarters, gives his address, and a small minibus comes to pick him up.

It also stops for other passengers; thus several people are sharing the vehicle and splitting the driver's wages, thereby reducing the price to a manageable amount. This has been hailed as a great innovation. Well, dial-a-ride is something that I know very well because I used to be part of a dial-a-ride system.

Here is how the system worked *circa* 1960. There was a group of drivers, including me, each with a motor vehicle manufactured by the Checker Company that would hold, in addition to the driver, four passengers comfortably and seven in a squeeze. The vehicle was equipped with a two-way radio. At the other end of the radio was a human being called a "dispatcher" who was intimately familiar with the community and its layout, and had a group of telephones whose numbers were painted on the sides of the motor vehicles, listed in the telephone book, and displayed in public places. In front of the dispatcher was a series of hooks, each labeled with the number of one of the motor vehicles. On a table with a microphone was a pile of little two-inch-square pieces of paper, each with a hole punched in it. When a prospective rider called, the dispatcher would write down on the little piece of paper where the pickup was to be made, what the destination would be, and what the fare was. He would look at the board with the hooks and read from similar pieces of paper where each of the vehicles had been and was going, would select the best-located vehicle for the ride, give the driver the information by radio, and hang that scrap of paper on the appropriate hook. In this way the dispatcher could keep track of every fare. At the end of the driver's shift the scraps of paper would be stapled to the driver's own trip record and this would constitute the records of trips and fares for that shift.*

When not being dispatched by radio, the drivers would congregate in places where fares might be generated—railroad sta-

---

* Another advantage of the company that I worked for was the "cash cut," whereby the dispatcher and the driver would split the receipts in cash at the end of the shift—no records and no taxes. For this reason I strongly suspect that the amount of taxicab usage in the United States is grossly underestimated in official data.

tions, bars, and other places of public assembly. While driving, the riders would occasionally get "flags" from people who hailed them on the street. The driver of the vehicle would get a fixed percentage of his fares, thus encouraging him to maximize the efficiency of his operation. The flexible hours made driving an excellent occupation for drifters, students, and other people who don't particularly like regular work.

Doesn't that sound like a good system—even though it lacks computers and systems analysts? What has been described is an ordinary suburban radio-dispatched taxicab operation. A single dispatcher can control up to twenty cabs; most of the taxi operations in the United States function in this manner. Both jitneys and dial-a-ride have thus been rendered obsolete by the radio-dispatched cab even before they have really been tried out. In other words, UMTA has been subsidizing "experiments" in a system that has already been operating effectively for over a generation.

The failure of attempts to promote car pooling is another grotesque example of transportation planners' lack of understanding of ordinary experience. Yes, merely joining a two-person car pool cuts operating costs almost in half and only slows the trip to work by the time it takes for one partner to pick up the other, but few people want to sacrifice the convenience and privacy of individual driving. Those who wanted pooling were already pooled.

UMTA does not give up easily. A recent venture into promoting urban mass transportation ventured far from rapid transit systems. UMTA bankrolled some experimental taxi designs. A taxicab is an automobile used by a lot of different people at different times. But UMTA dislikes automobiles, so it thinks that a taxicab should be as different as possible from a car. Thus it invested several million dollars in taxicab prototypes through —can you believe it?—New York's Museum of Modern Art. One hopes that the art buffs at MOMA loved the cabs, because they clearly cannot possibly go anywhere. There is not a sufficient market for taxicabs in the United States to justify tooling up for any of these machines. Some very interesting designs were produced by Volkswagen, Volvo, American Motors, AMF, and a West Coast firm. While they were better than the Dodges and Checkers used for most taxi work in America, they would be much more expensive, even in mass production. And the writers of the criteria for the prototypes forgot that taxicabs are not just used for fares—they are usually the off-duty transportation of owner drivers. No one is going to wheel his family around in those specially—and narrowly—designed machines. So another couple of million dollars of your money went down the drain, courtesy of UMTA.

These adverse judgments may be dismissed as the ill-tempered opinions of the author; that could be the reader's opinion. So let me make a last shot at the great transportation counterrevolution. Like all counterrevolutions, it has been a failure. As the federal, state, and local governments have been pouring money into collective transportation systems, the ridership has been declining (see Table 5). The only fvaorable sign is that the rate of decline is slowing, possibly because it is bottoming out. The automobile seems to have reached its saturation level in terms of percent of households owning cars, and the residue must be forced to use collective transportation.

There was a tiny gain in ridership during the energy crisis, but it is falling back. Worse from the point of view of the rapid transit enthusiasts is that despite the opening of BART, transit ridership has continued to drop. The gains have been in bus ridership (see Table 6). The most important effect of the transportation counterrevolution has been to use public money to buy buses—mostly from General Motors.

But to any right-thinking mass transportation advocate, GM is an evil organization bent on foisting automobiles on a gullible public. The auto giant has long dominated the bus business because of the huge savings of volume manufacturing—the cost per passenger seat of mass-produced buses is less than a quarter of custom-built rail cars. American Motors was encouraged to go into the bus business in competition with GM and Rohr-Flxible

Table 5: COLLECTIVE TRANSIT TRENDS

	1950	1955	1960	1965	1966	1967	1968	1969	1970	1971	1972	1973	1974	1975
Revenue Passengers (*Millions*)	13,845	9,189	7,521	6,798	6,671	6,616	6,491	6,310	5,932	5,497	5,253	5,294	5,606	5,626
Employees	240,000	198,000	156,000	145,000	144,000	146,000	144,000	141,000	138,000	139,000	138,000	141,000	153,000	160,000
Passengers/ Employee	58,000	46,000	48,000	47,000	46,000	49,000	45,000	45,000	43,000	40,000	38,000	38,000	37,000	29,000
Average Earnings/ Employee (*Constant $1975*)	$7,780	$8,770	$9,960	$11,335	$11,435	$11,640	$11,955	$12,335	$12,795	$13,310	$13,530	$13,980	$14,025	$13,995
Average Fare (*Constant 1975¢*)	22¢	30¢	32¢	34¢	34¢	36¢	35¢	36¢	38¢	40¢	40¢	38¢	35¢	33¢
Operating Revenues (*Millions $1975*)	$3,246	$2,866	$2,557	$2,463	$2,451	$2,508	$2,418	$2,387	$2,366	$2,314	$2,223	$2,178	$2,117	$2,002
Operating Expenses (*Millions $1975*)	$2,900	$2,567	$2,344	$2,344	$2,362	$2,468	$2,514	$2,562	$2,622	$2,711	$2,738	$2,931	$3,386	$3,535
Profit or Loss on Operations (*In Percentage*)	11%	10%	8%	5%	4%	2%	-4%	-7%	-11%	-17%	-23%	-35%	-60%	-77%

Table 6: COMPARATIVE COLLECTIVE TRANSIT MODES
(*Millions of Revenue Passengers*)

	1950	1960	1970	1971	1972	1973	1974	1975
Rail	2113	1670	1574	1494	1446	1424	1435	1385
Trolley	4051	782	300	268	247	218	174	150
Buses	7681	5069	4058	3735	3561	3653	3998	4081

(which uses GM components). Since UMTA is now paying 80 percent of the cost of all buses, it decided to promote bus improvement and cost savings by encouraging transit operators to form a consortium to make a mass purchase of an upgraded bus model. GM and Rohr have come up with advanced designs to meet the new specifications, while AMC, which has been losing money and cannot affort the investment in r & d and new tooling, is understandably miffed and has gone to court against the consortium, GM, Rohr, and UMTA. Because nobody knows what sort of buses can be sold, American bus production is shut down as I write this. So UMTA has been considerably less than successful at promoting the least inefficient collective transit mode.

The public has enough sense to know what is wrong with collective transit: it is slow. Although the top speed of a rapid transit train can be in excess of eighty miles an hour, it is the average speed that counts. The theoretical speed is reduced by the loss of speed in decelerating, stopping, and accelerating back to speed. Since the individual rider only needs two stops—where he gets on and gets off—he must spend his time waiting for other people. New York's subways average twenty miles an hour; even with stations a mile apart, an average speed of only thirty-five to forty mph is the best possible, regardless of top speed.

Furthermore, calculations of the average speed of collective transit systems rarely include waiting time, transfer time, making connections, or access time in getting to and from the transit stop. Unless congestion is really frightful, automobile point-to-point time (which is the time that counts to the traveler) must be less.

This assumes, of course, that the collective transit system is going where the traveler wants to go, which is rarely the case. Not only is the traveler obliged to adjust his time of leaving, time of arriving, and speed to the needs of others, he must also adjust his route. He can go only where the designers of the system permit him to go. Either he adjusts his plans to their design (in the case of railroads built a hundred years ago) or he must find other means. To be sure, the driver must do the same, but except where bridges and tunnels determine the route, the ubiquity of highways permits an effectively infinite choice of travel paths and destinations. No matter how well designed and competently operated, a collective transportation system must aggregate its riders. To the individual, aggregation is aggravation.

The rider of collective transit must share it with dozens of strangers, enough of whom stink, paw members of the opposite sex, or are otherwise obnoxious to make the experience occasionally unpleasant. There is just enough crime to make fear real and to require the hiring and cost of police. The collective transit system also increases crime outside the system by giving mobility to urban punks who would otherwise be confined to their native turf. When Co-op City was begun in the northern Bronx, its prospective residents were promised a subway extension; now that the complex is complete they no longer want one—with no subway the goons cannot get at them.

Collective transit systems are complex and centralized. If they are on fixed guideways, the failure of a single unit blocks the line. With centralized power sources, an outage cripples an entire section. Another drawback of collective systems is that they require professional crews who must be paid. This is a cost the driver of a car does not charge himself. Worse, these drivers are organized into unions that behave as if they have a monopoly position. Their wages are much higher than their skills would indicate. Certainly the responsibilities of controlling a vehicle with dozens or hundreds of passengers deserve a premium, but operating a rail vehicle is easy—all that is required is to operate one stop-start speed control and to watch signals. It is simpler than driving a car and much simpler than driving a truck. Nevertheless, a New York subway motorman is paid $300 a week, plus fringe benefits far in excess of most private industries.

Collective transit systems are regularly struck. This infuriates the public, but their suffering is justified—since most collective transit systems are now government owned, the citizens are the shareholders, and it is proper that they suffer in a dispute with the workers. Unfortunately the public ridership does not take such a sanguine view of the issue. When strikes occur, most people manage to get where they are going anyway, casting into doubt the need for the system in the first place—and when the strike is over, ridership invariably drops. Why should people subject themselves to the mercy of an unreliable system?

The economic costs of the interplay of transit unions with incompetent management, vacillating political leadership, growing subventions, and a resigned public are appalling. Table 5 tells the story. By 1975 wages alone are more than fares.

And although the public does not know it, the alleged benefits of "mass transportation" are specious. It does not burn less fuel—because collective transportation vehicles operate at only part of capacity, their fuel consumption per passenger mile is only slightly better than the private automobile.

Mass transit does not relieve congestion or pollution—the availability of collective transportation permits and requires more intensive land use that "generates" more truck and auto traffic. Urban places with rapid transit systems are the most polluted. And "the law of congestion" applies—there is "latent demand" by drivers who would use road space during rush hours but are dissuaded by congestion; the few cars pulled off the highway by the transit system are then rapidly replaced by others until the maximum tolerable level of congestion is once again reached.

Mass transit does not help the poor. The rural poor are almost entirely dependent on the automobile—to tax them to support affluent urban dwellers is regressive. And even within urban areas, the most impoverished do not work, and they make little use of mass transit. Rapid transit has the most extremely regressive effect. Only high-density office areas have sufficient density to justify it. Blue-collar and service workers have jobs in widely scattered locations that can be adequately reached only by cars. Subsidizing mass transit systems from gasoline levies or general revenue funds amounts to a system of taxing the less prosperous to subsidize affluent commuters.

The federal government has spent $6.5 billion on "mass transportation" in the last fifteen years, an amount more than matched by state and local government. Congestion has not been relieved, pollution has not been alleviated, mobility has not been improved. The American public has the good sense to recognize that the automobile is a superior mode of transport—yet we are told we must dump billions more into "mass transportation." Why?

8.

The War Against the Automobile

Up to now, I have made a strong case for the automobile, raking its critics over the coals. If my arguments have been as persuasive as they were meant to be, you might legitimately wonder, "If this fellow is right, why have all of these myths and misconceptions about mass transportation been so widespread?" Why have our leading journalists, social commentators, and politicians been promulgating so much misinformation? These are very good questions, and I hope this chapter will provide some plausible answers.

Fashion is one important element contributing to anti-auto sentiments. In many circles, being in favor of "mass transit" has become a sign of enlightenment, public spirit, and virtue—even for those who regularly drive and would never dream of using a public system. People whose view of the world is heavily influenced by the media can hardly be blamed, since almost all popular as well as highbrow journalism is anti-automobile and pro-"mass transit."

Let me give an example, plucked almost at random from my files. The *New York Times* ran an editorial (21 March 1975) claiming that "for City Hall to continue its present temporizing [in establishing a transportation control plan] is to fly in the face of the National Academy of Science's warning that automobile pollution in urban areas is taking a toll of some 4,000 lives a year." New York City has about 8 million people—5 percent of the urban population in the United States—so even if the figure cited were correct, automobile pollution would thus kill 200 New Yorkers annually, far fewer than casualties from practically every other form of death.

As I pointed out earlier, the National Academy of Sciences did not say that some 4,000 lives a year were being taken by automobile pollution. What it did say was this:

> It is suggested that automobile emissions may account for one quarter of one percent of the total urban health hazard. For the whole U.S. urban population, effects of this magnitude might represent as many as 4,000 deaths and four million illness restricted days per year. Four thousand deaths is about one-eighth of the deaths from bronchitis, emphysema, and asthma combined or one-twelfth of the deaths of automobile accidents. Four million days of illness is nearly equivalent to one-tenth of the total number of days lost from work each year because of respiratory illnesses.

These are scientists writing—note the qualifications: "it is suggested that," "may," "might," "as many as." This quote is from the summary. The full report indicates that the figure of 4,000 deaths is the maximum possible. Moreover, as I also pointed out earlier, public health officials have never been able to attribute one single death to automobile air pollution.

We all can make mistakes, and even editorial writers for esteemed newspapers are entitled to slip from time to time. But seen in the context of the position taken by the *New York Times* against the automobile, that editorial was no mere slip. The people who publish and control that newspaper do not like cars, and they have some very good reasons not to, in terms of their own self-interest. For our existing mass-transit system—the auto-highway system—is bad for the "better sort," those powerful interests that make up the so-called elite in America.

The sources of their opposition are worth examining. The automobile has been one of the greatest blessings to mankind, providing the masses with the mobility and therefore the freedom previously reserved for the rich. Yet Western society has always had doubts about the car. The horseless carriage may seem romantic to us, but we forget that it originally was a toy for the rich. Its early image was racy—that of irresponsible playboys tearing up roads, raising dirt, creating a racket, scaring horses, and killing chickens, dogs, and people. The initial reaction of the masses was hostility tinged, of course, with envy. Woodrow Wilson has been quoted as saying in 1906, "Nothing has spread socialist feeling in this country more than the automobile. To the countrymen they are the picture of the arrogance of wealth."

The democratic character of American society is apparent from the early appearance of speed laws. The traffic cop was the response of rural populism to the aggression of urban cosmopolitans. By contrast, there were no speed limits in Europe and few regulations on the automobile until the last decade; it did not matter there what the peasants thought.

Furthermore, the responsible elements among the privileged orders in the U.S. also were originally extremely leery of the car. The early decades of this century saw an orgy of speculation in automobile companies shares, which were the uranium stocks of that day. Bankers and trustees wrung their hands in despair at their clients' profligacy in such crazy ventures. (And rightly so—of the original 2,000 or more American automobile manufacturers, only four remain.) But cars were soon widely used by members of the middle class, and therefore became respectable. With the introduction of the Model-T Ford, every farmer could own a vehicle; rural hostility to the horseless carriage virtually ceased. In fact, farm boys eagerly embraced the automobile.

In the 1920s, a different sort of hostility arose from a new elite. "The Roaring Twenties" were a boom time of cheerful materialism, and the leading edge of the consumer economy was the automobile industry. Cars and car manufacturing were glamorous to most of the nation. Henry Ford symbolized American entrepreneurial ingenuity, and General Motors exemplified American managerial and marketing skills. But to a small but growing group of academics and literary intellectuals such symbols and the values they represented were loathsome. The car incarnated the crass vulgarity of the American middle class. That classic attack on bourgeois values, Sinclair Lewis's *Babbitt*, lampooned Babbitt's affection for his Buick and its cigar lighter as illustrative of the triviality and coarseness of this unfortunate American type. Of course, Buick sought to establish a product with an image attractive to people like Babbitt, and it has been incredibly successful in doing so—but the more it succeeded with Babbitt, the more abominable it became to those who despise him and all that he stands for. Even today, it would take a good deal of moral courage for an academic to buy and drive a Buick—and God help him if he should show up on campus with a Cadillac.

During the 1930s and early 1940s, Americans of all classes were worried about how to get the money to buy and operate a car, or how to get gasoline and tires on the black market—and not about the symbolic importance of the automobile. But in the post–World War II period, the anti-auto sentiments broke out again, this time much more vigorously and vociferously.

The passage of the National Defense Highway Act was the high-water mark of the auto culture. But it had scarcely been signed when the counterrevolution began. In 1958 appeared two fundamental anti-automobile tracts: Lewis Mumford, the renowned social historian and architectural critic, published an essay "The Highway and the City," which laid out the fundamental theme that the highway and the car were "anti-city." On a lower level was John Keats's *The Insolent Chariots*, a broadside attack on Detroit and all its works, caricaturing the car as a pathological symptom of American depravity.

Nineteen fifty-eight also saw a local political race which was

ultimately to have national repercussions. Governor Averell
Harriman of New York was facing a formidable challenger and
needed some issues to differentiate his candidacy from his opponent's. A young political advisor, one Daniel Patrick Moynihan, had fallen in with William Haddon of the State Health
Department, one of the leading theoreticians of the "secondary
collision" school of auto safety. Ribicoff's antispeeding campaign
in Connecticut had gained him much publicity, and it was hoped
that promoting an alternative "safety" scheme would do the
same for Harriman. Despite these efforts, Harriman lost.*

Moynihan published his research in two widely read essays—
"Epidemic on the Highways," which kicked off the "auto safety"
campaign, and "New Roads and Urban Chaos," which laid out
the case for the adverse effects of the national highway program.
In the works of these three men can be found almost all of the
common charges made against the automobile-highway system—
but, of course, none of the obvious benefits. These are the basic
texts for the great anti-auto crusade.

Soon thereafter appeared Nader † and the torrent of anti-auto,
antihighway writing and legislative attacks on American auto-

---

* This was the race Nikita Khrushchev described as "between two
millionaires, and the richest one won." No doubt it is purely by coincidence that the New York auto safety campaign was dropped when
Harriman (railroad money) was defeated by Rockefeller (oil money).

† The link from Keats to Nader is exemplified by Nader's use of
the term "Japanese lantern" (in *Unsafe at Any Speed* and in his anti-
Volkswagen study)—the very same term used by Keats to describe the
structural strength—or lack thereof—of a presumably unsafe car. Keats
has not changed his opinions over the years. Writing in early 1976
he reiterated his diatribe against Detroit in the *New York Times,*
making the point that a new Ford Granada costs $4,000 while he
was getting perfectly satisfactory service from a Volkswagen he
bought for $1,200 in Rome eleven years ago. But in the past eleven
years there has been 70 percent inflation and the price of new cars has
been pushed up by compulsory federal safety and emissions standards.
A new Volkswagen Rabbit also costs $4,000—the same as the larger,
more comfortable, and faster Ford Granada. That $4,000 Volkswagen
also has a notoriously bad maintenance record; Keats would be well
advised to hold on to his old model as long as he possibly can.

mobility that served the interests of three important groups in our society: the "New Class" of "intellectuals," academics, journalists, bureaucrats, and nonprofit professionals; the "downtown" banking, real estate, and newspaper interests; and the broad upper-middle class, largely in the suburbs. Let us examine these one by one.

New Class hostility to the automobile must be understood in terms of both ideology and self-interest. It has long been dominated by what the literary scholar Lionel Trilling called the "adversary culture," opposed to the established values of most of the society. The New Class does not like "materialism," and considers most of the achievements of our society as childish and foolish. More to the point, through its consumption patterns it seeks to differentiate itself from the rest of society. It does so, for example, in clothing fashion: when I met a former director of Nader's Center for Auto Safety, his first comment was on my clothing. I was clean shaven, with short hair, wearing a lounge suit, which he took to be a business uniform; he was mustached and long haired, wearing crumpled slacks, a corduroy jacket, and a knit tie—the uniform of the New Class. (He is a graduate of the elite Hotchkiss School, Yale, and Harvard Law School.) The New Class prefers restorations to new houses, antiques to modern items, sailing to power boats, backpacking to cross-country motorcycling, and in general rejects all of the cultural artifacts of the industrial revolution, save only the electronic ones—stereo, computers, and the like.

It is most instructive to examine the social background of the most renowned critics of the automobile, as revealed in their other writings. John Keats warmed up for his *Insolent Chariots* with his earlier *The Crack in the Picture Window,* a broadside against suburbia. Keats's other works are equally elitist and "anti-American." For example, he somehow turns a book about the guerrilla resistance in the Philippines during World War II, one of the most heroic episodes in our military history, into an indictment of the United States. His autobiographical *The New*

Romans reveals his shabby genteel origins, his disappointment at not maintaining high social status, and his utter opposition to American democracy and mass prosperity.

Lewis Mumford's writings are shot through with his hatred of modern civilization in general and American democracy in particular, which he would prefer to destroy in favor of some sort of idealized medieval, decentralized "nonmaterialist" society —where the peasants and workers would presumably know their place. Moynihan, the Clausewitz of the war against the automobile, is no friend of the rich, but he has another constituency— political power-holders. His omnifarious career has a common theme—the aggrandizement of state power.

The implacable war of Ralph Nader (Princeton and Harvard Law School) against American institutions is too well-known and well documented to elaborate further upon. It is noteworthy that "Nader's Raiders" are almost all rich kids from "the best schools."

But perhaps the most striking example of the social class of the anti-automobile forces is provided by Emma Rothschild, author of *Paradise Lost: The Decline of the Auto-Industrial Age,* a composite of almost every anti-automobile cliche. Miss Rothschild—or more properly, *The Honorable* Emma Rothschild—is one of *the* Rothschilds, daughter of an English nobleman of immense wealth. She is technical writer for the *New York Review of Books,* the leading "radical chic" periodical, bankrolled by New York millionaires and published for an audience of eastern academics.

Some politicians are charter members of the New Class. The original Congressional critics of the federal highway program were two former professors—Paul Douglas of Illinois and Eugene McCarthy of Wisconsin.

It is important to recognize the social background of these critics because their anti-auto bias is inseparable from their class prejudices. Consider, for example, Keats's description of the typical car owner, "Tom Wretch":

Tom is a member of the great middle majority that reaches from the upper-lower through the lower-middle class. In a word, he doesn't have much money and he is not too bright.

Here is Ralph Nader, self-proclaimed spokesman for the public interest, speaking to a college audience in New Jersey: ". . . this country is populated by people who fritter away their citizenship by watching TV, playing bridge and Mah-Jongg, and just generally being slobs."

Nader's writing was favorably reviewed in the *New York Review of Books* by Lewis Mumford, who clearly shares Nader's contempt for Middle America:

> In short, the crimes and the misdemeanors of the motor car [note the anglicism] manufacturers are significant, not because they are exceptional but because they are typical. . . . The insolence of the Detroit chariotmakers and the masochistic submissiveness of the American consumer are symptoms of a larger disorder: a society that is no longer rooted in the complex realities of an organic and personal world; a society made in the image of machines, by machines, for machines; a society in which any form of delinquency or criminality may be practiced, from meretriciously designed motor cars or insufficiently tested wonder drugs to the wholesale distribution of narcotics and printed pornography, provided that the profits sufficiently justify their exploitation. . . .

The M.I.T. economist Robert Solow has similarly sneered at

> the sort of person whose idea of heaven is to drive at 90 miles an hour down a six lane highway reading billboards, in order to pollute the air over some crowded lake with the exhaust from 220 horsepower outboards, and whose idea of food is Cocoa Krispies.

Journalist John Burby, former Neiman fellow at Harvard and former special assistant to the Secretary of Transportation, considers the United States a "sloppy society" because of the "unlimited freedom to drive cars"; he of course favors an "ordered society" where such abominations would not be permitted.

> Americans would have to accept the fact that nothing in the bill of rights says they are free to drive automobiles wherever and whenever they please.

Our politicians are not much better. Here is that great champion of the people, Senator Hubert Horatio Humphrey, sniping at the people's preferred mode of transportation in the course of telling us why we need "national economic planning":

> And may I say that what we have done is let the automobile industry decide where we are going to live rather than let the country decide. The whole development of outlying factories in the countryside is a product of the automobile industry. This is a peculiar time. People who live in the cities work in the country and people who live in the country work in the cities. Many of the industrial workers in the Twin City area live in the center of the city and work 30 miles out of town. The bankers, stockbrokers, insurance salesmen, and the real estate agents live 30 miles out in the country and work in town. The automobile has done this. We have permitted ourselves to be victims of four wheels with a 400 horsepower motor at a time when we shouldn't require four wheels for every trip, and surely we don't need 400 horsepower cars.
>
> What can government do about it? Government can do a lot about it. For example, the size of automobiles, and consequently energy consumption, can be influenced a great deal by taxing cubic displacement, horsepower, or weight.

In other words, instead of letting us buy the kind of car we want and choose where we are going to live, Senator Humphrey would let "the country decide"—i.e., allow the politicians to determine where and how we all will live. We are not to be permitted the modest satisfaction of having 400 horsepower, a trivial amount compared with the insatiable power requirements of politicians.

An UMTA administrator, defending the notorious "diamond lane"—which was reserved for the use of "mass transit" vehicles, thus choking the Santa Monica Freeway—granted nonetheless that it would have no significant effect on smog effect or energy conservation, but was justified because it would make a city work better and add to the use of bus service. Reflecting on why the diamond lane was promoted so vigorously, the editorial writers of the *Los Angeles Times* wrote:

> the answer lies in a purely ideological commitment that pervades the California Department of Transportation and some elements of the Federal transportation bureaucracy. These public servants are gripped by the notion that Los Angeles's dependence on the car is excessive, and indeed rather sinful. They would teach us a lesson, these latter day prohibitionists; we should be weaned from our dependency, and a little force in this process would do us good. Lest you think this characterization is exaggerated, talk with some of the officials in the state and federal agencies and count the number of times you hear the pejorative phrase, "Los Angeles's love affair with the car."

And to give a sample of the lunatic fringe, consider the official who wrote New York City's transportation control plan:

> My plan was a tool for social change. Very few people grasped that. My crusade is not air pollution: it's the fucking automobile, and what it's doing to the country.

His ideal city is Peking, the capital of Communist China, where everybody walks—everybody, that is, except the big bureaucrats.

As usual, it is Ralph Nader who sums up these attitudes best: "I'm in favor of zero automobile growth."

Correlating political and social attitudes with hostility to the automobile, particularly the large American car, is not just idle theory. When I wrote that academics had an aversion to Buicks in a magazine article two years ago, the dean of the college of social sciences at one of our most prestigious universities wrote to

ask where was my supporting evidence; I had to reply that my
statement was based on personal observations of campus parking lots and the professoriat in general, and I doubt that such an
answer was convincing to a "social scientist."

Fortunately, this subject has since been surveyed in detail by
the political scientist Everett Carll Ladd and the sociologist

Table 7: FACULTY ATTITUDES AND CAR OWNERSHIP PATTERNS

	ONLY U.S. CAR	U.S. + FOREIGN CAR	ONLY FOREIGN CAR	NO CAR
1972 Vote				
McGovern	55%	64%	81%	87%
Nixon	45	36	18	13
Attitude to Gerald Ford				
Positive	36	32	17	15
Neutral	32	30	28	25
Negative	33	38	55	60
Political Views				
Most Liberal	15	17	30	31
Liberal	19	22	25	28
Middle	19	15	19	23
Conservative	22	22	17	11
Most Conservative	26	24	9	7
Church Attendance				
Once a Month or More	49	43	25	21
Concert Attendance				
Once a Month or More	26	22	34	31
Athletic Event Attendance				
Once a Month or More	28	21	18	5
Discipline				
Humanities	21	20	33	39
Natural Sciences	27	30	26	25
Social Sciences	19	21	26	19
Education	8	9	5	2
Business	8	7	4	4
Engineering	6	7	4	4
Agriculture	3	2	1	1

Seymour Martin Lipset, who polled American professors about what cars they drove, correlating the responses with other information (see Table 7). The results are startling. According to Ladd and Lipset, "Car purchases turn out to be almost a proclamation of a social-political-religious orientation or style of life." To begin with, academics have a strong propensity to own foreign-made cars. Forty-two percent of them own imported cars, although only 19 percent of all cars on American roads are foreign made. Here is the breakdown of auto-ownership in academia:

American cars only	56%
Both American and foreign cars	19%
Foreign cars only	23%
No car	2%

This represents a major deviation from the American norm. And Ladd and Lipset found even more fascinating correlations:

> On question after question, those who owned one or more American cars are the most conservative, conventional, and least involved in "high culture." Those who own a foreign car as well as an American one are somewhat less conservative, followed in a more liberal direction by faculty owning one or more foreign cars. A small category of those who do not own any car are the most liberal or non-conventional of all.

In other words, the more liberal * or left wing a professor is, the more he is opposed to existing American institutions, and the less likely he is to own an American car.

* It is not intended here to use "left wing" or "liberal" as pejoratives. Socialism is not necessarily incompatible with an auto-mobile civilization. Renault, Volkswagen, Alfa Romeo, and Leyland (Jaguar, Triumph, MG) are government owned, and all but the last make superb products. Several years ago I had occasion to do considerable driving in Polish- and Russian-made Fiats, the former was an excellent car, and the latter junk. What is worth noting is this peculiar form of contemporary *privileged* leftism in America—the most successful, prosperous, and highly regarded professors are the most left wing. A similar pattern of "limousine liberals" and "Porsche populists" can be found in our major urban centers.

There is also a surprising degree of variation among different cars. Even among owners of American cars, small car owners are much more liberal than big car owners (see Table 8). The Ladd-Lipset data break down the most important makes of cars in the U.S.; there is a remarkable variation in the political views associated with different models (see Table 9). The pattern is straightforward: The more conservative you are, the more likely you are to own a GM car, with those slightly more liberal owning a Ford, Chrysler, or AMC. Look at that degree of leftism correlated with ownership of a Volvo. Saab owners are even further left. Is this correlation connected somehow with Swedish socialism or with a marketing and design strategy that eschews styling and flair in deference to utilitarianism, longevity, and safety? These preferences seem to suggest a particular form of self-identification on the part of the professoriat. Rather than indulge in the sort of "conspicuous consumption" that they claim to abhor, many of the professors opt for a conspicuous form of "inconspicuous consumption."

The complaints of the professoriat against the automobile are particularly poignant. Academics often complain about the "ir-

Table 8: FACULTY ATTITUDES AND SIZE OF PRIMARY CAR
(*U.S. Cars Only*)

	SMALL CAR	LARGE CAR
1972 Vote		
McGovern	68%	53%
Nixon	32	46
Attitude to Gerald Ford		
Positive	30	37
Neutral	31	31
Negative	39	32
Political Views		
Most Liberal	22	13
Liberal	21	18
Middle	21	17
Conservative	20	24
Most Conservative	16	28

Table 9: POLITICAL VIEWS AND AUTO OWNERSHIP

	1	2	3	4	5
		← MOST LIBERAL			
		MOST CONSERVATIVE →			
GM	12%	18%	18%	23%	29%
Ford	15	19	20	22	24
Chrysler	19	22	18	21	20
AMC	21	17	12	23	26
Japanese	22	22	17	20	18
VW	26	26	16	17	15
Fiat	27	18	30	11	13
Leyland	27	31	15	15	12
Mercedes-Benz	32	19	21	17	11
Volvo	32	19	18	18	14
No Car	31	28	23	11	7
All Faculty	20%	20%	20%	20%	20% = 100%

rational" and "unplanned" nature of our economy and society, our addiction to growth at any cost. This indictment may or may not be true of America at large, but it is certainly true of the universities. In the post–World War II period there was an orgy of breakneck expansion: campuses were covered with new buildings, enrollments skyrocketed, and affluent students brought their cars with them. By the mid-1960s, one of the major issues of most American campuses was the fight over parking places.

Furthermore, because the academic community desires to concentrate a number of activities in a small area, major university towns and the "college towns" in major cities are among the highest density, therefore most congested parts of the country. Cambridge and Berkeley have densities in excess of 100,000 people per square mile—higher than Manhattan. It is no accident that Berkeley is at the forefront in its efforts to keep cars out of the city.

Other New Class centers are also jammed. Washington is one

of the most crowded cities in the United States because every ambitious bureaucrat wants to be at the center of the action. For generations governments have tried decentralization, pushing offices into outlying centers, but it does not work. The centripetal forces are too strong. Washington is building a $6 billion subway (with your money) because of the increased congestion resulting from a huge block of new federal buildings in Washington's southwest, expanding Congressional offices, and adding new federal buildings elsewhere in the District of Columbia. Faced with these conditions, businesses decentralize to the suburbs, but government officers feel that they must cluster around the political center.

Another important element of "the New Class" are the independent intellectuals, largely drawn from refugees and other relatively recently arrived families from central Europe. They have no tradition of land ownership and personal mobility, and expect to live in apartments and use public transportation systems and taxicabs. Their view of urban life is not an unattractive one (see Jane Jacobs's fine book *The Death and Life of American Cities*), but it is not shared by the bulk of the American population, who have different origins and are motivated by different values.

Given this background, we can better understand the motivation behind the editorial pages and news departments of the *New York Times* and the *Washington Post*,* with their consciously shrill anti-automobile stance and promotion of mass transit; the New York publishing industry, which has put out dozens of anti-auto and antihighway books (and not, to my knowledge, a single procar book before this one); the favorable reviews of Nader's contemptible book in the *New York Review of Books*, and of Helen Levitt's silly *Super Highway–Super Hoax* on the front page of the *New York Times* book review section; the anti-automobile articles and casual comments circulated in

---

* The film *All the President's Men* depicted the *Post* journalist Bob Woodward (Yale) driving an old Volvo—this was sociologically brilliant.

"liberal" journals such as *Progressive, Nation,* and *New Republic,* the cheerful predictions of the death of the family car found in mass-circulation magazines like *Time*: the vulgar slanders against Detroit by columnists like the cynic Russell Baker and the nihilist Nicholas von Hoffman; and the nonsense produced even on television, that opiate of Middle America.

Although the professoriat and the intellectuals in general have important influence in establishing opinions, ideas are not enough. What they believe does not much matter unless there are substantially wider interests at stake.

There is what I call "the downtown interest," which takes several forms, depending on the region of the country and the part of the city. In the Northeast, our old high-density cities are gradually losing their importance and prosperity. While their fiscal and economic difficulties are grossly exaggerated by the press and by their politicians, the problems are real, and these cities are no longer as healthy as their suburban areas. There are vast vested interests in these cities—in banks, real estate, and department stores; "suburban sprawl" threatens these investments. Falling central city department store sales are of particular concern because these stores have historically been the major advertisers in big city newspapers. Small wonder then that newspapers howl about the evils of suburbanization and its vehicle, the automobile—after all, it is obvious that the move to the suburbs has been made possible by automobiles and highways.

Newspapers are not merely mercenary. Their publishers are important men, usually of high community spirit; they are in contact with bankers and other local fat cats. The automobile presents a grave threat to their city as they know and love it.

In the older cities, the aging mass transit facilities are rapidly losing riders and for the most part are enduring operating losses that cannot be borne locally. Understandably, such places are crying out for subsidies from the national government merely to keep them alive. Among these decaying northeastern cities are Boston, the academic capital of the country; New York, the media capital; and Washington, the political capital. The problems and interests of these cities are thus imposed upon the nation.

The downtown interest also favors collective transit in the growing cities of the South and Southwest, but for quite different reasons. Although these cities exemplify "suburban sprawl," they have promoted concentrated high-rise office and commercial centers very much in the traditional eastern pattern. The very admirable freeway systems will soon be unable to provide workers with easy access to these burgeoning downtowns. Congestion is still trivial by northeastern standards, but it is growing, and the people who run cities like Atlanta, Houston, Dallas, and Denver can see the point when the freeways will no longer be able to bear the burden.

Clogged freeways could be disastrous to the real-estate interests. On the expectation of further expansion, undeveloped real estate on the periphery of downtown areas has been driven up by speculation to great heights. If that land cannot be developed, its value will collapse. Billions of dollars will then be lost by bankers, realtors, and other speculators. But this self-sustaining, inflated development is threatened; more high-rise office buildings cannot be built unless some sort of collective transit system is installed—highways alone cannot provide access to large high-density areas. Thus more profits for the fat cats requires a massive public investment in mass transit, a key element in the central-city development spiral. Some unsympathetic souls, like me, would argue that it is a misallocation of public funds to tax everybody in the country to provide mass transit facilities that merely guarantee the investments of speculators.

Some of the desire for collective transit in these Sun Belt cities is less rational, merely reflecting the wish to have the symbolic attributes of a big city. The men who run our growing Sun Belt cities have a high degree of civic spirit. They want their towns to be in the big time, and big-time cities, as everybody knows, have rapid transit facilities. If Atlanta, Houston, and Dallas are to be in the same league as New York, Philadelphia, and Chicago, they must have subways. Don't sneer at this prestige motivation —it is the reason that underdeveloped countries build jet airports and big international hotels. In the late nineteenth century a growing mining camp had not made it without an opera house. Every society has its symbols of success, and a rapid transit transport system is one of ours today.

But the "downtown interests," however powerful and vocal, are not enough to explain the great anti-automobile crusade. After all, the car makers, the unions, and tens of thousands of subcontractors—not to mention service station owners, oil companies, and garages—are more than enough to overwhelm them politically. The great war on the auto could not have gotten off the ground without a powerful constituency—made up of people like you.

Up until about 1950, having a car in America was really great and always getting better. The roads were improving, the cars were becoming more reliable, easier to drive, and cheaper. It was fun to go driving on Sunday. But in the 1950s it became apparent that too many *other* people were beginning to have cars. The ideal system is one in which all the roads are paved, all of the gas stations are built, mass production is keeping car prices down—and nobody else is on the road but you.

From 1945 to 1955, the automobile expanded from its previous middle-class and rural constituency to include the bulk of the urban working class. To the urban dweller, the automobile was no longer a middle-class perquisite. The middle classes now had to share the road with the workers, and they did not like it very much. It is no coincidence that both the agitation against the automobile and the promotion of mass transportation began when the urban workers switched from mass transit to the car. At its most vulgar level, the anti-automobile crusade is simply the attempt to drive the other guy off the road, particularly when he is not as sensitive, educated, or prosperous as we are. That lower-class slob has some nerve jamming highways in his junky old Chevy with his wife in curlers and his squalling brats beating on the rear window. People like that belong in mass transportation, in subways or buses, not clogging our roads and slowing us down.

So what are we going to do? Well, just what we've already done: convince ourselves that our interest is not selfish, but high minded. We are not cynical people like those nasty Europeans who do not mind stepping on the faces of the working classes—we are Americans, we believe in democracy, we have noble intentions. So to drive the rabble off our highways we must divine elegant justifications—that cars are unsafe, that they are polluting, that they are chewing up the landscape, etc., ad infinitum.

We should raise large amounts of public money by taxing the lower orders, to provide them with facilities appropriate to their station in life. Of course, *we* will continue to drive, except when we are commuting from long-distance suburbs and have jobs that require a lot of paper work. In that case, we will tax the working man to subsidize commuter railroads for us. After all, what more appropriate use is there for the tax dollars levied from the factory worker than the equipping of air-conditioned bar cars for the run to Westport or Lake Forest?

Moreover, we should force our taste in cars on the nation. Federal legislation should mandate that all Americans must drive the sort of cars preferred by the "New Class"—the purely utilitarian vehicles blessed by the safety regulations. The great bulk of the American people must be denied the vulgar pleasures of powerful or aesthetically pleasing automobiles. A federal requirement for small cars also protects the interests of the prosperous in general—no longer will it be possible for the slobs to load up their family in big cars and jam up the national parks or recreation areas.

The quality of life in our bohemian neighborhoods, university precincts, and nice suburbs is being threatened. As auto ownership grows we find it more difficult to find parking spaces. The flow of the rabble out from the city is overrunning our suburban paradise. We can stop this by blocking highway construction. The transportation control plans of our EPA will halt the expansion of metropolitan areas.

But our most important tactic to reduce the auto-mobility of the average American slob is to make driving too expensive for him. One of the most unattractive aspects of contemporary American civilization, recognized by all "enlightened," "concerned," "thinking" people is that mass prosperity is a vile thing. It is shocking that ordinary working people have enough money to live almost as well as we do. Indeed, some of them are so crude that they cannot distinguish between their worldly goods and coarse pleasures and our superior preferences. Worse, we are constantly exposed to their vulgarity—there is no way we can escape the sight of a Chevrolet Monte Carlo or a Cadillac Eldorado. Clearly, the standard of living has to go down. We should push the cost of driving up. We will put in compulsory insurance to squeeze them a little bit. Safety inspections are merely an annoyance to us, but dollars of hard-earned money to them. We will put safety equipment on cars to run up the prices a few hundred dollars, and require emissions controls to make cars run less economically and smoothly.

Over and over again I have emphasized that the safety and emissions question involves not so much technical capability but cost. We could probably have safer cars, and we could certainly have lower emission cars, but they would be much more expensive—by definition, limited to a much smaller portion of the population. But wouldn't that mean that the more prosperous must also pay more to drive? True enough, but we can afford to pay. Doesn't the problem result from cars and gasoline getting cheaper relative to income? Push up the cost to prewar levels—get the working class back into buses and subways and leave the roads to the middle class. After all, we can afford higher prices—don't we buy Oldsmobiles, which are really the same as Chevrolets, and pay hundreds of dollars extra just for the privilege of distinguishing ourselves from the masses? Don't we buy Volvos and Peugeots, which are inferior products to "Detroit iron," just to differen.iate ourselves from the rabble? Isn't it better to drive a Chevrolet in a world of walkers than a Rolls-Royce in a world of Chevrolets?

Given who runs the country, it is understandable that Congress has emphasized fuel conservation in those activities that are most important to the average citizen—housing and automobiles. The reader is probably unaware of the Federal Energy Conservation Act of 1975, signed by President Ford in December of that year. This law requires that all new cars average 27.5 miles per gallon by 1985. Gasoline consumption is partially a function of engine efficiency—high-performance engines and emission-free engines are gas guzzlers—but since we must assume that efficiency is kept low by the emissions regulations, the principal factor controlling gas consumption is thus vehicle weight. (Aerodynamics hardly matter at highway speeds under sixty miles an hour, and only really become significant at speeds over eighty.)

A car with consumption of 27.5 miles per gallon must be a small car. Automobiles *can* be made somewhat smaller and lighter, with the same interior space and almost as comfortable a ride, but a good-sized, comfortable car can only be made to average 20 mpg—not 27.5. So by 1985, according to the new law, the average car made in America is going to be the size of a subcompact Vega or Pinto. Consider the cars on the road today. What size car do you drive? This law really indicates that Congress is absolutely out of touch with the country. Do they seriously believe the American people will squeeze into cars that small? Of course, when millions of consumers go down to the showrooms and discover that there is nothing larger than what they regard as kiddie cars, they will howl to heaven, rudely reminding Congress once again that the "New Class" is not the entire electorate. All this nonsense will then be swept away to oblivion—but meanwhile, Detroit will have invested billions of dollars tooling up for smaller cars. And all the costs of retooling at the last minute will be passed on to the poor crying consumer.*

All the above strikes me as a reasonable program for "an elitist

---

* Canada has been a little less silly in this regard, by mandating cars that cannot weigh more than 3,500 pounds. This is pointless, but less stupid than the American regulations. An adequate four-door sedan or station wagon can be built within a 3,500-pound limit. It cannot be built to get mileage of 27.5 miles per gallon.

bastard." Now, I am not claiming that anyone has consciously thought it out along the lines I have indicated. Instead, we are experiencing what Weber called "elective affinities," whereby peoples' values coincide with their interests. Major social movements—like the anti-auto crusade—do not happen unless they are in the interest of powerful elements. No one can honestly claim that there is a widespread *public* benefit in screwing the average American on the basis of false or exaggerated claims.

Those who are opposed to the automobile and who have been howling about its "faults" for a generation are the same people who are trying to block suburbanization, halt the production of new energy sources, and promote measures to run up the cost of driving. As the Marxists say, "it is no accident" that they will profit as individuals, and as a class, from the curtailment of auto use.

The class aspect is the foundation of the war against the automobile. In his book *Cities on the Move,* the distinguished English historian Arnold J. Toynbee wrote that the 1930s were "the golden age" of the automobile. In the 1930s, only the upper-middle classes in England owned automobiles. The 1960s, when the skilled workers became automobile owners, was presumably a period of decay and decline. Depending on the national density, the optimum situation for an automobile is roughly when half of the households have it. The U.S. is up to 85 percent—and that is a killer for the people on top. To satisfy the dominant elements in this country we must cut back on automobile usage.

However, the correct transportation policy is the line of least resistance; the policy that is most democratic, egalitarian, and useful is to expand the auto-highway system and adapt the rest of the transportation network to and around it. That is not difficult to do.

9.

What Is to Be Done?

The establishment of a sensible and democratic personal transportation system must involve recognizing that the key to effective policy is not so much what is to be done, as what is *not* to be done. Individual Americans have had the intelligence to select the automobile as their mode of transportation. Although it is conceivable we might select some other mode at some time in the future, public policy in the meantime must be directed toward promoting the automobile-highway system.

So, "what is to be done" is to *stop* doing things that have the effect of driving Americans off the road. From this follows the need to reconsider the principal thrust of national and, to a lesser extent, state and local transportation policy as it has developed over the last fifteen years. Principally, there must be a review and probably selective modification of the programs that are alleged to promote automobile safety, emissions controls, fuel economy, and so-called mass transportation. However, we must also continue to recognize that automobile safety, emissions, fuel supply, and mobility for the nonautomobile are and will continue to be costs of the predominant auto-highway system, and all

193

reasonable efforts should be made to minimize them. But the real emphasis should be on maximizing consumer choice and reducing the direct financial costs of auto ownership and operation.

There are many ways of cutting these costs. As indicated earlier, I am by no means convinced that safety inspections have any validity whatever; this can and should be determined. If no correlation between automobile safety inspections and auto safety is found, inspections should be terminated forthwith—despite the howls of the garages that are now cashing in on the compulsory business.

Another candidate for review is compulsory auto insurance; it is not absolutely clear that it provides a public benefit. Cautious drivers will have liability protection and will guard themselves against uninsured drivers, anyway. It would not be difficult to compare the states having compulsory liability insurance with those not having it to discover what effects it had on accidents and accident costs.

One promising possibility to cut insurance costs is what is now called "no-fault" insurance. Although I agree with critics who maintain that it has the effect of weakening individual responsibility, I think this single cost must be weighed against the possible benefits. The existing automobile insurance litigation business is a racket for lawyers, particularly the worst sort of ambulance-chasers. Anything that can reduce this kind of litigation is desirable.

But there is a most peculiar aspect of existing no-fault insurance: in states where it has been established, there is also obligatory self-insurance. In New York, for example, an auto owner is required to have "personal injury protection" (PIP). But this is a serious abuse of state power—requiring people to have liability insurance to protect others is one thing, but there seems to be no reasonable justification for forcing people to insure themselves. Most people have other forms of protection for themselves, particularly Blue Cross, Blue Shield, and major medical insurance at their place of work. Obliging motorists to carry PIP coverage is basically a means of making business for insurance companies. So before we get too deeply into no-fault we should examine other options.

A big chunk of the insurance expense is personal liability, which is run up by sympathetic juries who operate on the faulty perception that suits pit an individual against a big, faceless, and rich insurance company. In fact, that fat insurance company must necessarily pass on the cost of the damages and the litigation to all its policy holders. One possible way of dealing with this problem is to establish fixed awards, very much like airlines on international flights, who will pay only a certain amount per head in case of a crash. It would not be at all difficult to legislate fixed awards for damages suffered in automobile accidents—medical bills, loss of earnings, and even arbitrary amounts for loss of limb, future earnings, or even life. Fixed awards would eliminate all need for litigation; the insurance companies would settle right on the spot. So-called pain and suffering should be no-fault. All this would cut well into the size of insurance premiums.

And premiums could also be reduced by other means. The maximum deductible for collision insurance should be increased. At present in New York State the maximum is $250 deductible; there should be $500 and $1,000 deductibles.

Another major way of saving on auto insurance is minimizing the amount of litigation among companies. The simplest way of achieving this has been done in some Canadian provinces, where automobile insurance has been taken over by the government. Those of us who have little faith in the competence of a government bureaucracy to adjust claims properly will be more than a little suspicious of the efficiency of such an arrangement—a prejudice reinforced by some accounts coming out of Canada. But perhaps there is something in the idea of states taking over coverage and engaging private insurance companies to provide service and investigate the claims.

The existing system of fixed rates established by the government gives no incentive for insurance companies to investigate more carefully the accuracy of claims, which are notoriously crooked. If they were really serious about reducing costs, they would have their own repair garages, or franchise private garages to do the job for them—at least in concentrated metropolitan areas. If the insurance companies were doing the car repairs themselves, you can bet your life the body-shop rip-offs would be minimized.

Another way of reducing costs is better law enforcement. The existing system of criminal justice in the United States seriously increases the cost of operating an automobile, particularly for poor Americans in urban areas. A car parked on the street in any of the inner cities is in perpetually grave danger of being stripped or stolen, a risk reflected in loss of mobility and astronomical insurance rates. We might consider devoting fewer police resources to the dubious benefits of maintaining the fifty-five-mile-per-hour speed limit, and more to patrolling the streets of our cities.

We should also think of maximizing the potential mobility of our older and younger citizens. Reducing car costs would help them most of all, but we should also consider making our licensing restrictions more liberal. Over the last twenty years there has been a steady tightening up of licensing for younger and older drivers, the groups most accident-prone and most appropriately objects of concern. Nevertheless, the social benefits of keeping the older people mobile longer might more than compensate for the slight additional risk that they create. In any event, most of them tend to be prudent. If they feel uncomfortable driving they drive less, and eventually quit altogether. Their judgment is usually, but not always, good. They certainly should not be harassed by government.

Nor should younger drivers—except that their judgment is not so good. As I suggested earlier, it would be very interesting to discover the trade-off between youth and experience in driving skills. An investment, if you like, in permitting younger drivers on the road might be more than returned by their safer driving record in later years.

Another way of reducing costs for our less prosperous citizenry is to cut or at least hold the line on license and registration fees, which have had an unfortunate tendency to creep upward. One reason is that these fees are supposed to support the operations of motor vehicle bureaus—which, if New York and Connecticut are typical of the nation, are among the more abominable bureaucracies afflicting the citizenry. Pennsylvania's system of "auto tag" service through local notaries is far superior.

It is very difficult to judge whether there is any point to a sliding scale of registration fees. Charging a higher fee for heavier and therefore presumably more expensive cars seems to be justified on the basis of equity, but one really wonders if it is worth the trouble to the motor vehicle bureaus—or even if it is effective. The slight differences among cars are certainly not going to discourage people from buying larger cars. A man paying $10,000 for a Cadillac will not be dissuaded by the need to pay an additional $20 or $30 per year to register it. The argument that a heavier car will wear the road more than a lighter one is certainly correct, but this difference is more easily taken care of by the gasoline tax than by registration—a heavier car will burn more gas and therefore pay more gasoline tax. It makes sense to transfer as much as possible of the taxing of autos from a fixed cost to a variable cost—that is, cut the registration fee and increase the gasoline tax.

A complete and impartial review of the effectiveness of the federal auto safety standards promulgated over the last decade by the National Highway Traffic Safety Administration is necessary. There is now a review underway that one hopes will be honest—but knowing bureaucratic inertia, one has good reason to be skeptical. If that report comes out saying something like "we see no need to change the standards"—watch out. This would mean that the reviewers have no clear idea whether the standards are any good, but they have not been shown that the standards are necessarily bad. A "zero-base" review is really what is needed: it must be demonstrated that the standards have value by some objective criteria—such as proving they prevent

10,000 crashes a year or save motorists $10 million a year or prevent 10,000 injuries a year or save a thousand lives. I very strongly suspect that none of the existing safety requirements (with the obvious exception of seat belts) will be able to meet any of those criteria.

I will wager that almost all of the existing regulations can easily be disposed of, resulting in considerable savings to consumers—how much would be very difficult to calculate. On the technical side, many of the standards probably have almost unnoticeable safety effects, but no longer cost anything because the ability to withstand crashes and whatnot are now already designed into automobiles. Apart from the cost of crash testing, which a prudent large-scale manufacturer should undertake in any event, designing a car that can crash a barrier at thirty miles an hour without serious injury to its occupants no longer costs significantly more than conventional designing. But other auto-safety details are essentially expensive add-ons that could be eliminated at a clear saving to the consumer. Among these are the little running lights on the sides of automobiles, buzzers and flashing lights inside, probably headrests, protruding knobs, and some of the lighting standards, particularly the compulsory backup light.

The compulsory "recall" programs may be worth keeping. Detroit pursued them anyway before they were mandated by the Feds—but not too aggressively, on the understandable grounds that it would not be commercially prudent to advertise defects, especially safety defects. However, the existing recall system fails to distinguish between trivia like a throttle that might stick open and serious flaws like brakes that are almost certain to fail—more selectivity would probably be desirable.

The "passive restraint" issue should be put on the back burner. Obviously, the Congress and the states are not about to pass compulsory seat-belt laws; equally obviously, the air bag is an expensive device of dubious value. There should be more investigation of other types of passive restraints. Volkswagen has devised an interesting seat belt that gives considerable protection merely by deploying when the door is closed.

But the best means of passive restraint is not any add-on to the car, but part of the necessary equipment of the automobile and its occupants. The single most important crash-protection device inside an automobile is the arms and legs of the passengers. More investigation should be done concerning what individual people do in crashes. One particularly promising direction followed by the safety engineers concentrates on the design of the steering wheel. It seems unnecessary for people to be impaled upon the steering column in a crash, since the principal protection afforded the driver is his grip on it, with his feet braced on the floorboards and on the brake pedal. This is the position taken by most drivers in most accidents, and it should not be difficult to design a car so that drivers could survive head-on crashes at relatively high speeds in that position without a seat belt.

The importance of the steering column for safety is evident from the fact that the right-hand front seat has long been known as the "death seat" because its occupant does not have the steering wheel to brace himself against. The passenger seat is by definition less important than the driver seat because it is far less frequently occupied—the latter is, of course, in use in any operating automobile, while the former is in use far less than half the time. Nevertheless, the passenger of a car needs something equivalent to the steering wheel, preferably a well-braced collapsible bar within easy reach. In the name of safety the current federal standards have perversely pushed the dashboard farther and farther away from the passenger, making it more difficult for him to brace himself in a crash and permitting his body to build up more speed before hitting the dashboard or windshield. We should not completely ignore rear-seat safety, but should not concentrate on it very much because these seats are so seldom occupied.

To prevent accidents, there seems to be very little that can be profitably accomplished in the design of a car. The single most important modification is one that has been talked about considerably, although precious little has been done. What the world needs from the safety engineers is a cheap and reliable nonskid device to prevent the wheels from locking under heavy braking. The average driver does not know how to modulate the brake pressure under emergency conditions to prevent skidding. There are any number of possible ways such a device could be designed. The requirement is obvious, and the technology should be fairly simple. The current attempts to regulate braking electronically have potential, if microprocessors can be effectively employed, but a simple servomechanism might be better.

But the principal effort for auto safety should not be aimed at the driver or the vehicle, but the highway. A little further on I shall talk about what needs to be done to highways—principally, improving the speed and convenience of movement. But anything that simplifies and smooths the flow of traffic is desirable for increasing safety as well.

Another step should be taken in the repeal of the federal fifty-five-mile-an-hour speed limit. Speed limits obviously should be left to the states and local governments. If the state of Connecticut feels it can cut traffic fatalities by making people drive fifty or fifty-five, let it try. If Montana and Nevada have other interests, they should have different speed limits.

But whatever the safety regulations are, it is absurd that they be exploited to reduce the consumer choices of Americans. Current federal law permits the Department of Transportation to exempt motor vehicle manufacturers of fewer than 2,500 vehicles per year from meeting some or all safety standards.* This gives too much discretionary power to the bureaucracy. The law should be modified to *require* the Department of Transportation to exempt manufacturers or importers of fewer than 2,500 vehicles a year from any and all safety regulations, except the requirement that seat belts be fitted. It is a disgrace that a work of art like a Ferrari should be crash-tested for the dubious benefits thus derived, and that Americans should be denied the opportunity of

---

* This is the so-called Bayh Amendment which was passed to protect the low-volume Avanti factory in Senator Bayh's state of Indiana —this was a desirable modification of the law, but nevertheless gives us a hint of how politics dominate such "safety" considerations.

buying more than three-quarters of the automobiles manufactured in the world. Even if the safety regulations were desirable, the tiny number of cars that would be imported or manufactured under such a revision would be unnoticed in the total safety picture. Furthermore, DOT should be given the optional discretion of exempting importers or manufacturers of up to 5,000 vehicles per year from the safety standards.*

The case of emissions control is much more clouded than safety regulation. We do not know very much about the effects of emissions, nor what needs to be done about them. While it is quite possible that we may never know the effects, the existing evidence suggests they are probably very trivial. What we do know for certain is that air pollution from automobile emissions is only perceived to be a problem in very limited areas of the country. It is absurd that a motorist in Montana should have to pay for an expensive and annoying emissions control apparatus merely because Los Angeles has a smog problem. There should be different standards for different parts of the country. Indeed, this is such an obvious step that it is surprising that the federal authorities are moving so slowly in this direction. The original scheme was to have a single national emissions standard, but this was first modified by California's demand for a more rigorous standard, and the recent development of the "high altitude" standard by the Environmental Protection Agency. In effect we now have three standards. But, unfortunately, the two modifications are more severe than the national standard. We need some easier standards for areas without an existing or potential pollution problem.

On the face of it, it is bizarre that air quality standards should be promulgated in Washington. Why should some bureaucrat (who is almost certainly a "New Class" enemy of mass prosperity) be qualified to determine the desirable air quality in

---

* Motorcycle and bicycle safety standards should also be eliminated altogether. Nothing significant can be done about the safety of a single-track vehicle. The efforts by NHTSA in this area have simply been a waste of the taxpayer's money.

Chicago, Cheyenne, or Chattanooga? The vicious and reactionary "transportation control plans" and controls on "traffic generators" should be stricken from the books immediately.

However, given the abysmally low quality of the state bureaucracies and legislators, it would be a grave error to let them establish their own standards unaided—because this would make the mass production of automobiles impossible and drive the cost of an automobile out of the reach of an average American. The principal function of EPA should be to offer the states information and staff support. This arrangement would doubtless be biased against the American people, but certainly would be less pernicious than unrestrained EPA power on the one side and the irresponsible actions of state authorities on the other.

The Federal Government should provide a variety of emissions standards from which states can select as they see fit. We now have three standards, and I suspect that five would be about the practicable maximum. The range should begin with one much stricter than any of the existing standards—for Southern California and other areas where it is at least believed that automotive emissions are a serious problem. The other extreme should be a relatively liberal standard, rather like the national standard of a few years ago—this would be almost costless to the motorist and the automobile industry because the technology needed to meet a tough standard makes satisfying of a much looser one very easy. (In all jurisdictions, the crankcase ventilation system should be retained on the grounds that it is practically costless.) Between these two extremes, there should be three or four standards of varying degrees of toughness.

Another step might be experimenting with the existing standards. In particular, the interplay between the hydrocarbons and NO_x needs to be better understood. It might be preferred in some places merely to have a tough hydrocarbon standard (which would also take care of the carbon monoxide), let the NO_x go, and see what happens. Depending on local atmospheric conditions, this may be more than adequate to deal with photochemical smog. It is worth looking into.

Such measures should deal with emissions in the short run,

but the long-run problem is even cloudier. Toward the end of the century we are likely to have approximately 150 million automobiles on the American road, and even a cut in emissions to a fraction of their current levels will mean that the total emissions from automobiles will begin to go up after 1990. We need a contingency plan for dealing with this problem if it arrives. This can be tricky. Given what we know now, or think we know, it looks as if emissions will be a growing problem then, but we cannot be sure. It should not be expected that the private manufacturers of automobiles, who work on short lead times (in corporations, five years in advance is called "long-range planning"), will invest on the basis of a prospective threat so far off in the future. This is a legitimate area for public policy to consider investing in advanced technology—not for the short run, but for the very long run.

I see no reason why the federal government should not employ nonautomotive engineers and organizations to work on alternatives to the existing internal-combustion engine. Detroit has great experience with the internal-combustion engine, but much less with the gas turbine, steam, sterling, and other potential modes. However, the existing organizations of the federal government involved with the automobile are simply not to be trusted with this sort of research. They are opposed to the automobile and this slants their analysis, just as much as Detroit's commitment to the internal-combustion engine slants its research. So what are we to do? Let me make a suggestion that may seem odd but has considerable weight behind it. Some of the fundamental research in the stratified charge engine was accomplished by, of all people, the U.S. Army. The Chrysler prototype for a new tank currently under evaluation has a gas-turbine engine developed under Army auspices. We tend to forget the military is a major user of motor vehicles—jeeps, trucks, tanks, and other tracked vehicles. The Army Ordnance Command has a strong and legitimate interest in improving propulsion systems; it could be given the job of researching in advanced technology in this area.

Work on the electric car might be attempted through NASA

or some other high technology agency. It seems fairly clear that merely developing existing technology further will not achieve the necessary power storage and transmission capability needed for an effective electric car. But this research should not be intended for replacing the internal-combustion engine, but for contingency purposes only.

Barring some major breakthrough in battery design, the most likely solution to the emissions muddle is some sort of constant velocity internal-combustion engine, with an infinitely variable transmission so that engine speed remains more or less constant and easily controlled and the ratio of engine speed to car speed can be adapted to road conditions. The most obvious way to achieve this is through the hybrid engine, whereby the internal-combustion engine drives a generator that transmits electricity to motors at the wheels—but this is complex, heavy, expensive, and entails serious power losses with each conversion from one type of energy to another. A mechanical or hydraulic system is probably a more practical way to go.

Now I am going to suggest another method of relieving pollution that might possibly strike the reader as bizarre—but I know of no other serious discussion of this possibility. The idea is to relieve pollution by dispersion. Remember that everything emits obnoxious effluents of one kind or another. We are all individual emitters, or rather excreters. But like any other emitting device, we are harmless so long as we pollute far enough apart. It is the concentration, the high density, of emissions that creates the pollution problem.

It seems to me that a very reasonable way of reducing air pollution in America would be continuing to permit our cities to spread out even farther. By lowering the density of the number of people or structures or activities per square mile, we lower the potential problem. But, it may be objected, if you spread things out more, people are going to drive more, and you will have even more emissions and pollution. No—lowering the density spreads out the area more than it increases the amount of driving. Let me make the point clear with a very simple model.

Imagine a typical planner's theoretical city. It is flat, perfectly round, and has a uniform distribution of residences, while all other destinations are concentrated in the center. Let us assume it has a radius of 10 miles and a population of 314,000. From high school plane geometry we know that something with a radius of 10 miles has an area of $\pi 10^2$, or 314 square miles, so the density is 1,000 people per square mile. A little more plane geometry tells us that the average person drives just a hair over 7 miles to work every day. Now let us double the area of our city and keep the population constant, thus cutting the density in half. Then the area is 628 square miles, so its radius is a hair over 14 miles and the average distance to work is 10 miles. If emissions are proportional to the distance driven, then the total emissions are increased by 10/7 or 43 percent—but the additional emissions are spread out over an area that is twice as large, so that the pollution or amount of emissions to air volume is down 29 percent $(1 - \frac{1.43}{2})$.

In practice, the gain should be even more than this example would suggest, because not all of the employment places and other destinations are in the center. As the metropolitan city spreads and densities drop, the destinations will tend to be relocated nearer to people's residences. Once a metro city has made the major breakthrough from collective mass transit to automobile transportation, the amount of emission-creating driving does not increase as fast as the density drops.

Of course, the process described is what has already been happening in every major metropolitan city in the United States (though not in the desert, which requires piped water, and thus inhibits spread). Since the automobile came into use, the densities have been dropping precipitously and seem to be moving overall toward a level of about 3,000 per square mile, which seems to be appropriate for an automobile city, such as Houston. By comparison, Manhattan Island has 70,000 people per square mile, New York City 26,000, and the New York metropolitan area about 5,500 per square mile.

The reduction of density also decreases congestion. The most congested areas in the country are those with the highest density. If we could reduce the number of people who are using downtown Los Angeles or New York or any other city, the congestion would be reduced almost equally. Imagine that every skyscraper in the country was cut in half. Think how much easier it would be to find a parking place and get to and from work. The only places hurt by such a scheme would be those with preautomotive rapid transit systems that rely upon the very high densities of those skyscrapers to generate enough traffic to make them economical.

The fuel issue is related to safety and emissions standards. Modifying the existing safety regulations will probably reduce weight slightly and therefore marginally help economy; but more significant gains can be achieved by incremental improvements in the quality of safety engineering. This is a learning process already far advanced, yet it certainly has much farther to go. A crash-proof car need not necessarily be a tank. Modifying the emissions regulations will have more of a positive impact upon economy. The relaxation of some standards will permit major gains in the fuel economy of the average car.

Fortunately, fuel economy is almost entirely a phony issue. We would not have to worry at all about it (so long as a wide variety of automobiles is available, so the consumer can choose whether he wants an especially economical vehicle), except for the political issues. As should be apparent from chapter 5, these are twofold: the balance-of-payments problem and the susceptibility of the United States to an oil boycott. To a considerable degree, the policy measures dealing with these two problems are contradictory. If we are most worried about the adverse effects of an Arab oil boycott, we should *not* promote conservation now; if a boycott should occur, we would thus have available for quick implementation all the easy ways of saving fuel. In other words, the easy means of fuel conservation should be avoided now. Fuel savings under a boycott would then be simple, because there is always a large amount of "discretionary" driving that can be eliminated. In a pinch, the average family could cut its driving by at least 25 percent, at the cost of only some annoyance. Under normal conditions, there is no need for even this minimal hardship. People will respond properly in an emergency —but it should not be expected that emergency-type measures can be maintained for long periods of time. So as far as the possibility of an oil boycott is concerned, it makes sense that we be wasteful now so that the fat can easily be trimmed later when necessary.

But an undisciplined use of energy under existing economic conditions means an outflow of cash to foreign oil producers and presumably a balance-of-payments problem. To my mind, however, the adverse effects of this outflow are grossly exaggerated. If the cheapest place to get oil or energy is from the OPEC nations, then we should continue to do so, concentrating our efforts on improving our comparative international advantage in other products. The United States of America is no longer the cheapest place in the world to get oil, but it is still the best place to get such raw materials as coal, cotton, soy beans, wheat, and many other types of agricultural produce, airliners, computers, microprocessors, earthmoving equipment, and any number of manufactured goods—not to mention all manner of skilled services in construction, etc., etc.

If the fear of the potential effects of an Arab boycott is serious enough to make us want to be free of blackmail and other pressures, we should then move to energy self-sufficiency, not by trivial attempts at conservation, which will only have marginal effects on total energy usage, but by improving our own output. This is not the place to get into an extended discussion of what our energy policy ought to be. But if we are interested in moving toward energy independence, we should have a policy; unfortunately, we have none today. The federal government, both the executive and the legislature, are pulling in all manner of different directions.

The desire for energy independence is confused and complicated by hostility to oil companies and automobile companies

generated by various local interests of all sorts, including the
"limits-to-growth" movement and other manifestations of elitist
hostility to the prosperity of the average American working
man. It does seem to me that we are in the business of cutting
off our noses to spite our faces. If the process of gaining energy
independence means that oil companies make a lot of money,
that should not bother us. After all, these are *American* oil companies, and this is a capitalist economy—and one of the char-
acteristics of a capitalist system is that corporations make a lot
of money that they then invest in other activities. If for some
reason or another we strongly object to their making a lot of
money, then by all means nationalize the oil companies. Most
countries in the world have national oil industries that are probably more inefficient and wasteful than private companies, but
they are successful in getting oil out of the ground, transporting
it, and marketing it. Beating the existing oil companies over the
head certainly does no one any good, except for the psychic
satisfaction it gives a few of our more demagogic Congressmen
and their claques.

There can be some wide agreement on what should be done
by a rational energy policy. For one thing, the price of natural
gas should clearly be allowed to rise to its market level, as was
made clear by the Northeastern gas crisis in the winter of 1976–
77. This would curtail demand to some degree, give incentives
to bring in more gas (including some that is probably already
located but that the gas producers are sitting on, waiting for the
price to rise—they all deny it, of course, but no serious person
believes them). Most important of all, a higher price would restrict the use of natural gas to those activities needing it the
most, pushing other uses to coal, of which we have plenty. A
higher price for natural gas will also encourage exploration for
oil since the two fuels are searched for together.

The price of oil should also be deregulated. This would not
cause it to rise to the free market price; in fact the free market
price would be lower then than the existing price. Deregulating
oil would rather cause it to rise to the OPEC monopoly price—

such a profitable situation that oil companies would then be encouraged to implement the more expensive and less efficient means of exploring and extracting oil. If deregulation would create a "windfall profit" for the oil companies, then by all means tax it back with some special windfall profits tax. But anything that pushes up the price of gas and oil helps the cause of energy independence by making alternative forms of fuel much more competitive, and therefore attractive. Oil at $12 a barrel means that we can afford to use coal, oil shale, tar sands, coal liquefaction and gasification, better nuclear power, currently marginal hydropower, and eventually even solar and fusion power.

These may be short-run solutions. Although I doubt that anyone alive today, however young, will see the day when we run out of fossil fuels, it is conceivable that some time in the distant future we might. If so, the more rapidly that we move to develop other sources, the better off we are, and raising oil and gas prices now will have the effect of hastening the day when alternative sources are available.

It can be argued that increasing domestic energy output will have environmental costs. But everything has environmental costs. In the case of energy production, these can be minimized almost to the level of zero by serious precautions in off-shore oil drilling, strip mining, and everything else. We should take great care of the environment while producing energy, despite —not because of—the howls of the "environmentalists" who, on the basis of their record, are clearly less interested in preserving the environment than in depressing the standard of living of the average American. It is no accident that the strongest opponents of the automobile—those who claim that it is exhausting our energy resources—are precisely those who are at the same time blocking the development of those resources. But we should not let the political exploitation of legitimate environmental concerns by such people prevent us from an intelligent approach to defending the environment from unnecessary risk and abuse. Clean air and water are impossible, because nature itself does not provide them, but we can keep the air and water and landscape almost free of unhealthy and unaesthetic abuses at a reasonable cost.

I recognize that discussion of energy supply is inconclusive. This is because there are so many different ways of dealing with our short-, medium-, and long-term energy needs; which solution we find will depend upon the politicians' perception of which aspects of the problem are most pressing. If we want energy independence, let's go get it and stop fiddling and fooling around. But let us not achieve it by cutting into the mobility and individual freedom of the average American family. The impossible requirement that all automobiles get an average of 27.5 miles per gallon by 1985 is ridiculous; it will never be enforced. The sooner it is dropped from the public law, the better.

Turning from what should be done less or not at all, let us consider what should be done by government. First is the continuation of highway construction, reconstruction, maintenance, and repair along the lines of the past two generations, but with some appropriate changes in emphasis to reflect the changing needs of the driving public.

One major change is in the most visible type of highway—the expressways mostly financed through the federal Highway Trust Fund. Almost all of the intercity expressways are already in place or under construction. The national highway network for the remainder of the century can be fairly well determined on the basis of today's layout. There are a few gaps that need to be closed, but these are trivial given the whole picture. In the Northeast, the major investment in intercity highways should be the buying up of the toll roads. Before the interstate highway program was instituted, the financing of the great turnpikes, parkways, and thruways of the Northeast with bond issues to be amortized by tolls was a sensible way of levying the costs of these roads on their users. But tolls are a very inefficient means of financing highways compared with the gasoline tax. Toll collection is labor-intensive; the need to control access unnecessarily limits the free flow of traffic; the toll plazas are sources of congestion and unnecessary pollution; and the whole procedure slows up everything. This is particularly true on tollways like the Connecticut Turnpike and the Garden State Parkway, which rely on many small collections at periodic intervals along the route—a terribly inefficient method of operating roads. Buying up these roads would be a good investment for the highway trust fund revenues; this would also have the effect ex post facto of leveling regional disparities in highway investment. Since the revenues were used to build new freeways, this program discriminated against the Northeast, where the toll roads went in before federal dollars were available.

Upgrading the physical appearance of highways would also be very desirable. Landscape architects and maintenance crews have unfortunately got into the habit of uniformly planting grass on the areas along expressway rights-of-way and interchanges. This is dull and inefficient. Wherever possible, highways should follow the lead of the Los Angeles freeways, where the berme is planted with flowers and shrubbery. Thicker growth along the roadsides would serve several purposes: in addition to being aesthetically pleasing, it would block and diffuse noise, have some impact on the diffusion of fumes (plants take in carbon monoxide and produce oxygen), and also have safety effects, shielding drivers from the glare of oncoming headlights and acting as a buffer to slow down vehicles that leave the road. (Thicker brush would also offer privacy for dire emergency calls of nature.)

Better information should also be provided motorists. In many of our larger cities, local radio stations are performing an extremely useful function with airborne traffic reporters who give valuable information regarding highways clogged by weather conditions, breakdowns, or road repairs. Radio stations such as WOR in New York are to be commended—especially since other stations monitor their reports and broadcast them without attribution or payment.

The most efficient way of providing this service would be by government action. In all metropolitan areas planes should be in the air at all times of heavy traffic—not just weekday rush hours but during weekends as well. The helicopters commonly used are expensive, difficult to fly, and not necessary, in any event; ordinary light fixed-wing aircraft are more than adequate.

Moreover, there should be a regular source of information concerning road conditions. I propose that there be a permanent service provided by a government body, such as the state police, notified of adverse road conditions by local police or citizen's band radio. The information could be made available to all radio stations, or franchised to a limited group of stations that would guarantee regular road reports. For example, it would be very nice if the traveler driving down the Connecticut Turnpike from Cape Cod to New York could know that something has happened to block the road so that he could stop for a meal or gas and wait for the obstruction to clear, or else take an alternate route. Such an information system would not be expensive, merely requiring concern for the problem and a little organization.

The intercity expressway system is nearly completed, and so are the intracity patterns. In many cities there are gaps that ought to be filled, and in many of these cities there is strong citizen resistance to filling them. So if the local people do not want the roads, then by all means do not build them. Instead, the most pressing need for urban expressways is in the outward extension of existing systems into the open country. These extensions should be laid out now; at least, the alignments and rights-of-way should be reserved for radial and circumferential roads in our growing metropolitan areas (which is to say, almost all of our metropolitan areas). This expansion of the system will provide the means whereby congestion and pollution can be diluted through "sprawl," as mentioned earlier. The retrofit of highways into existing urban areas is always difficult and clumsy, with potentially dislocating factors. Hardly anybody objects to building highways where nobody is, and then the development patterns evolve around the highways.

Within the urban areas, the most pressing need is for the upgrading of existing arterial roads. In most metropolitan cities, despite the expressways, the most heavily traveled highways are

the boulevards and avenues built before the expressway age—
usually during the period 1920–1950. These usually have four or
more lanes of traffic, but with multiple crossing roads, traffic
lights, and nearly continuous commercial strip development.
Highway engineers do not like this design very much, and such
roads are no longer built. But by concentrating on expressways,
the engineers have disregarded the potential of upgrading the
volume, speed, and safety of these highways. Almost all of our
arterial routes could be substantially raised toward expressway
standards by relatively straightforward modifications.

These changes would be fairly simple and cheap, but would
require a good deal of intellectual ingenuity to fit in the reconstruction to the existing pattern. For improving highway congestion, speed, and safety, the elimination of any traffic light, any
cross street, any curb cut, any telephone pole, or any other obstruction is a plus. Driving along these arterial roads reveals
numerous opportunities for improvement. Abutting streets can be
closed off and the remainder of the street turned into dead ends;
those that cannot should be turned into one-way streets. Traffic
lights should be eliminated and overpasses installed instead.
Acceleration and deceleration lanes should be provided. Highways can be widened selectively, perhaps only in sections, from
four to six lanes.

Perhaps most important, the number of "curb cuts"—places
where vehicles can enter or leave the highway—can be substantially reduced. In most places, the setback for commercial strip
development is deep enough that the parking lots can be linked,
creating in effect a service road with access to the commercial
establishments, thus freeing the highway of unnecessary amounts
of traffic getting on and off.*

* Let me give some examples of highways that I mean: in New
Jersey, Routes 4, 17, and 22; in Philadelphia, Roosevelt Boulevard,
the Westchester Pike, and the approaches to the Benjamin Franklin
Bridge; in Los Angeles, parts of Wilshire Boulevard; in Dallas, parts
of Mockingbird Lane; in Washington, parts of the Lee Highway; in
Vancouver, the Kingsway. None of these roads can be brought up to
full expressway standards, but as they are upgraded, circulation and
safety are improved.

Another important highway need is reconstructing the streets of our major metropolitan areas, which are often in miserable condition, particularly in older cities. They are plagued by heavy traffic and have been temporarily patched for fifty years or more. Some need to be torn out right down to the base so that a much more solid foundation can be installed.

The quality of traffic engineering varies wildly—in some places it is incredibly sophisticated; in others, very crude indeed. One detail that particularly annoys many motorists is leaving traffic lights on all the time—almost every signal should be turned into a warning flasher late at night.

In very high-density urban centers a systematic reduction of the amount of street furniture would be a plus. There are altogether too many telephone poles, power poles, street lights, traffic lights, parking meters, parking signs, fire hydrants, mail boxes, telephone booths, etc. In New York it is common to see two street lights side by side on a corner, and there is an endless clutter of other signs and lights that could be combined on fewer standards. For example, there really is no need whatever that every parking meter have its own post; they can be mounted in pairs. This is a trivial concern, but it would greatly raise the aesthetic standards of our streets and highways, have a small positive effect on accidents, and perhaps most important of all, improve pedestrian circulation on our sidewalks.

The forgotten man in the highway system has been the pedestrian. In altogether too many places his proper use of the thoroughfares has been neglected. While I scarcely support those misguided plans to bar automobiles altogether from urban centers —on the grounds that vehicular access is absolutely necessary for the benefit of the operators of facilities in these areas, as well as potential users of the areas—it does seem to me that in a few places the balance should be shifted from the side of the automobile to that of pedestrian. Achieving this does not require fancy malls or exotic planning, merely widening sidewalks and narrowing roadways. If the roadways are narrow enough, two things happen: automobiles are far less likely to take the risk of getting caught in such a trap, and narrow roadways make pedestrians much more willing to use streets for walking, further discouraging traffic. The greatest example of this effect on this continent is downtown Manhattan; Wall Street does not bar cars, but few drivers use the streets there because these narrow roadways (which follow the wanderings of early Dutch settlers' pigs) are wholly unsuited for auto traffic. If a driver absolutely must enter the Wall Street area, he can—but in practice the streets belong to the pedestrians.

The complex and impractical plans for discouraging traffic in cities and pushing people onto mass transit should be thrown aside. The only reasonable exceptions are in those places where water crossings create congestion. Water crossings both create congestion and provide the means to deal with it. Where there are bridges and tunnels, traffic can be easily controlled by the careful adjustment of tolls. One of the most striking testimonies to the lack of imagination on the part of whoever supposedly controls traffic in this country is the system of fixed tolls on bridges and tunnels. If there is perceived to be a rush-hour congestion problem and the alternative of collective transportation is available, it is absurd that a fixed price should be charged for bridge or tunnel use at all times of the day or night. Take New York as the best example. Commuters can reach Manhattan from New Jersey by crossing the Hudson River in a variety of ways, using either collective transit or cars: the Hudson Tubes operated by PATH, a subsidiary of the Port Authority of New York and New Jersey, which parallel the Authority's Holland Tunnel; the Pennsylvania Railroad as well as buses using the PA's terminal, which both parallel the route of the PA Lincoln Tunnel; and buses that use the PA George Washington Bridge. Most of these rush-hour commuters are headed for highly concentrated office employment centers in Manhattan, which are destinations best served by collective transit service. Conversely, the Port Authority bridges from New Jersey over to Staten Island are almost entirely used by rush-hour commuters and shoppers going to widely scattered locations, not well serviced by mass transit.

But PATH recently raised its tolls on all crossings at all times across the board. A more sensible policy would have been to jack up rush-hour tolls only at the Holland and Lincoln Tunnels, keeping an intermediate toll at the George Washington Bridge (because it is the route from New Jersey to the Bronx and Long Island), and leaving the Staten Island bridges at a lower rate. The effect would have been to discourage rush-hour tunnel traffic by those who could thus be encouraged to use the mass-transit facilities already available to them.

On the east side of Manhattan the situation is even worse. There are seventy-five-cent (each way) tolls on the Triborough Bridge, the Queens Midtown Tunnel, and the Brooklyn Battery Tunnel, which provide the best access into the city—but the other East River crossings are free. Yet it is the free crossings, like the 59th Street Bridge and the Brooklyn Bridge that lead into heavily congested areas; their use should be discouraged. The toll structure is exactly backward. If there were a toll on the now-free Willis Avenue Bridge to the Bronx, and a lower toll on the Triborough Bridge, the result would be to divert traffic to the Triborough Bridge, which can funnel it into the East Side Drive more efficiently.

Similar modifications of the toll and traffic pattern can be made in a few other cities where water crossings permit this type of control—Philadelphia, Baltimore, Washington, Cincinnati, St. Louis, Kansas City, and San Francisco. (Los Angeles also has some potential because of the narrow mountain passes that funnel much of the freeway traffic.)

Nobody much likes tolls, but the use of tolls during rush hour (and particularly against trucks) forces the traffic that does not have to drive during rush hour to divert to other times or other modes of transit, thus relieving congestion and other adverse effects.

Now let us turn to collective transportation. The first rule to understand is that mass transit as understood today should be used as little as possible. Collective transit facilities are inherently inferior and inefficient; just about any alternative sort of transportation mode should be encouraged instead.

The first and most obvious alternative is walking. There is very little that can and should be done to improve it. One possibility, mentioned before, is widening sidewalks in denser urban areas. Another is lowering the height of pedestrian overpasses. It is absurd that people must climb up twenty feet to use an overpass, just because of the highly unlikely possibility of an extra-high load on a truck. Overpasses should be constructed at normal truck height; any trucker with a load more than fourteen feet high should take an alternate route. There also need to be more pedestrian islands.

The next step up is the ubiquitous bicycle. Again, very little needs to be done. In fact, any major investment in improving bicycle circulation is almost certain to be wasted. Today, bicycling is a major fad. The market is becoming saturated, and will almost certainly soon collapse. Already in New York, apartment balconies are littered with rusting bicycles bought by people who thought it might be fun to go cycling, but found there was less entertainment than hard work out in the sun, the rain, or the cold. Bicycling is well suited to countries that are not very prosperous, with temperate climates and flat terrain. We must expect that bicycles will continue to be used somewhat more than they were in the 1950s, but principally by kids and by college students. When the bicycle fad fades, it will then be more practical to allow them onto footpaths and other pedestrian thoroughfares where they would not be safe today because of their large numbers.

The best that could be done by government for or to the bicycle is nothing at all. There should be no regulation of any kind, no registration, no licensing, and no safety nonsense.

The next step up, the motorcycle, deserves to be encouraged on the basis of cost, convenience, and safety. The motorcycle will only be attractive to young men. It is a very nice means of transportation for not-very-well-paid younger workers, and deserves public support on that ground alone. Some readers may be startled to hear the motorcycle defended on the grounds of safety, because it is reported to be three times as dangerous per mile as the automobile. This comparison is a little misleading, because the principal reason the motorcycle is hazardous is that it is ridden by the most aggressive and risk-prone young men. Half of motorcycle fatalities are to males under twenty-five. This, I argue, is a positive safety phenomenon. It is better that these types be on motorcycles rather than in cars—because on motorcycles they can kill only themselves, but do not (usually) risk the lives of passengers or the occupants of other vehicles. The trade-off here is a difficult one for society to make, but if our most dangerous young drivers want to split their own skulls, we should not object too much, so long as they do not hurt others. The motorcycle is an excellent vehicle to divert these aggressive energies into a socially innocuous pursuit.

Much more important in any transportation system is the taxicab. Fortunately, it is attracting more attention these days as a mode of transportation. A cab shares the flexibility of an automobile, but does not require a capital investment by the rider, nor does it demand that the rider have driving skills. In most places the cab also needs only a modest investment by the potential owner, which is minimized because the typical owner-driver uses the vehicle as his transportation to work, as well as his family automobile.

Unfortunately, maximizing taxicab use has been severely restricted by municipal franchising and licensing. The relations between the Chicago taxicab companies and the city government are notorious. In New York, the attempt to establish a *de facto* monopoly by the city sale of taxi "medallions" has led to a huge quasi-legal dual system, with unlicensed "gypsy cabs" to serve the black and Puerto Rican areas of the city. Similar patterns are found elsewhere.

Little or no positive public purpose is served by limiting taxicabs. Licensing should be as simple and straightforward as possible, preferably by state governments, which are less sensitive to corrupt pressures than municipal governments. Regulation should be limited to a few minor details; most important the prior notification of fares to the passenger. Having been a cab driver, I know how easy it is to rip off a customer, particularly late at night when no other means of transportation is available. The best way to let the passenger know the fare is to post rates on the outside of the cab, or in lieu of that, on the inside. Beyond that, it is hard to see any other legitimate reason for prohibiting any taxicab from operating anywhere within a state.

Limiting the number of taxicabs might be desirable only in high air-pollution areas, where cruising taxicabs are a major contributor of emissions. But a better way of reducing the emissions, particularly in Manhattan, might be to imitate Tokyo by requiring taxicabs to have special propane fuel. Another possibility in such areas are diesel cabs. These are more expensive than conventional engines, but many less prosperous countries employ diesel cabs. If Israel can move people around in expensive long-wheelbase Mercedes diesel cabs, it is hard to see why the United States cannot as well.

Another method of bringing down costs is to repeal all regulations that require that a single passenger be carried in taxis, preventing sharing. This is another example of the prosperous enforcing their standards on the less prosperous. If people want a private cab, they should pay a premium for it, but this should not be the standard or only type of service available.

In low-density areas, radio dispatching will be the principal means providing service, with streetside hails or "flags" secondary. In denser urban areas, the reverse will be true. With taxicabs, we must include all other types of non-regularly-scheduled hired vehicles—jitneys, dial-a-ride, and minibuses; all amount to the same thing. There is no need to design special vehicles for taxi use. While an ordinary passenger sedan may not be the optimum design, it is certainly adequate, especially considering the enormous cost of building special taxicabs, as in London. When a sedan is not adequate for taxi work, adaptations of mass-produced vans for multipassenger use are perfectly satisfactory, particularly for meeting trains at suburban stations and other types of light work. Regardless of equipment, taxis could and should provide the bulk of the nonprivate automobile movement in America, if permitted to do so by law.

Finally, we get into the area which is commonly called "mass transportation." These collective transit facilities cannot under any reasonable circumstances be expected to provide more than 5 percent of the intraurban travel in the United States at any time in the next half century. Nevertheless, 5 percent is a lot of people, including these groups for whom we have special concern on grounds of social equity—the old, young, crippled, and poor. Also, we must maintain most of the existing collective transportation systems in our large older cities. To abandon mass transit in places like Chicago and New York is in effect to throw away these cities. They were built around the rapid transit systems and cannot function without them.

But outside of the few major urban centers, the predominant collective transit facility is and will continue to be the motor bus. Its advantages over other systems will continue to be overwhelming. It does not require a separate guide path; it is flexible in its routing; it can swing around an obstruction; a breakdown of a single unit does not immobilize the system; it is relatively cheap to operate; the capital cost is lower; and the passenger is out in the sunlight, not stuck in a hole in the ground.

The low capital cost is probably the most important aspect of bus operations. Buses are mass produced (largely by the General Motors Corporation) and the cost per unit is relatively low. Most have diesel power, and will last at least a million miles. With air conditioning, they are reasonably comfortable in the summer.

The best thing about the bus is that it shares the highway with the automobile, but this can also be a drawback, when the highway is congested. In many places, local officials are taking steps to give priority to buses. This can be justified on the basis of equity—a bus holding sixty passengers deserves priority over an automobile holding one or two. But giving buses priority is not easy—it requires detailed attention to the highway pattern. In some places, special bus lanes are desirable, in others perhaps reserved ramps on or off expressways.

Other innovations in bus operation, such as the "park-and-ride" facilities for suburban commutation, need to be more widely imitated. A particularly promising scheme is to provide parking lots in the median strip of expressways, offering easy pickup for commuters (not to mention good security for the parked cars).

Suburban bus lines should more often use the parking lots of major shopping centers as their major transfer points. It is in the interest of the shopping center owners to have bus stations on their premises, and the parking fields on the periphery of these centers are usually unused during the day because the major business is on weekends and evenings.

Since most buses are now diesel powered their economy and emissions are relatively low—though doubtless more improvements should be made. The increasing use of automatic transmissions in buses is getting rid of the notorious gear whine, but the engines themselves remain noisy; much more progress is needed in noise abatement. Another drawback is now being corrected: the General Motors "kneeler" bus will cut down the climb to the main floor of the bus.

The details of operations also need improving. Bus stops are not as well marked as they could be, and they have no schedule information posted. Even printed schedules are hard to find, and worst of all, maps of bus routes are extremely difficult to get. Several years ago, I was contemplating commuting into New York City from New Jersey by bus and naively went to New York's Port Authority Bus Terminal to find a map of the bus routes. No such map existed, nor was there a common schedule—only individual schedules for individual routes, sometimes with primitive little sketch maps. Every metropolitan area should have a master map of all of the collective transportation routes, and every bus stop should have a schedule posted of arrival times.

Most buses in America are not for public transportation, but for use by schools. The three hundred and fifty thousand school buses are terribly underutilized, in use only for a few hours a day, 180 days a year. It would not seem at all difficult to combine school bus fleets with transit bus fleets, especially since most schools open after and close before rush hours. Of course, the primitive (and relatively unsafe) school buses, which are now fitted on truck chasses, are unsuitable for general use; regular buses should be substituted for them whenever possible. Combining school buses with transit buses would require some detailed planning, but should not be very difficult. Either an integrated transit-school system could be assembled, or schools could contract with transit operators for service, as they do in big cities. A typical system might have commuter runs early in the morning, followed first by school bus runs, and later by shopping runs. Such a system would also offer an advantage to students who want to participate in extra-curricular activities after school, but are discouraged from doing so, finding it difficult to get home afterward because their buses have already left. Merging school bus and regular bus operations would probably create substantial financial savings to both systems, but more important, would greatly improve service to students and other riders.

Perhaps the less said about the trolley the better. It is an obsolete transit mode, and the current revival of interest in "light rail transit" is seriously misguided. There is nothing a trolley can do that a bus cannot do better. That is the general rule, with only minor qualifications. In a few places, particularly in Boston and Philadelphia, trolleys are currently in service in tunnels. It would be very expensive to convert these systems to buses, so they should remain in service. And there might be some advantage somewhere in installing sections of line in places so narrow that rails are needed. In such cases, instead of investing in a new rail system and buying a custom-made and therefore expensive vehicle, buses should be adapted for rail use. A single rail with an appropriate fitting on a bus should be adequate for almost all purposes. Since the bus would be running on its own tires, the rail would only act as a guide; it would be inexpensive and long lived. After passing through the narrow part of the system where the rail is required, the bus could fan out into normal roads as desired.

If tunnels and other enclosed spaces are too long for riders to endure the diesel exhaust, by all means go to electrics, but not to expensive trolleys. Although the number has been dropping in recent years, there are still "trolley coaches," or electric buses. These are merely ordinary buses without diesel engines and transmissions, fitted with electric motors and gears, and with electric pickups added to the roofs or underbodies. This kind of conversion is straightforward and takes advantage of the mass-produced aspects of the rest of the vehicle.

Now for "rapid transit": it follows from all the arguments above that the first rule of rapid transit operation is *not* to get involved in complex, expensive, unreliable, and inefficient rail systems in the first place. No city in the United States currently without a rapid transit system requires a new one. The real need is to improve the operating quality of the existing transit systems, which are on the whole abominable.

Much the same things should be done with rapid transit as with buses. There should be readily available maps and schedules posted in stations. But the pressing need of all existing mass transit systems is improving their handling of pedestrians. Apparently their designers had little or no interest in how people gained access to them or made transfers between lines. Examples of such shortcomings are legion. To make a connection at the George Washington Bridge between the Port Authority bus terminal and the Eighth Avenue Subway line, it is necessary to walk through a long tunnel. Eyeballing the layouts suggests that two stops could have been closed and a single one put directly under the bridge. Transferring between trains at Times Square, Grand Central Station, Union Square, or the World Trade Center is a nightmare. In many places it surely would be possible to cut through existing walls and lay out stations more rationally.

It also should not be difficult to make simple surveys determining which end of rapid transit stations people favor, and to stop the trains accordingly. A particularly annoying experience in the New York subway system is walking to one end of a station and finding the exit has been barred; entrances and exits are often closed in off-peak hours, but there are not adequate indications of this to the riders. There need to be more gates that can be operated without a token clerk present.

There should also be more imaginative adaptations of scheduling and station location. Most of New York's stations were built more than fifty years ago. Certainly some of them can be closed, or skipped by many trains. Every station that can be eliminated saves personnel costs, but more important the time of the riders on that train.

We must make a major attack on labor costs of rapid transit systems. The unions have gotten quite out of hand. It is incredible that a token clerk in New York, who merely performs the simple operation of selling a single item at a fixed cost, is paid far more than a department store clerk or even a bank teller, who both have many more decisions and responsibilities. One way to reduce the number of token clerks is to charge for use in only one direction. Many bridges charge tolls only one way, thus delaying the motorist once instead of twice; likewise, some rapid transit systems might make certain stops free and charge twice as much at others. Since the largest amount of the traffic volume in the system is headed toward the center, it might make sense to collect fares only at the downtown stations and leave the rest of the system "free." This might be done only for certain periods of the day, or at certain stations. Another possibility is leaving the station unmanned at night (providing safety is not a consideration). Any such possibilities would have to be juggled and adjusted to fit local conditions.

Another saving of personnel cost is the elimination of two-man crews. Having another man just to operate the train doors, as in New York, is clearly unnecessary. In Boston the situation is even more grotesque, where double trolleys in underground lines have two-man crews. It would not be any problem at all to equip the driver with a switch to operate all the doors.

Another potential saving would result from doubling up the functions of the subway personnel. There is no special reason why the token clerks, transit police, and motormen could not be more or less interchangeable. I doubt we would want to pay a token clerk a policeman's wage. But all too often policemen are lounging around the token booth anyway; it would be easy to train policemen as token clerks.

Now, I realize that the operators of rapid transit systems would dearly love to enforce these reforms, but are prevented by the unions. In New York, union rules require a three-month training period for motormen. Operating a train is far easier than driving a truck, a taxi, or a bus; one really wonders why a three-month training period is necessary to be "licensed."

As I pointed out before, the principal effect of the massive federal investment in collective transit facilities has been an income transfer from the public at large to the employees of the system. There is nothing that can be done about this at the local level until some politician gets up enough guts to break a strike. This is a tough-minded approach, but the gains for cities and their transit systems are potentially enormous. It would not take a particularly ingenious management to work out detailed contingency plans for taking over and operating the system, and then provoke a strike. Except for the maintenance personnel in the yards, everybody in the transit system is easily replaceable, particularly in a time of high unemployment. A broken strike would save the system enormous funds in potential pensions and would permit an immediate across-the-board wage cut of at least 20 percent. Perhaps cities do not want to follow such a plan of action, but then they should not expect their systems to be subsidized by the good people of Idaho and Oklahoma.

Commuter railroads are even less desirable than rapid transit systems. The railroad is archaic, expensive, and inefficient. Fortunately, there is a growing pattern of converting commuter railroads into rapid transit operations. Raising station platforms to the level of the car floors to facilitate ingress and egress, putting larger doors in the middle of cars rather than at the ends to achieve the same goal, eliminating conductors and the collection of fares at stations, and selective electrification—all of these are now being done and should be accelerated.

Except for a few, such as the Long Island line and the Southern Pacific line south of San Francisco, most commuter railroads really are not very necessary. They handle a trivial amount of traffic that could be moved in other ways. In any event, these lines cannot make money on normal operations and must be supported by government funds. Since they carry some of the most prosperous people in the metropolitan areas, this amounts to subsidizing the rich—making it difficult to justify their continuation but making it politically impossible to abandon them. So commuter lines should be kept more or less as they are, as a trivial supplement to the total transportation system.

Despite the strong case against building mass transit rail lines, I realize it is quite possible that those who run the world will probably not be impressed by my arguments, and that the social and political pressures to construct them will continue.

So let me make some modest suggestions concerning the design and operation of these lines, if they must be built. First, keep them simple—no fancy "advanced technology." Have one-man operated trains with standardized cars on the customary track gauge. Lay out stations with the platform between the tracks so the motorman can see and control the doors and so riders can transfer easily. Whenever possible, use existing rights-of-way. Every U.S. city has unnecessary railroad trackage that can be devoted to rapid transit use.

So that the systems are much less expensive to taxpayers at large, major steps should be taken to make them financially self-supporting. One obvious way is for the system to cash in on the speculative gains in the value of real property around the stations. Instead of letting local landowners make an unearned profit, the system should purchase the land within a decent radius of the station, and lease it long-term to developers. Part of the conditions of the lease should be that the developers build the station. At the end of the term the entire property would revert to the ownership of the system, thus completely eliminating the cost of building the stations. Using existing rights-of-way would minimize the cost of obtaining the thoroughfare, so that the expenses of the system would include merely the cost of re-tracking, the few new sections, the signaling, and the rolling stock. The cost of the rolling stock could be minimized by operating buses on these lines rather than custom building new cars. Diesel or electric buses would provide adequate volume in almost all cases.

No attempt should be made to provide rapid transit service for an entire metropolitan area or even for an entire city. The system should feed the downtown and link it to a few other major centers. This kind of partial service would provide for the transportation needs of the non-auto-mobile in the metropolitan city because they would tend to live in places thus served, and would thereby have access to the other major points of the area.

For downtown sections and other new additions to the system, tunnels should be avoided at almost all costs. They are incredibly expensive to dig and build. Instead, elevated systems should be reconsidered. Elevateds rightly have a bad name on account of their noise and ugliness, but advanced technology can reduce these to a minimum. If buses were operating on rubber tires on these systems, the rail noise would be reduced; modern reinforced concrete permits much less bulky and therefore more elegant structures. One problem with elevated systems, as with subways, is the long climb up or down. Therefore, cities, particularly in the Southwest, should consider very low elevations, just enough for pedestrians, cars, and light trucks to pass under. A clearance of ten feet would permit normal pedestrian and automobile circulation and would bar only large trucks. This design, particularly if it were in the shape of a loop, as in Chicago, would have the advantage of providing physical control of truck access to the downtown area. Of course, the tracks could be raised at limited points to permit large trucks to get through.

The purpose of improving the existing mass-transit systems

should not be to attract people away from the automobile, though doubtless substantial service improvements would have some marginal effects. The real purpose should be to make them better for the people who ride them. Improving collective transportation is a legitimate end in itself—it need not have any "higher" social justification. Such systems are merely appendages, anyway, of the real mass transportation system consisting of the automobile, the highway, and the driver.

All the above suggestions would seem to make for an expensive program. How are we to pay for it? Basically by continuing the same system used in the past—taxing gasoline and using the revenues for construction. We might, however, consider extending the principle much further. It appears to me that critics of the existing highway trust fund make two legitimate points: first, the fund is a means of encouraging excess investment in one particular type of transportation facility—new highways, and by so doing favors rural and developing areas over urban and established areas. Second, the fund is inadequate to pay for our entire highway bill. The roads are on the whole subsidized by a few billion dollars a year from general revenues. It seems fair to me that the entire direct cost of highways should be levied directly on the highway users. It has already been advocated that we hold the line or cut the fixed costs of transportation; so the other side of that is to increase the variable costs, especially the tax on gasoline.

The federal tax on gasoline has been four cents since 1959. Inflation has reduced the real value of that tax by half. While nobody likes higher taxes, the tax on gasoline should at least keep up with inflation. The simplest way of achieving this is substituting for the existing flat rate a percent of the wholesale price of gasoline. The current (late 1976) wholesale or "tank wagon" price of gasoline delivered to the service station is forty cents a gallon. The existing tax is 10 percent of that. Locking the gasoline tax at 10 percent of the wholesale price would provide for automatic increases of the tax revenue as the price went up. (The percentage tax might also have a four-cent minimum, just in case the price collapses.) But let me advocate an even higher rate. An argument can be made for pushing the gasoline tax up to ten cents, or 25 percent of the wholesale price. Why? Because the real price of gasoline, until very recently, has been steadily dropping and the tax revenues have not kept up with the pace of all other prices. A gasoline tax of ten cents a gallon today would pay for a formidable transportation system.

To deal with the second reasonable objection to the highway trust fund—that it promotes overinvestment in new highways—let me propose that the fund be made available to local governments for any sort of highway use. If the local jurisdictions wish to build more highways, fine. If they wish to use the money to upgrade existing roads, great. If they wish to use funds for ordinary maintenance, street lighting, or any other highway related use, terrific.

The correct formula for the allocation of the highway trust fund revenues to local government is a political question, and would inevitably be subject to ferocious log rolling in the Congress. Having the doubtless naive notion that simple solutions are the best, let me suggest a straightforward way of handling revenue allocations. Take the bulk of the trust fund revenues, say 80 percent, and distribute it to counties on a straight per capita basis. If a county has .5 percent of the population in the United States, it gets .5 percent of the revenues. The counties are to be preferred to the states or the municipalities as the units of allocation because there are so many municipalities having different constitutional arrangements with the states, while the states are too large to properly take local needs into account. Allocating to the counties would also facilitate most of the necessary regional transportation planning, because most metropolitan areas are included in a single county, and formal regional transportation agencies are confederations of counties. Many of our larger cities are themselves counties or the equivalent of counties—New York, Philadelphia, Baltimore, Washington, St. Louis, San Francisco, Miami, Jacksonville, Nashville, and New Orleans. The three thousand counties in the United States are for the most part large enough and sophisticated enough to handle this money. Let them decide which municipalities get what cut of the funds.

The remainder of the highway trust fund, say 20 percent, should be allocated to the states on the basis of how much of the gasoline tax revenue they generate. If Tennessee collects 1 percent of the total revenues, it should get 1 percent of the distribution to the states. This arrangement would help those states having more traffic than population, including those that are the major corridors for through traffic, such as New Jersey; those that have a lot of incommutation by residents of another state, such as New York, Pennsylvania, and the District of Columbia; and those that receive a lot of out-of-state traffic for touring, such as Florida, California, and Colorado. Whatever is the exact formula, revenue allocation should take into account both population and road usage as reflected in gas tax collections.

But what about states and counties with existing mass-transit facilities? Here is the next part of the scheme I would suggest the Congress consider: permit the states and counties to use their share of the funds not just for highways, but for other types of transportation as well. If they want to use the money for railroads, commuter lines, rapid transit, buses, or whatnot, let them do so. Does this amount to raiding the highway trust fund? Hardly. The highway trust fund is already being raided, but in an incredibly irresponsible way by the federal bureaucracy. Remember that the modified highway trust fund described here would have the decisions on spending made at the county level. Of the three thousand counties in the United States, precious few would use their money for anything but highway work, since the automobile is the American mass transportation system.

Only a very few large cities would use significant amounts of their allocation to build or maintain mass-transit lines. And it can be argued that such a "diversion" of highway trust fund monies aids the motorist—by pulling the other guy off the road. The guy who drives benefits from the guy in the subway. So some diversion is equitable—so long as it is not pushed artificially from Washington. The decisions on whether a given city should have a mass-transit system should be made in and by that city, not by Washington bureaucrats of doubtful competence and dubious intentions.

The scheme described above has a very nice political advantage: on the whole, it should be acceptable to the "highway lobby" because almost all the money would be used for automobile related purposes anyway, and even the asphalt and other construction interests could not seriously object to diverting some of the funds from building new highways to reconditioning old roads. Either way, a lot of asphalt and cement is used.

In order to acheive these democratic transportation objectives, the interests of American motorists, which is to say almost all Americans, must be better protected in the political process; we need an effective lobby. The automobile manufacturers and the rest of the "highway lobby" have let the driver down badly. Their methods of proceeding have been primitive, and all too frequently counterproductive. The insolence, arrogance, and insensitivity of the automobile manufacturers are partly responsible for our present fix. Just as an example, at the time of writing, no automobiles can legally be produced in the United States in the 1978 model year. When revisions to the Clean Air Act failed to pass the Congress in 1976, the President of General Motors announced that the law *had* to be changed and that General Motors would go ahead and violate the law. But the most elementary rule of politics is that you do not hold a pistol to the head of the Congress. Even if the Clean Air Act is eventually amended, Congress will retaliate against the automobile industry for that arrogance, and we will all pay.

For twenty years the automobile industry has misunderstood the nature of its opposition. As early as 1958, the journalist Eric Larrabee quoted the complaints of Detroit executives concerning "effete Eastern aesthetes" who bought foreign cars; the car makers did not understand that their own middle American style matched that of the great masses, but not that of coastal cosmopolitan elites. Imagine, businessmen complaining that some people don't like their products! But instead of behaving in a businesslike way—responding to this different kind of demand by providing products, advertising, and dealer networks suitable for this important and growing segment of the population and the automobile market—Detroit chose to spit in the eye of "the New Class" and its political representatives.

We now have a twenty year record of the incompetence of the automobile industry in the political arena. We cannot count on car makers effectively to defend the interests of the automobile public. The alternative is a motorists' lobby. Several years ago there was an attempt, Miles Brubacher's "Motorists United" which could not get off the ground. Once upon a time, the drivers of America did have an extremely effective lobby—the American Automobile Association. In recent years it has been almost quiescent on the legislative front, largely because its principal function is selling insurance—and the interests of the auto insurance industry are not necessarily those of the public. Our interests now require that the AAA be resuscitated and/or a new organization be built to defend us from those who would drive us off the roads.

The American mass-transportation system—the auto-highway complex—has made real the ancient dream of personal mobility that was reflected in the myth of the centaur, giving every man the liberty of movement once afforded only the rich, and permitting the masses a quality of life previously inconceivable. We must not let it be destroyed by the machinations of the new plutocrats and demagogues.

Postscript

While automobiles, highways, and the ways the Americans use them change very slowly, the politics of transportation veers so rapidly that it is difficult to keep up with it. Since this book was written over the winter of 1976-7, there have been many important new developments, not the least of which is a change of administration.

The new Secretary of Transportation, Brock Adams, immediately began mouthing ten-year-old clichés about the need for more "mass transit," and for his trouble was stepped on by the White House—the Office of Management and Budget and the Congressional Budget Office are now aware that these are bottomless fiscal pits. A further expansion of transit subsidies will ultimately result in New York motormen driving Rolls-Royce.

While endorsing Adams's appointment, now-Senator Daniel Patrick ("New Roads and Urban Chaos") Moynihan made a pitch for Manhattan's Westway highway project, a wholly unnecessary billion-dollar boondoggle benefitting only the New York real estate interests who supported his candidacy. Moynihan is also pushing for a federal buy-out of the Northeastern toll roads—an idea which I fed into his staff.

Joan Colebrook, Ralph Nader's chief lieutenant, has been made traffic safety czar. This is rather like appointing Joan Baez as Secretary of Defense.

On a more positive note, the nomination of Theodore Sorenson as Director of the CIA was squashed—Sorenson was the smart lawyer that advised General Motors to roll over on its back for Nader.

GM stepped in it again. Unlike the other major auto manufacturers who produce "corporate engines" for all their brands, GM has proudly advertised that each of its divisions makes its own engine. With the increasing difficulty of designing for emission standards, those engines now only have detail differences. Because Oldsmobiles have been selling very well, GM started slipping Chevrolet-made V8s into them. The corporation thought nobody would notice, but got nailed—and now has another multi-million-dollar payout.

It looks like the 1978 emission standards will be slipped only one year—we will go through a cliff-hanger again next year.

But the most important news is the new "energy policy" of the Carter administration. As one would expect, the emphasis is on conservation. Indeed the policy provides for *discouraging* production of energy; instead, the administration has recommended higher gasoline levies as well as taxes on "gas-guzzling cars." These will have little effect on consumption. A man who raised four kids in rural Georgia ought to know how necessary a big car is to American families. The cost of gasoline relative to income will still be far below levels in Europe, where automobile usage continues to grow. This will not cut energy use, but is merely what used to be called a sumptuary tax. It won't work— nor is it intended to work. The purpose of the policy is propaganda—to convince the American people that they must use less energy, i.e., have a lower standard of living. This will be followed by more draconic measures in the future.

A federal judge has ordered New York City to implement a

transportation control plan by putting tolls on all bridges into Manhattan. The City is resisting, claiming that toll plazas will *increase* air pollution.

And my little Honda CVCC has turned out to be a particularly rotten lemon.

June, 1977

Sources

This is not an academic work, so a full bibliography and annotation would be inappropriate. In any event, they would be impossible to provide because the book draws heavily upon my reading about the automobile for twenty-five years and a clipping file accumulated over the past decade. That estimable magazine *Road and Track* has always been of particular value.

But the principal source has been my use of the American mass transportation system—especially driving some 100,000 miles—mostly in the northeastern United States, but also elsewhere on the continent and in a dozen foreign countries—and regular use of collective transit facilities in and around New York, Philadelphia, and Washington, and occasionally in San Francisco, Chicago, Boston, and foreign cities, as well as a brief stint as a taxi driver.

The following published materials were particularly useful:

Most of the statistical data are derived or calculated from publications of U.S. Census Bureau, Federal Highway Administration, National Highway Traffic Safety Administration, National Safety Council, American Public Transit Association, and the Motor Vehicle Manufacturers Association. Public opinion data are from Gallup Poll, the Roper digest of *Current Opinion*, Department of Transportation, "Nationwide Personal Transportation Study," and the elegant work of the late John B. Lansing of the University of Michigan Survey Research Center, especially his "Automobile Ownership and Residential Density."

While there is a vast literature of automobile history, unfortunately, there is no single comprehensive work on the role of the automobile in modern civilization. The best is John Rae's thin *The Road and the Car in American Life* (Cambridge, Mass., 1971). For the early period see Ralph C. Epstein, *The Automobile Industry* (Chicago, 1928) and for more recent history, Lawrence J. White, *The American Automobile Industry Since 1945* (Cambridge, Mass., 1971).

The fundamental book on urban transportation remains the RAND Corporation study: J. R. Meyer, J. F. Kain, N. Wohl, *The Urban Transportation Problem* (Cambridge, Mass., 1965). This is far preferable to Lyle C. Fitch, ed., *Urban Transportation and Public Policy* (San Francisco, 1964) which is the text for the theory that more investment in mass transit would stimulate major shifts in passenger demand. Also see the works of Wilfred Owen of the Brookings Institution, who nicely reflects establishment opinion in transportation. His most recent volume is *Transportation for Cities* which backtracks somewhat from his earlier emphasis on collective transportation. Also see "Where Transit Works: Urban Densities for Public Transportation," *Regional Planning News*, August 1976, and Melvin M. Webber, "The BART Experience," *The Public Interest*, Fall 1976.

On poverty: J. F. Kain and J. R. Meyer, "Transportation and Poverty," *The Public Interest*, Winter 1970; J. M. Goering and E. M. Kalacheck, "Public Transportation and Black Unemployment," *Society*, July/August 1973. On the highway trust fund: Gary T. Schwartz, "Urban Freeways in the Interstate System," *Southern California Law Review*, March 1976.

On emissions: U.S. Public Health Service, "Control Techniques for Carbon Monoxide, Nitrogen Oxide, and Hydrocarbon Emissions from Mobile Sources"; Lawrence J. White, "The Auto Pollution Muddle," *The Public Interest,* Summer 1973; National Academy of Sciences, "Report by the Committee on Motor Vehicles"; National Academy of Sciences and National Academy of Engineering, "Air Quality and Automobile Emission Control"; Southern California Air Pollution Control District, "Air Quality Trends in Los Angeles County, 1975"; A. P. Altshuller, "Evaluation of Oxidant Results at CAMP Sites in the United States," *Air Pollution Control Association Journal,* January 1975; Environmental Protection Agency, "Progress in the Prevention and Control of Air Pollution in 1975"; F. P. Grad et al., *The Automobile and the Regulation of Its Impact on the Environment* (Norman, Oklahoma, 1975).

The fuel chapter drew upon energy studies by the Hudson Institute. There is a useful summary in chapters 3, 4, and 6 of Herman Kahn et al., *The Next Two Hundred Years* (New York, 1976). The Brown study on Gulf of Mexico methane is summarized in *Fortune,* October 1976. See also Robert U. Ayres and Richard P. McKenna, *Alternatives to the Internal Combustion Engine* (Baltimore, 1972). On the economic effects of higher gasoline prices see my "Gasoline Prices and the Suburban Way of Life," *The Public Interest,* Fall 1974.

On the safety "crusade": Andrew J. White, *The Assassination of the Corvair* (New Haven, 1969); Charles McCarry, *Citizen Nader* (New York, 1972); Simon Lazarus, *The Genteel Populists* (New York, 1974); Ralph de Toledano, *Hit and Run* (New Rochelle, 1975); David Sanford, *Me and Ralph* (Washington, 1976); and interviews with involved individuals, including Ralph Nader (who unconvincingly denies anything the least bit unfavorable to him). See especially D. F. Huelke and J. O'Day, "The Federal Motor Vehicle Safety Standards: Recommendations for Increased Occupant Safety."

The Hilton quotes in chapter 7 are from his "Federal Transit Subsidies" (American Enterprise Institute Evaluative Studies #17, 1974). The Nader quotes in chapter 8 are from *Citizen*

Nader, the Humphrey quote is from *Challenge* Magazine, Solow from the *New York Times,* and the "crack-pot" quote from *Human Events,* 13 March 1976, with the obscenity kindly provided by the perpetrator of the remark when the quotation was verified by telephone.

The most renowned of the anti-auto works are: John Keats, *The Insolent Chariots* (Philadelphia, 1958); Lewis Mumford "The Highway and the City," *Architectural Forum,* April 1958; Eric Larrabee, "Detroit's Great Debate: Where Did We Go Wrong?" *The Reporter,* 17 April 1958; Ralph Nader, "The Safe Car You Can't Buy," *Nation,* 11 April 1959; D. P. Moynihan, "Epidemic on the Highways," *Reporter,* 30 April 1959, and "New Roads and Urban Chaos," *Reporter,* 14 April 1960; Ralph Nader, *Unsafe at Any Speed* (New York, 1965); D. P. Moynihan, "The War Against the Automobile," *The Public Interest,* Spring 1966; Jeffrey O'Connell and Arthur Myers, *Safety Last* (New York, 1966); Lewis Mumford, "The American Way of Death," *New York Review of Books,* 28 April 1966; Helen Leavitt, *Superhighway–Superhoax* (Garden City, N.Y., 1970); Kenneth R. Schneider, *Autokind vs. Mankind* (New York, 1971); R. Buell, *Dead End* (Englewood Cliffs, N.J., 1971); John Burby, *The Great American Motion Sickness* (Boston, 1971); John Jerome, *The Death of the Automobile* (New York, 1972); W. H. O'Connell, *Ride Free, Drive Free* (New York, 1973); Emma Rothschild, *Paradise Lost: The Decline of the Auto-Industrial Age* (New York, 1973); Terence Bendixson, *Without Wheels* (Bloomington, 1974).

The Ladd-Lipset materials are from *The Divided Academy* (New York, 1975), *Chronicle of Higher Education,* 5 April 1976, and computer printouts kindly provided by Professor Ladd.

Index